THE LOST LADIES

ROD WELLS

Fulton Books
Meadville, PA

Published by Fulton Books 2023

ISBN 979-8-88731-634-5 (paperback)
ISBN 979-8-88731-635-2 (digital)

Printed in the United States of America

To my beautiful wife, Dr. Diane Schill Wells.

Without your encouragement, support, and valuable editing

skills, this novel would likely not have been published.

PROLOGUE

The author is hopeful that this novel will alert people of a certain older age that they could become victims, such as those described in this novel. People, due to loneliness or just naïveté, can invite awaiting human predators to enter their lives and cause them harm.

The reader will note the absence of cell phones. The time frames in this novel can best be described to have occurred in the middle to late 1980s, before the soon-to-be proliferation of cell phones. DNA, as it is used in today's crime fighting, was comparatively only in its infancy during the events in this novel.

CHAPTER ONE

S he went way faster than he thought she would. She was seventy-nine years old, a tall slender woman who, surprisingly, just looked into his eyes as he stepped from the back of the boat and wrapped his hands around her neck. She put up her hands on his for a moment, but seemed to give up easily. Then she was gone.

He removed the tarp covering the bag of cement which he had hidden there previously. He began tying the cement around her lifeless body as he struggled to muscle her over the side of the boat, finally watching the bubbles appear on the surface, and then, she disappeared.

He remembered back ten days ago at the senior citizen's dance. He had seen her across the dance floor, sitting between two older women. He had sauntered across the floor wearing his pearl-buttoned Western shirt, Wrangler jeans, and cowboy boots, carrying his Stetson.

"Excuse me, ma'am," he said, looking only at her, "would you care to dance with me?"

She looked surprised and seemed to seek approval from her friends. With nods from both she said, "Well yes, I certainly would." As she got up, he placed his Stetson on her chair. He held her at an appropriate distance as the band began playing Glenn Miller's "Moonlight Serenade."

Neither spoke for a few moments, when she said, "My name's Dottie."

He said, "It's a real pleasure to make your acquaintance, ma'am, er, I mean Dottie. My name's Carl Johnson, but I go by CJ."

"I have to tell you, CJ, I have not danced in over seven years, not since I lost my husband, Harvey. I occasionally come to the dances here, but you are the first man to ask me to dance. You are a wonderful dancer, CJ."

"I was just about to tell you the same thing, ma'am, whoops, Dottie. You're as light as a feather. If you don't mind, can we keep on dancing a few more?"

He had noticed that the moment she stood, Dottie was a large woman. Not overweight, but tall and big-boned. She must have been close to five ten or eleven. He was being truthful, as she seemed light on her feet. When the band took a break, he walked Dottie over to her friends.

They said, "Dottie, you haven't looked so happy in a long time."

Dottie introduced CJ to her friends and told them CJ was going to treat her to coffee and pie at Denny's. Dottie told them that since she and CJ had their own cars it should be okay. It seemed a bit out character for her, but Dottie seemed to be happy.

At the restaurant, they were mostly discussing Dottie's past. Her late husband, Harvey, died from lung cancer over seven years ago. She had three children, all of which lived many states away. She admitted to being lonely but did have some friends. All of this chatter was very boring to CJ; however, he pretended to be interested. His eyes brightened when she told him Harvey had left her a large insurance policy, her home was paid for, and she had a nice pension from teaching elementary school for over forty years. "But I still miss Harvey so very much."

Dottie's parents were a part of the great dust bowl migration West. She and Harvey met in high school when she was a sophomore and Harvey a junior. They immediately became a couple "going steady." They were considered by most classmates as "most likely to be married." Most didn't realize that both Dottie and Harvey held true to their Southern Baptist upbringings of no sex before marriage. They spoke of marriage before he was drafted. He immediately enlisted in the Marines, planning to wed when he returned.

Those years were most difficult for Dottie. After she graduated high school, she worked for a dentist as a receptionist, anxiously waiting for Harvey's return home. They corresponded by mail and professed their love for each other. When he returned home, he told her she was all that kept him going while serving in the Marines overseas. They married soon thereafter.

Dottie told CJ, "You seem to be a real cowboy."

"Well, shucks," said CJ. "I guess that's what I've always been. Ever since I was a little boy, I have pretty much been cowboying, always working as a wrangler on ranches. I did some rodeos, mostly riding broncos and bulls. Got myself broken up a few times, but did make a little money. In fact, I got me my own spread south of town. I have some horses and a few head of cattle, but I mostly raise alfalfa hay." They parted with CJ saying, "Maybe we could have lunch tomorrow."

Dottie seemed a little surprised, but, "Sure, where?"

"Do you like Mexican food?"

"I love it," replied Dottie.

They met the following day at a very popular Mexican restaurant, dining on the best tacos Dottie had ever eaten. They also talked a bit about CJ being a cowboy. He told her he would like for her to see his spread sometime. It was then that Dottie said that she had a few questions. She told him that she was too old for a romantic relationship, "If that is what you have in mind." She said, "First of all, I am seventy-nine years old."

CJ seemed shocked. "Dottie, I am completely surprised about your age. I thought you might be a few years older than me, but you are a pretty girl, more like a filly to me. I am sorry, I don't think age makes a difference, especially if two people like each other."

"Well, CJ, I am not interested in romance or sex or any of those things younger people do." CJ began to respond, but she cut him off. "I do have a question for you, CJ. Are you married? My friends you met bet me that you are."

CJ said he was no longer sure whether he was married.

"What does that mean?" she asked him.

He told her about five years ago, he was out on the west end of his property fixing some fences and had ridden his horse, Junior, out there. He saw a dark-colored car or SUV pull into the front of his house. It wasn't there but a minute or two and left. He didn't think much more about it as he had work to do. When he finished the fences he rode back to his house, unsaddled Junior, brushed and fed him, and left him in his stall.

He went to the front of his house and found the front door standing open. He had a strange feeling when he called out, "Melba, honey, are you okay?" No response. He began walking through house, calling her name. He noticed a kitchen chair was knocked over. He saw Melba's purse in its usual place, along with her keys. She never left her purse behind when she left the house. He became frantic.

Since he lived in the county, he called the sheriff's department. A deputy came out and he told him what had happened. The deputy began quizzing him about whether they were having marital problems or had been arguing. He told the deputy they got along just fine and was very worried something bad had happened to Melba.

He mentioned the dark-colored car and thought his wife had been kidnapped. The deputy took the report and was leaving when CJ said, "Wait a minute! My wife is likely kidnapped, and you're just doing a report? Can't you do an APB or whatever you call it?" The deputy told him he was doing all he could for now. He was going to check with any neighbors who may have seen something, but for now it was all he could do. The report would go to Detectives in the morning, and CJ would be contacted. Melba's description would be put into the system.

"CJ, that's just horrible, you poor man," said Dottie. "Have you ever heard from her?"

"No, Dottie, never any word. I just keep on a praying and worrying. I have come to believe that I'll never see her again. The detectives are now calling it a cold case. Every time I go talk to them, they begin asking me if I had something to do with her disappearance. I sometimes break down and cry, telling them over and over I loved her so and would never do her any harm."

"I am sure you had nothing do with her disappearance. Why won't the detectives leave you alone and try to solve the case?"

"I am completely perplexed, if that is the right word? It seems they have done very little to find whoever did this to my Melba. Anyway, I hope you understand better now why I don't know if I am still married or not. I sure hope that won't cause us to no longer be friends."

"Of course not, CJ, it just makes me want to be your friend even more," she said.

"That makes me feel better. I still want to show you my spread."

"I really look forward to that," she told him.

"Dottie, we will do that real soon. Do you think we can go on a picnic tomorrow?"

"That sounds like fun," replied a surprised Dottie. "There is a nice little park in Layton. I used to go on picnics with my husband, Harvey, but have never been to this particular park. How about I make some fried chicken and potato salad?" she said and gave him her address and phone number.

"Okay," replied CJ. "How about we meet at the park about 12:30?"

"Is there a reason why you can't pick me up?"

"Well, Dottie, I'm just not sure how it will look to your neighborhood folks, me showing up at your house."

"Do you feel they might not approve of a cowboy coming to my home?" asked Dottie. "I'm sorry, CJ, that wasn't a nice thing to say. Sure, you do look like a cowboy, a look, by the way, I believe is quite handsome. But you are probably right in my not revealing we know each other. My girlfriends are terrible gossips, and if they knew

I have actually seen you since coffee after the dance, it would create more gossip than I need."

"Well, it is probably good we're not telling anyone because I don't think your friends would approve of me," said CJ.

"You are most likely right about that," she replied. "I am, however, a grown woman and am free to make my choices of friends."

"All right," said CJ, "we'll keep up the secret for the time being. All I want is to keep seeing you, even if it is nothing more than being very good friends."

"Sounds like a good plan for the time being," replied Dottie.

"See you at the park tomorrow," said CJ.

CHAPTER TWO

·　●　●　○　●　●　·

"That's about the best fried chicken and potato salad I've ever had," said CJ.

"Well thank you sir," said Dottie. "My grandmother was from Germany, and this is her recipe. The fried chicken I'll take credit for," Dottie said. "This little park is great for a picnic. I suspect you have had some picnics here with Melba." CJ sadly shook his head.

Several minutes went by in silence when Dottie asked him, "Are you okay? You seem a little down today."

"Sorry, Dottie, I have a bit of a problem, but I don't want to trouble you with it."

"CJ, for goodness sakes, I thought we were friends. Are you in trouble with the law?"

"Oh no, ma'am. Sorry, Dottie. I am a little embarrassed to tell you or anyone, but it is awfully serious." Minutes went by when he said, "I'm about to lose my ranch."

"What?" said Dottie. "I don't understand."

"Well, since we are friends, I'll tell you. It is not a very nice story, so here goes: When Melba disappeared, I couldn't do anything but think about her. I put up missing-person signs everywhere. I didn't take care of my hay business and just grieved about Melba. Well, the second year, the hay business really dropped in price; in fact, I didn't even break even. I am not trying to make excuses, but I have fallen so far in debt due to taxes, the tax collector is filing to take my spread. I have spent about everything I had trying to find Melba. Now with the tax collector wanting to take my property, I am beginning to feel lost," he told her.

"Believe me, CJ, I completely understand. This can happen to anyone. How much do you owe, if I may ask?"

CJ hung his head and said, "Twenty-eight thousand dollars."

"Oh my, that is a lot of money," said Dottie.

"Well," CJ told her, "I have tried for a loan from banks and anywhere they loan money. No one will help me. Believe me, Dottie, I really didn't mean for this to happen. You know, Dottie, my grandaddy in Tennessee is very, very wealthy. He's ninety-eight years old and in bad health. His mind is still good, though. I've asked him for help, but he told me that me and my younger brother, Lester, will get all of his money when he passes, but for now, he is not going to help. I have explained that to the tax collector who said, 'That's just pie in the sky, your taxes are still due, and they can't be paid with wishful thinking.' I'm sorry, Dottie, I don't want to burden you with this, and I'm truly sorry I told you. I hope this won't change anything between us."

"Of course not, I feel you are a very humble man, and this must be difficult for you to tell me. What about your younger brother?"

"Lester is mentally retarded. He has been this way since he was born. He barely gets by on SSI and welfare. My grandaddy told me when we get his money, his will is set up for me to get the money, and he has made something called a trust in which I take good care of Lester for the rest of Lester's life." CJ said, abruptly, "Dottie, I would rather talk about our new friendship right now."

* * * * *

The next morning, they met again at the same park. CJ brought doughnuts and a thermos of coffee. Dottie said, "You seem a bit more upbeat today."

"Well, the more I thought about my ranch problem, the more I thought what a lucky man I am."

"What do you mean by that?" she asked.

"Dottie, even though I may lose everything I own, I feel fortunate to have you for what I feel is my very good friend. Now, I'm afraid it may be becoming something a little more than friendship. I know you said that you are not interested in romance, but I think I have really fallen for you."

"But, CJ, there is such a difference in our ages. I also told you how much Harvey and I were in love, and I miss him so very much," Dottie said. "I must, however, confess that I have developed some feelings for you, but as a friend, feelings which I feel very strongly."

CJ interrupted and tried to say something when Dottie said, "I am not finished. You must understand that Harvey was the only man I have ever been with, and I plan to keep it that way."

CJ said, "Dottie, I must confess that Melba was the first and only woman I have ever been with, and I don't need that from you, as long we care for each other. When I get my money from my grandaddy's will, things will be so much better."

Dottie said, "I am so happy you understand that our relationship is as very good friends. Anyway, you have somehow captured a bit of my heart," she said. "And on that note, I have a gift for you."

"What?" said CJ. "You have a gift for me?"

Dottie handed him a large envelope. CJ curiously opened the envelope to find nothing but $100 bills. He looked up when Dottie said, "Twenty-eight thousand dollars."

CJ seemed overwhelmed and said, "This is too much for you to do."

"Well, since we have become such good friends, I find it my duty to help in any way I can. Plus, I know you will pay me back when you have the money. One condition, CJ, this must be our secret. If my friends found out about this loan, they would give me a very hard time."

"Then it is our secret," replied a delighted CJ. "I'm just so thankful, Dottie. This means so much to me. I can't hardly believe that you are being so good to me. I can save my ranch, start raising alfalfa again, and the hay market is up, so that will help me pay you back even before my grandaddy's money. I'll also pay you interest."

"Nonsense," said Dottie. "I completely trust you, and there will be no interest."

"You have made me a very happy man. Tell you what," proclaimed CJ, "how about tomorrow I take us up to the lake? You'll see how pretty it is, and I'll teach you how to fish. Then, I'll take you to my ranch and show you around. Meet me at Denny's. I'll pick you up tomorrow morning. Right now, I'm going to go visit the tax collector. Let's plan to go to the senior center on Saturday and do some dancing."

"That sounds great!" replied Dottie.

Dottie went home feeling a little giddy, thinking that CJ seemed so happy and upbeat again. She wondered, *Can I really be in love again? He is such a fine man. Uneducated, but truly a wonderful man that I have made so happy.*

* * * * *

CJ watched the last of the bubbles as Dottie went to the bottom of the lake. He looked around, saw no one, and said out loud, "Dottie, you were a fine woman, who has made me twenty-eight thousand dollars richer," as he patted his tackle box containing the money. Her purse had another $200. He took the money, her house and car keys, placed some fishing weights into her purse, and tossed it into the lake. Next, he would pick up his brother, Lester, drop him at Denny's, and give him the car keys to take away Dottie's car and make it disappear. Lester had been very good at this.

CHAPTER THREE

Detective Sergeant Bill Burris of the Layton Police Department was reviewing the missing-person report involving Dottie Lambert and was troubled by what he was reading.

With a population of nearly 300,000, Layton was the largest of the ten incorporated cities within Center County, as well as the county seat. Their police department was generally well thought of. The detective division was top notch with Bill Burris, one of the best.

Detective Sergeant Bill Burris was fifty-three years old and nearing retirement. He was a big man, six two, two hundred pounds. He spent twelve years in the army, mostly working in the Army's Criminal Investigation Detail as a sergeant. While in the army, he had been responsible for solving many very well-known cases.

The most memorable for him was the kidnapping of a United States Army general in Iraq. While the military was negotiating with Al Qaeda for the general's release, CID's Sergeant Bill Burris was frantically, but patiently, trying to find the general. Sergeant Burris knew that, despite whatever deal was made with Al Qaeda, the general would be beheaded before his release. Burris's tenacity as an investigator prevailed when he found the general was being held in a local neighborhood in Iraq. The sergeant had led a squad of special forces into the captive's compound. The raid resulted in safely rescuing the general, along with several previously captured US Marines, while capturing two dozen Al Qaeda insurgents. No one was seriously injured during the raid.

As a result of Sergeant Burris's excellent job of investigating and saving many lives, he was presented The Silver Star by the President of the United States. After the White House ceremony, he took some leave and returned to his hometown, Layton, to visit family and friends. He was met with a hero's welcome. A parade was held in his honor, followed by several speakers, and the Layton Mayor presented him a key to the city.

After twelve years, Sergeant Burris was now faced with reenlisting in the army. He did not possess the necessary education to be considered for promotion to a lieutenant. He knew if he left the army, about all he had learned over the years was investigation.

He stopped by the police department to say hello to his old friend, Police Chief Henry Graham. After catching up, they discussed Burris's dilemma about reenlisting in the army. He was asked by the chief if he had considered becoming a police officer. Burris was only thirty-three years old and shouldn't have any problem with testing or physical abilities. The chief mentioned that he was currently recruiting for officers. Burris made the decision then and there to become a police officer.

He successfully passed all of the tests and was offered a job with the Layton Police Department. He left the army with an honorable discharge and moved his young family to Layton. Bill quickly was promoted to detective sergeant, a position which he loved and was not interested in further promotions. Over the years, Sergeant Burris became a well-known, respected investigator and worked cooperatively with other agencies at the local, state, and federal level. He had received many commendations for his service.

He was now trying to make some sense out of the disappearance of a seventy-nine-year-old woman. Sergeant Burris found very little helpful information in the missing-person report.

Dottie's son, Harvey Lambert Jr., had flown out from Memphis to offer whatever help he might provide. The son was also troubled that his mother's car was missing. The son described his mother as a very stable, no-nonsense type of woman. He had visited her during the past Christmas. She was in good spirits and told Harvey that, other than missing her late husband, she was doing fine. Her son was also administrator of Dottie's estate. He discovered his mother had withdrawn $28,000 at about the time she went missing. He found, in talking with the manager of his mother's bank, they had felt compelled to talk with her about the large cash withdrawal. Dottie had explained the cash was necessary for a family medical emergency. The son couldn't find any evidence of a family medical emergency, unless his mother might have been ill and was trying to be treated privately, with cash. Harvey Jr. explained that his mother was comfortable financially, but far from wealthy. Harvey Jr. left contact information with Sergeant Burris and returned to Memphis.

Burris had done a survey of residents in Dottie's neighborhood. Two neighbors saw her leave in her car on two occasions before she went missing. One lady, who boldly stated, "I'm not the neighborhood snoop," but noticed Dottie the last time she saw her leave in her car, having a spring in her step and whistling. She never saw her or her car again.

Burris followed up on the two friends who attended the senior dance with Dottie. They described her dancing with a cowboy-looking man who Dottie introduced as CK? Or something similar. Dottie explained that she and this cowboy were taking separate cars for dessert at Denny's. That was the last time they ever saw their friend.

The manager of the senior dance remembered Dottie and her friends as regulars of the dance but never danced, just seemed to have a good time watching. He remembered a cowboy attending the dance a couple of times, who he described as a very good dancer. He did not know his name but would check around and call Burris if he found a name. Two days later, the sergeant received a call from the dance hall manager and was told the only cowboy anyone could think of was Carl Johnson, a former rodeo cowboy, who had a ranch in the southern part of the county.

Sergeant Burris drove into Carl Johnson's driveway and was met by a tall lanky man coming out from a barn. Burris introduced himself and shook hands with Carl Johnson, who asked, "Is there a problem?" When it was explained the purpose of the detective's visit and whether Carl knew a Dottie Lambert, he immediately said, "I met a lady named Dottie at the senior dance a while back, what about her?"

"Did you and Dottie leave the dance together?"

"No, sir, we decided to go to Denny's for coffee and pie, but we took our own cars. I have to tell you, she was an elderly woman who told me she hadn't danced for some years, and I guess I had some pity for her; plus, she seemed like a nice person. I could see she was lonely and missing her dead husband something terrible. In fact, he was all she talked about. We had our coffee and dessert and she thanked me and we left. I've never seen her again. I felt a little uneasy because she told me, a complete stranger, that she just was so lonely she thought, at times, about driving her car into a river. What is going on?" asked CJ.

Sergeant Burris explained that he was investigating a missing-person report regarding Dottie Lambert. He thanked Carl and told him he would be in touch if he needed to talk further.

Carl said, "I go by CJ."

As he drove away, the sergeant was thinking something was off with this CJ. He noticed that CJ, at no time, made eye contact with him. Something about this Johnson guy that the veteran sergeant just couldn't put a finger on.

He recontacted Dottie's friends, who both were in agreement that Dottie would never harm herself. *What now?* thought Burris.

CHAPTER FOUR

• • ● ○ ● • •

Three years earlier, CJ was feeding his livestock when a large SUV drove up his driveway. He saw an older, very fit-looking woman exit the vehicle. She was wearing jeans and boots.

He walked over and asked, "May I help you?"

"Are you Mr. Johnson?"

"That's me," he replied.

"You don't know me. We have never met. My name is Sylvia Robinson, and I live in Oakview."

Oakview, CJ recalled, was in a very upscale community in the unincorporated area of Center County.

"I knew Melba when I was taking riding lessons from her, when she taught at the junior college. That is until that terrible thing happened to her. I did send you a sympathy card at the time. Melba was a great lady and excellent riding instructor. I cared very much for her, and then this tragedy struck. Has there ever been any word about her?"

"No, ma'am," he replied. "It has been over two years now. I still have hopes, but I have to tell you that the cops really haven't tried very hard to find her."

"Well, I'm sorry to hear that. Perhaps they may have been trying harder than you think."

"I don't know about that, but I miss her every day."

"I'm sure you do," she replied.

"Anyway, what can I do for you, Ms. Robinson?" asked CJ. "By the way, my name is Carl Johnson, but I go by CJ."

"Please call me Sylvia. Shortly after we lost Melba, the riding program at the college was canceled. I underwent some fairly major surgery. It took some time to recover, and other things in my life took me away from riding. I am now interested in riding again. Do you, by any chance, give riding lessons? Before you say no, I'll tell you I'm prepared to pay you very well. Melba used to mention what a great horseman you are."

"Ma'am, I haven't taught riding in some time. I mostly been trying to make ends meet here with my ranch."

"I understand," said Sylvia. "I'm a business owner."

"Are you any relation to the Robinson Petroleum folks in Oakview?"

"Yes, I actually still own the business. I took the helm when my husband, Jack, passed away. It keeps me pretty busy."

This information brought a sparkle to CJ's eyes. "What level were you riding when Melba was teaching you?"

"I would say advanced beginner, if that makes any sense. I was feeling pretty comfortable at whatever level I was. Actually, let me explain what I'm seeking regarding riding. I have friends that live in Oakside. They have a large ranch and raise cattle. You have probably heard of the De Luccas?"

"Oh yeah, they are big in the cattle business," replied CJ.

"Well, I am sure you're familiar with the big combined cattle drive each year, bringing the cattle down from the Sierras to the Oakside area for the winter."

"Yeah, that takes several days and is sort of the way it was done in the old days," he said.

"It sure is," she said. "The drive has become such a very popular event; many celebrities are now participating. I'm no celebrity, but they have, in fact, invited me to join them. Mr. Johnson, I want more than anything to be able participate in this cattle drive. As I said earlier, I will pay you very handsomely to get me ready."

"This is very interesting," he said. "Tell you what, Ms. Robinson, since you are dressed for riding, if you have the time, we can saddle up my horses and take a little ride around my property. That'll let me take a look at you."

Sylvia rode Louise. He told her it had been Melba's horse. They rode for about a half hour, when he said, "Okay, I'll help you."

She thanked him and expressed how grateful she was.

"In my opinion, you already ride well enough for this drive. The people, especially celebrities, probably don't ride any better than what Melba has trained you. We have to toughen you up a little, get you stronger, and learn to handle unexpected problems. It will take some time for you to get saddle tough. Actually, I have worked cattle most of my life. I know a few of the cowboys who work this drive. I'm sure they charge you a lot of money to go. I have to be honest with you, Ms. Robinson, this is a little bit like a dude ranch, except you put in a full day's work. The cowboys will provide you with well-trained horses who will mostly do the work for you."

"Please call me Sylvia."

"It will be fun though, camping out, eating great outdoor campfire cooking, and listening to cowboy tales. Sleeping in tents and starting the whole thing all over again the next morning. Maybe you'll meet some movie stars."

"That's not what I'm interested in with this drive. I'm sixty-four years old," she said. "I have wanted to do this riding trip for years. I work very hard with the petroleum business and need some different activities including this cattle drive. Jack, my late husband, left me very well-off. Despite the opportunity to be a woman of leisure, I chose to take Jack's place in running the business. Now I realize it's time to have a little fun before it's too late. Jack and I had a cabin built in the Sierras. It's high up a mountaintop with awesome views. We used to go up there when we had a chance. Jack and I soon learned, despite our wonderful views, it is extremely dangerous driving down the mountain. It is terribly steep and often icy. I tell friends, if my brakes should ever fail, I'm probably finished. The view, however, is almost worth the danger. It's another place for me to relax. Then Jack passed away, and I took over running the business. We now have over two hundred employees."

In describing the location, CJ knew the area. *It is steep*, he thought.

For the next several days, he taught her some techniques, particularly knowing what to expect riding up and down rough terrain. He told her, "It isn't likely you will actually be doing much herding cattle; the cowboys don't want anyone getting hurt, but it should be fun. By the way, those cowboys will do all they can to keep you happy. Their tips depend on that."

After the training was finished, he had her riding for lengthy periods of time around the ranch, getting her "toughened up" for long rides in the saddle. Spending so much time together found them becoming pretty close. They had some lunches and one nice dinner together, all Sylvia's treats. CJ had, early on, told the story about Melba's kidnapping. As usual he was pretty convincing as he told Sylvia the story. He made sure to mention that he had not been with another woman since he lost Melba.

Sylvia's response to that was "Don't look at me" in an almost joking, sort of manner. "I'm sorry, CJ," she said, "it isn't that you are not appealing and handsome, you certainly are. My situation is similar to yours in that after Jack, I will never be interested in another man."

Sylvia continued to ride, while CJ continued to plot. Finally, he thought it was time. While Sylvia was taking a break from riding, CJ approached her and said, "You probably can't keep riding here much longer. I'm very sorry."

"What on earth is wrong, CJ?"

"I'm a little embarrassed to tell you."

"Come on, what is it? I think we have become close enough friends that we can share each other's problems."

"Okay, here goes. When I lost Melba, I also lost her income. The hay and cattle market have also been way down the last two years. My mama, back in Tennessee, has been really sick and is not expected to live. I have sent her what little I had to try and make her comfortable. My brother, Lester, and I are her only children."

"I didn't even know that you have a brother. Does he help you out with your mother?"

"No, he isn't able. He is several years younger than me, but Lester is mentally retarded and barely able to take care of himself. I intentionally have not had him meet you, because I'm a little embarrassed about him," he told her. "I also help him out financially, which adds to my current difficulties. So now I have fallen way back on my property taxes and they are threatening to take my ranch for unpaid taxes."

"I'm so sorry to hear that, CJ," she said.

"It isn't your fault," he replied. "It is just that finally, hay prices are way up and I have a really nice crop coming up for harvesting. Plus, a couple dozen steers just about ready for market, but they won't be ready in time either. I never thought it could ever be so bad. I've tried the banks for loans. They won't help me."

She had never seen him be so low, he wasn't a complainer.

"How much do you need?" asked Sylvia.

"I figure about thirty-five thousand dollars will take care of the taxes and leave enough to take care of Mama until the end. She's going very quickly."

Sylvia began to speak, "Well, I—" when CJ interrupted, saying, "Sylvia, don't even think about helping me, if that's what you are about to do."

"That's exactly what I am thinking about doing," she said.

"If anyone found out you loaned money to me, my reputation would be shot," he said, sounding shamed.

"CJ, I know you are a very proud man, but right now you need some help," said Sylvia. "I can easily loan you thirty-five thousand dollars and no one even needs to know. I trust you to pay it back; we don't even need a contract. We will do it the old-fashioned way: we'll shake on it. How about it?"

CJ's heart was beating rapidly, and he had some heartburn discomfort. He was doing his best to stay calm. "I just can't think this is proper for me to accept your being so kind and generous."

"Nonsense," she said.

The following day, Sylvia returned to his ranch. CJ saw she was carrying a briefcase.

"Good morning, CJ!" said Sylvia. She opened the briefcase, and CJ saw nothing but $100 bills. An astonished CJ stood with his mouth hanging open, as Sylvia said, "Thirty-five thousand dollars in cash."

"I don't know how to thank you," he said.

"Well, fortunately I have the means to help you," she said. But then Sylvia said, "This a loan which you must pay back as soon as you sell your hay and cattle, so I expect full payment in sixty days with eight percent interest. Don't forget, I am a businesswoman. I have not revealed any of this to anyone, so you can keep your pride intact. Let's shake on the loan," which they did.

"That's all fine, Sylvia. Now I can pay my taxes and help my mama. You have saved my ranch. Thank you from the bottom of my heart."

Shortly after, he told her she was ready for the cattle drive. Sylvia thanked him for all the great riding instruction. She announced, "I am going up to the cabin tonight. I need a few days off and some quiet time for myself."

"Do you have dogs you take with you?" he asked.

"No, I don't have dogs," she replied.

As she was leaving, she called to CJ, "Don't forget to pay back the loan as promised."

"I won't," he replied. "And thank you again, you are really helping me."

CJ called Lester. "Get over here, we have to take a little trip."

CHAPTER FIVE

S ylvia arrived at her cabin and was grateful the road was clear of
ice. She planned on going shopping in the village the following
day, thinking of buying a gift for CJ, since he had been so helpful.
She was pleased CJ had made an exception in her case and helped
her get ready for the cattle drive. The cattle drive had been going
for many years. It was extensively covered by the media, both on
the ground as well as aerial coverage. Sylvia knew that her ego was
mostly what made participating in this so important to her. Just driving large herds of cattle many miles, sleeping and eating outdoors,
driving the herds through the middle of small towns, seemed just
what she needed. Meeting some celebrities, she admitted to herself,
could be the chance of a lifetime. More importantly, she had plenty

of money and counted on doing the cattle drive as something of a vacation.

While sitting cozy by the fireplace, she reflected on her life with Jack. He had taken a great risk in buying into a small petroleum business. With Jack working countless hours, and with his business acumen, the Robinson Petroleum Company was born. It was now one of largest of this type of business in the state. Jack had been the very best husband, partner, and father she could imagine. She missed him so much.

* * * * *

As Sylvia slept soundly, CJ and Lester quietly drove up the hill near Sylvia's cabin which, in the moonlight, looked more like a mansion than a cabin. Her car was parked out front.

CJ dropped off Lester near where she was sound asleep. CJ already knew that she didn't have dogs. Lester very quietly crawled beneath her car. He was carrying two different types of side cutters. Lester proceeded to cut all four brake lines, then quickly ran down the road to where his brother was waiting.

"That was easy work for five hundred dollars. Thank you, CJ."

* * * * *

The following morning, Sylvia, for some reason, felt something was just not right about CJ's story. It had begun bothering her the night before. She decided to call the county tax collector, whom she had known for years. In fact, she had contributed to her election campaign.

Rita O'Conner said, "Hi, Sylvia, nice to hear from you." They exchanged some pleasantries. "I hope we haven't done anything wrong with your tax bill."

"Oh, nothing like that, Rita," she said. "I'm calling regarding someone who is very delinquent on his taxes."

"Well, it is a matter of public record. Give me a name and I'll check it out."

"Carl Johnson. He has a ranch south of Layton."

"Oh, you must mean CJ."

"Yes."

"I can tell you without looking he doesn't owe any back taxes. He and Melba, well, before she disappeared, have never owed any back taxes. In fact, CJ doesn't believe in banks, always pays his annual taxes in cash. I am looking at his file right now, and he is paid in full. He always grumbles when he comes in to pay, but that is all. He is completely paid up."

Sylvia managed to contain her anger long enough to thank Rita. They agreed to have lunch together soon. When she recovered from the shock, she was outraged. CJ had always paid his taxes on time and was not delinquent. She had been bilked. At first, she felt sick to her stomach, then her anger returned. How could she have been so stupid? She had considered herself to be a very astute businesswoman. She should have known better. Her judgment had been caught up in pity and sympathy for CJ. Well, she no longer had any nice thoughts about him.

As she sat, fuming, she called her longtime friend, Sheriff Tom Gentry. She and Jack had been friends with Tom for many years. They had contributed heavily to his campaigns for the office of sheriff. He had proven himself to be a great sheriff.

"Hi, Tom," she said when he answered.

"Hello, Sylvia," said the sheriff. "It has been a while, what's up?" he asked.

"Tom, I am embarrassed to say, I have been bilked."

Tom chuckled softly. "That is very unlike you, my friend."

"It's true, I have never been so stupid."

"So, what happened?" he asked.

"I would rather discuss it with you in person. I'm up at the cabin, and as soon as I close it up, I will be down to see you."

"Okay," he said. "You need to be careful. That downgrade is pretty steep, especially for someone as upset as you are, Sylvia. As you remember, I tried to talk you and Jack out of building up that road."

"I know, Tom, I'll be careful. See you soon then, and thanks, Tom."

Sylvia closed up the cabin, wishing she could stay longer, but knew she couldn't rest until she discussed this matter with Tom. She started her SUV, which was pointed toward the road. She coasted to the road and turned down the hill. She was grateful there was no ice. As she approached the first curve, she depressed the brake pedal, which felt very soft and spongy. Next, as she gained speed, the brake pedal went to the floorboard. Sylvia felt immediately, her deepest fear about this road was brake failure.

After she made it through the first curve, she tried downshifting, but the vehicle continued developing speed. She now was exceeding sixty miles per hour and gaining speed. Sylvia and Jack had developed a plan in the event something like this happened. They had picked a spot on the right side of the road to crash in order to stop the car. She realized, too late, she had already passed that spot.

She saw the next, almost-hairpin curve approaching. Continuing to pump the brake pedal, she was gripped with panic and terror and knew she was going to die. As her vehicle went through the curve, she was suddenly airborne. Her last thoughts were of Jack and her family while she plummeted in space, screaming the entire fall. Her vehicle, landing on its top a thousand feet below, burst into flames. Then all was quiet.

*   *   *   *   *

Sheriff Gentry asked his watch commander to dispatch a deputy up to Mrs. Robinson's cabin. The sheriff explained she didn't meet with him as scheduled and didn't answer her phone. This was unlike her. The next couple of hours were anxious for him while he awaited news. The cabin was some distance, being in the easternmost part of his county.

"Sheriff," his watch commander said, "we think we have some bad news. Our deputy up there reports there is a burned-out vehicle of some sort below Mrs. Robinson's road. It is still smoking. There isn't anyone at her cabin."

"Oh no," said Sheriff Gentry. "What type of vehicle?" he asked.

"Can't tell, Sheriff, I have already put together our search-and-rescue team. It will take some doing just to get down there. As you know, it is very difficult terrain."

"Yes, it is. Please keep me posted, Lieutenant."

The sheriff pondered the call he had earlier received from Sylvia Robinson. She seemed distraught when she told him she had been bilked. What on earth did she want to discuss with him that she wanted to talk in person? He decided he needed to drive up to the scene and see for himself. He and the watch commander, Lieutenant Jim Watkins, drove up to the accident scene. They observed the search-and-rescue team had made it down to the burned-out wreckage.

The search-and-rescue team leader was standing on the roadway near several sheriffs' vehicles. He greeted the sheriff and lieutenant, saying, "Sorry, Sheriff, there isn't much of anything left of the car. We have found what appear to be traces of human bones. This fire was extremely hot, leaving nothing much recognizable."

Sheriff Gentry told the lieutenant, "Have our pathologist brought up here, along with our crime scene team."

Lieutenant Watkins asked, "Do you believe this is something more than a vehicle accident, Sheriff?"

"I am not sure of anything right now," said Sheriff Gentry. "Let's go up to Mrs. Robinson's cabin, Jim," he told the lieutenant.

Her cabin was secure. They didn't find anything seemingly wrong around the cabin and were preparing to leave when Lieutenant Watkins said, "Wait a minute, Sheriff, look at this." He was pointing to four, uniformly placed, liquid appearing spots on the driveway. The lieutenant put a finger on one of the spots, sniffed it, and held his finger for the sheriff to smell. "Brake fluid!" they said together.

"Oh my god!" the sheriff cried out. "Get the crime scene team up here fast. Get in touch with Captain Broadmoor. I want our homicide team up here as soon as possible. Sylvia may very well have been murdered."

They found four empty buckets behind Sylvia's cabin which, after taking photos of the brake fluid, they placed over the spots, hoping to keep them from evaporating.

It took a great deal of effort to finally remove Sylvia's SUV or what little was left of the car. They enlisted the aid of a nearby rancher who came in from below with a team of draft horses and dragged the remains of the vehicle some distance to the road to an awaiting tow truck. The vehicle's remains were taken to the county storage facility. It did very little to resemble the beautiful vehicle it had once been. Fortunately for the detectives, Sylvia's license plate had broken free on impact and was found nearby. Without the plate, it was unlikely they could have identified the vehicle, as every part had melted from the intense heat of the fire.

CHAPTER SIX

aptain Broadmoor's homicide investigators were pretty much stumped. The only physical evidence had been what was established as brake fluid by the crime laboratory. There was nothing left of the vehicle to determine whether the brake lines had been tampered with.

The investigation was mostly met with statements from Sylvia's friends; all of whom thought she didn't have an enemy in the world. Sheriff Gentry received a call from a banker friend, Cornell Thompson. "Tom," he said to the sheriff, "this may be nothing, but you should know."

"Know what?" asked the sheriff.

"Just before Sylvia's death, she withdrew a sizable amount of cash. You know I can't share the amount without a subpoena. I can tell you, however, it was not uncommon for Sylvia to withdraw sizable amounts of cash, usually for business purposes. We both know she was very wealthy."

"Of course, Cornell. We will get a subpoena right away. Thanks very much, my friend."

"I can only hope it will help in some way," said the banker. "Sylvia was a great woman."

Chief of Detectives, Captain Broadmoor, assembled his homicide team. "As you all know, we searched Mrs. Robinson's bank account by using a subpoena and found, shortly before her death, she withdrew thirty-five thousand dollars. She was a very wealthy businesswoman, so this transaction only mildly, if at all, caused any suspicion. Any ideas what Mrs. Robinson did with the thirty-five thousand she withdrew?" he asked. There was no response.

"We have been tracking her activities up until her death," said Lieutenant Jeff Travis, homicide team leader. "We have just learned Mrs. Robinson had been taking riding lessons from a cowboy south of Layton. We haven't any idea who he might be. We are following up on this after our meeting. This is a tough one, Captain," said Lieutenant Travis.

Lieutenant Jeff Travis was a veteran of seventeen years with the Center County Sheriff's Department. He was born in Oklahoma in 1945 and lived there until his high school graduation, at which time he enrolled in The University of Oklahoma. Beginning his sophomore year, the Vietnam war was starting to rage and he received his draft notice. Being part of a very patriotic family, he joined the army.

Those two years of his life, including one tour of combat, changed his outlook on life dramatically. He watched a friend die in his arms, realizing there was nothing he could do to save him, all the while wondering, *Why not me? I was standing right next to him.* His final year was spent in Washington State working as a military policeman, which he thoroughly enjoyed. On his discharge, he returned home for a while and reenrolled in the university for a year. One day, he found job openings in Center County for the sheriff's department, some fourteen hundred miles away. He applied, tested, interviewed, and was accepted.

He truly loved his job as second in command of the detective division, although lieutenants were not usually bureau chiefs. Center County had an unusual number of violent crimes. Due to gang fights and murders, they were way above the norm. Since the other bureaus such as property crimes, auto theft, arson, and drug enforcement were supervised by sergeants, Jeff spent most of his time managing the major crimes bureau. He had, in fact, declined to take the Captain's Test, as he, being a lieutenant, was able to take an active role in investigations, which he thoroughly enjoyed.

Jeff had been happily married to the same woman, Pakuna, for over twenty years. They had five children. Pakuna was Native American and held true to her culture, her name meaning "deer running downhill." She taught indigenous studies at the local junior college. Pakuna remained in contact and active with her tribe, which still numbered at nearly four thousand people. Their oldest son had made the decision to involve himself with their tribe, which made both Pakuna and Jeff very proud. Jeff's father had been raised in Oklahoma and had been part of the Kiowa Tribe.

One of the detectives mentioned, "The only real cowboy in that area is Carl Johnson, CJ as most of us know him. He's the guy who reported his wife, Melba, as being kidnapped a couple of years ago. It's been a very suspicious case. He's been a real pain in the ass, accusing us of not doing enough to find her," said the detective.

"Jeff," said Captain Broadmoor, "set up a visit with this CJ the cowboy. As a suggestion, you might want to use his reported kidnapping case as a ruse to get him a bit more comfortable by your sudden

---

visit. If, in fact, he's the guy who has been giving Mrs. Robinson riding lessons."

"Good idea, Captain," said Lieutenant Travis.

"Of course, it is," said the captain jokingly. "I *am* the captain."

* * * * *

Lieutenant Travis and his homicide detectives met to strategize their approach to visiting Carl Johnson. If he had been the person giving the riding lessons, where do they go with that information? As Detective Sergeant Bill Morris was the case officer on the alleged kidnapping of Melba Johnson, he selected Detective Lynn Hoover to assist him with the visit to see Carl Johnson.

* * * * *

Bill Morris was a local product being born in Center County. His parents were responsible hardworking people. His father worked in a local manufacturing plant for most of his adult life. He had retired several years ago at age sixty-eight. With Social Security, plus a small pension, they got by.

Bill's mother was the same age as Bill's father. She was primarily a homemaker, raising Bill and his two younger brothers. She did augment the family income over the years with seasonal employment at the canneries. Both the mother and father provided a stable life for their three sons.

As Bill was growing, he could have been described as average. He received average grades. He played several sports while in high school, but only as an average player. Upon graduating high school, he wasn't interested in college, so he enlisted in the Navy, where he proved to be an average sailor. That is until one fateful day.

Bill had the watch on deck of a Navy Destroyer. They were at sea doing training maneuvers when a massive fuel line, which fed the ships engines, ruptured. Soon, the spewing fuel caught fire. With all of the pressure of the fuel which was still pumping, the situation was critical. Many seamen were soon to be roasted alive. Seaman Bill Morris remembered seeing the turn off wheel valve, but to get to it he put his life at great risk, running through the intense flames. He found the wheel valve which required two men to turn it off. With his hands being burned, he somehow found the strength to turn off the fuel supply. Seaman Morris saved the lives of a great number of men and women and quite likely the ship itself. He spent the next several weeks in a burn unit recovering from severe burns to his hands and arms. On release from the hospital, Seaman Bill Morris was summoned to the White House where he was awarded the Navy Cross. He returned home to a similar ceremony as had been given to Bill Burris, a parade, and the key to the city. Layton and Center County truly knew how to welcome home their heroes. Bill received an above-average honorable discharge from the United States Navy.

He had thought over the past few years of becoming a police officer. After the Navy, he enrolled in the local community college, taking courses directed toward law enforcement. In college, he began dating Peggy Martin. They had grown up together but were never close. Their romance blossomed rapidly. They were soon engaged to be married.

Bill began looking into different law enforcement positions in the local cities and county. He additionally looked into the Highway Patrol. In talking with the sheriff, Bill was convinced he wanted to be a deputy sheriff. He applied, tested, and was hired. His first year was spent working in the county jail. He would later frequently remark, "Working in the jail gave me a greater perspective of many different types of personalities."

Bill and Peggy married and, in a couple of years, had their first of six children. Bill worked patrol for several years and did above-average work. He was scheduled to be transferred on rotation to the Detective Bureau.

While off duty, in plain clothes, he was in line at his bank, when two armed men came into the bank both yelling, "EVERYBODY FREEZE! THIS IS A HOLDUP!" The frightened looks on the customers told Bill he better just stay quiet, until the elderly unarmed bank guard touched his insulin pump. The first gunman must have thought the man was reaching for a weapon as he shot and killed the bank guard.

Bill dropped into a crouch shouting, "Police, drop your weapon!" The first shooter turned toward Bill, who shot the gunman in the chest, dropping him to the floor. Bill stood and faced the other gunman who began firing at Bill. He shot Bill through the knee. The pain was excruciating, but as he was going down, he got off a shot, killing the other gunman. Two customers suffered non-fatal gunshot wounds from the second robber. As he was lying on the floor, in great pain, Bill Morris was hoping the knee injury would not be career ending for him.

His knee injury was bad. The bullet passed through the knee cap, taking bone and ligaments as it exited. He received the medal of valor. He was offered a medical disability retirement. When he declined, the sheriff made an exception and allowed him to remain with the department. Although he would walk with a limp for the rest of his life and would not likely be chasing people on foot, he was to become an exceptional investigator. When he recovered from the knee wound, he was transferred to Detectives.

He began as a detective, later was promoted to detective sergeant where he enjoyed a stellar career. More than twenty years later, approaching retirement, he was now working a case of a possible psychopathic killer named Carl Johnson.

Lynn Hoover was a former juvenile detective whose excellent investigative abilities soon caught the attention of Captain Broadmoor. She gladly accepted the transfer to the homicide team and was doing a first-rate job in her new assignment.

Lynn was thirty-five years old. She had grown up in Orange County, California, living most of her early years in Anaheim.

Her mother had worked as a probation officer for the Orange County Probation Office. At age thirty-six, when she was a supervising probation officer, she developed breast cancer. Despite her courageous fight against this terrible disease, she died on her thirty-seventh birthday. Lynn, the only child, was eleven years old when her mother passed.

Lynn's father was a detective sergeant with the Los Angeles Police Department. As a workaholic, it caused him a great deal of grief suddenly becoming the only parent to an eleven-year-old daughter. He did his best for Lynn. Slowing down his pace at work proved to be difficult.

Lynn was grief-stricken by the loss of her mother. Things an eleven-year-old girl had to deal with, such as puberty, proved awkward discussing with her father. Having been raised Catholic, and attending Catholic schools, made her discussions with her father a bit easier, as she had the good fortune to meet Sister Josephine. The sister worked with her during these awkward times in Lynn's life.

Sister Josephine was there as Lynn matured. Her school subjects came easy to Lynn. She graduated high school with honors and scholarship offers. During her high school junior year, she met a boy named Troy. He was a senior, a year ahead of her. They seemed to be in love. Lynn sought advice from Sister Josephine who insisted that Lynn remain a virgin. Virginity was very difficult for Lynn to strive for, with the constant pressure from Troy. One particular night of passionate necking, Lynn gave up her virginity to Troy. Six weeks later, Lynn knew she was pregnant. Her father nearly had a heart attack. Sister Josephine was deeply hurt. She and Troy decided to get married.

Despite her father's reservations and Troy's parent's reluctance, they were married in a civil ceremony at the courthouse. Troy's parents agreed the young couple could live with them. Lynn's father chipped in enough that their kids could remain in school. It wasn't long before things became oppressive to all involved. Troy wanted to hang with his friends; Lynn wasn't happy with the situation of living with Troy's parents.

One day, Lynn was going down the stairs with a load of laundry when she tripped and fell down almost the entire flight of stairs. No one was home when Lynn began bleeding and lost the baby. Everything went very quickly. An annulment sought by the unhappy couple was granted, and they went back to where it all started. Lynn graduated high school and entered college with a major in criminology. In her senior year, her father retired, and within a year he died of lung cancer.

After graduation, Lynn joined the Los Angeles County Sheriff's Department. After a few years of working patrol, she felt a need to move to a quieter environment. Quite by accident, while at the laundromat doing her laundry, she was reading a newspaper someone had left. She found the Center County Sheriff's Department was recruiting for deputy sheriffs. It was several hundred miles north, likely quieter, which is what she was looking for. She applied and was hired.

She found it be the best decision, a smaller community with a greater sense of individuality. Center County wasn't Los Angeles, with thousands of officers, but it wasn't Hicksville either. The sheriff's department had several hundred deputies and correctional officers. The sheriff believed in training and education, which fit her profile. While working in patrol, she distinguished herself with her investigative abilities. It wasn't long before she was transferred to Detectives. She found herself working many sex crimes and putting away sex offenders, including pedophiles.

She was transferred to the major crimes unit and began what seemed to be a career working the Carl Johnson case.

* * * * *

CJ was working in his tack room when he saw what he knew to be a detective undercover car. He recognized Sergeant Bill Morris but didn't know the attractive woman with him.

"Hello, Mr. Johnson. How are you, sir?" said Sergeant Morris. "I'd like you to meet Detective Lynn Hoover." CJ ignored her outstretched hand.

"Do you have news about Melba?" asked CJ.

"Sorry, nothing new. We just thought maybe you may have heard something which we could follow up with. We realize it has been two years now since she disappeared."

"Well, as far as I'm concerned, you haven't done a damn thing," said CJ, the visible anger rising in his voice.

"You know, Mr. Johnson, your attitude against us doesn't make things any better," said the sergeant. "We have done everything we can do; in fact, we have just assigned Melba's case to Detective Hoover here. She is an outstanding investigator and will give a fresh look into your case."

"Is that a fact?" said CJ.

"I was just given your case, Mr. Johnson, and hope we can work together. At least give me a chance," Detective Hoover said, convincingly.

"Well, you can't do any worse than this guy," said CJ, referring to the sergeant.

As they turned to leave, Sergeant Morris asked, "By the way, were you, by any chance, giving riding lessons to a Mrs. Sylvia Robinson?"

They both saw CJ's face turn pale, as he swallowed hard.

"Yes, I am, why do you ask?"

"You haven't heard?"

"Heard what?" asked CJ.

"It is our sad duty to tell you, Mrs. Robinson was killed recently in an auto accident," said Lynn.

After a pause, CJ said, "Oh my god, no! I can't believe it; how did it happen?"

"Her SUV went off of a cliff near her mountain cabin," said Lynn.

"That's just terrible. She was such a nice lady," he said. "Was she alone?" he asked.

"As far as we can tell she was alone," said Detective Hoover. "It was a very gruesome accident," she told him.

"Have you been up to her cabin?" asked Sergeant Morris.

Before he answered, CJ felt that painful heartburn again. "No, what reason would I have to go to her cabin?" he asked. "I didn't even know she had a cabin."

"No reason, just thought she might have mentioned it to you," said the sergeant. "Well, we need to get back to work. Just wanted you to meet Detective Hoover. As I mentioned, she will be taking over your wife's case."

"Thank you for your time, Mr. Johnson. Here is my card," Lynn offered. "Call if you hear of anything new." As they drove away, Lynn said, "It could just be my female intuition or detective intuition, but something about that guy scares the hell out of me." They returned to the office where Detective Hoover began reading the Sylvia Robinson case file.

The file contained a number of crime scene photos, including the video recording of the burned-out vehicle and the crash site, the four liquid spots from the victim's driveway, and the cabin which had been thoroughly searched. The only fingerprints found in the cabin were from Mrs. Robinson. Lynn Hoover felt, for a homicide case, the file was very sparse.

Lynn was assigned the Sylvia Robinson homicide. She tiringly worked the case. Lynn spent several days interviewing Sylvia's friends and employees. For some reason, she kept coming back to Carl Johnson. "What was it about this guy?" she asked herself. Soon, however, she was assigned other cases, and the Robinson file became buried under other, more current, cases.

CJ, on the other hand, spent the next three years fully expecting more visits from the detectives about Sylvia Robinson which, to his relief, never happened.

Then he met Dottie.

CHAPTER SEVEN

---•—•—○—•—•---

The Center County detectives were milling around, awaiting Monday morning roll call and briefing. Suddenly, "Attention new Skipper on board."

"As you were," said Captain Ron Willis, their new detective division commander. "As my first order of business, there will be no further saluting unless, as an example, we are dressed in our Class A uniform or some other special circumstances. Is everyone on board with this?"

"YES, SIR" was the response.

"I also hold to the chain of command; however, my door is open to personal issues or complaints which cannot be resolved with your supervisor. Any questions?" Silence. "Okay, you recently lost your former commander, Captain Larry Broadmoor, from a massive heart attack. He seemed to be the fittest man I've ever known, but we never know. As you may know, I said his eulogy, as we were the best of friends, having started with this department on the same date. I assure each of you I'll do my best to try and fill his shoes. I did spend several years in Detectives as a detective sergeant, so I do bring considerable investigative experience to you. I know many of you; some, however, we have never worked together. So, let's begin with each of you bureau supervisors. I want, on Friday, a summary of your cases, especially those which need immediate attention. Additionally, as new budgets are upon us, what you need and what you wish to have, including new technology. I'm looking forward to working with all of you. By the way, beers are on me tonight."

"Way to go, Captain!" was the unanimous reply.

Captain Willis felt strange occupying his old friend's office. They went way back, beginning their careers, working in the county jail together, an assignment required for new deputies. His friend's sudden death had truly bothered him. They had been friends for many years.

He spent the day settling in. He reviewed many files and statistics regarding crime reports and how they stood with crimes solved. After work they met at Elroy's, the local cop watering hole, where more than a few careers had come to an abrupt end for cops from many different agencies within the county, usually because of booze and related problems such as women. The captain paid attention to how his new crew handled their drinking. Most only had one or two beers, while some seemed to be heavy drinkers. Alcoholism, along with marital problems, was not uncommon in police work.

Captain Willis had lost his wife several years ago to cancer and lived a pretty good bachelor life, raising their sixteen-year-old son. He had worked several other command assignments over the years, including uniformed patrol, incarceration facilities, and administrative services. He was looking forward to being chief of detectives. He was presently romantically involved with a local physician, Dr. Cheryl Patterson, a radiology specialist, who had also lost her husband to cancer. They enjoyed each other's company and thought it may lead to something more serious, but for the present they lived apart, she with her fifteen-year-old daughter. Their romance was exclusive.

When Ron had lost Wendy, it was more than he thought he could take. Having a young son as well made it even more troubling. His son, now sixteen, was a great young man. A good deal of the way they accepted their loss of Wendy could be attributed to their

Catholic faith. Father O'Brien had spent countless hours working with both him and his son, Greg. Ron felt the help which he and Greg received from Father O'Brien had, in fact, helped the three of them to become very good friends. The priest was from Ireland. He was a former first-rate soccer player in Ireland. He was great in encouraging Greg with his participation in various sports and his studies as well. "A father could never be more proud," Ron said of his son, Greg.

As to Dr. Cheryl Patterson, despite the loss of her husband, she felt she had found a kindred spirit in Captain Ron Willis. Their children seemed to like each other. Ron was a great lover. She knew she was hopelessly in love with the guy, so, if he didn't pop the question soon, she would do it; she loved this guy so much.

Captain Willis spent the rest of the work week reviewing performance evaluations, statistics, and many case file data, getting a feel as to how well his detectives were doing. His career had been a success. After working the county jail for a year, he began working a squad car for a couple of years. This was followed as a Bailiff to an incredibly great superior court judge. From there he went to Detectives. His first detective cases were burglaries. His outstanding case clearance came to the attention of the chief of detectives. He was then sent to special crimes against person training, which included homicide investigations. From there he began his successful career in the investigation of these types of cases.

He and his late partner, Henry Marshall, had successfully solved the case, referred by the media as "The Midnight Rapist," a case of national notoriety. Since he and his partner had actually solved the case, they were part of the task force assigned to make the arrest. When the arrest warrants were issued for the suspect, Darrel Evans, he had been tipped of the pending arrest and was waiting for them. Evans had set up a bunker at his home, where he ambushed the arresting officers using a high-powered, scoped rifle. Henry was struck in the head and died instantly. Two other officers were also hit, but survived. Evans fatally shot himself with a handgun. Willis suffered severe depression over the loss of his friend and partner, but some great counseling brought him back successfully.

By Friday, he was ready for feedback from his bureau chiefs. He saved the homicide/crimes against persons chief for the last interview. This bureau was responsible for the investigation of major crimes: homicide, rape, kidnapping, armed robbery, and aggravated assault. The supervisor was Lieutenant Jeffery Travis, who had been an excellent investigator for many years and had the respect of Captain Willis.

"So, Jeff," said the captain, "you seem to have your bureau in pretty good shape. As always, however, you are way over budget on overtime."

"As you know, our success in solving homicides require we go full on with a new homicide and try to solve them within forty-eight hours," replied the lieutenant. "That eats up lots of overtime."

"I understand," replied Willis, "which leads me to begin seeking two additional detectives to your bureau. Anyway, I'm still getting my feet wet with my new assignment. I think with some additional investigators, we may try to establish a cold case unit. With all the things we see occurring with DNA, we have a good opportunity to solve some of these older, cold cases."

"I'm pleased to hear that," replied Lieutenant Travis. "Captain Broadmoor tried with last year's budget to increase our staff but, as you remember, it was a tight budget year. Hopefully, this upcoming budget will be a little better," said the lieutenant. They talked some more when Lieutenant Travis mentioned a troubling case.

"So tell me about it," said Willis.

"We have a guy who has a ranch south of town who reported his wife kidnapped about five years ago. He's now about fifty-five. He just appeared suspicious to us when he made the report. There has been no trace of her. Her family told us they had been having marital problems when she went missing. She told her sisters that her husband had been knocking her around, and it was getting worse. Melba told her sisters she was going to leave him just prior to her disappearance. Her late father left her some money. She opened a bank account, in her name only, which really upset this guy. We have talked with him several times, but he claims she was kidnapped. Here is the file, Captain, we hope you'll take a look at it."

"Sure," replied Willis. "What's this guy's name?"

"Carl Johnson, goes by CJ" was the reply. "Carl Johnson had also been mentioned three years ago in the homicide investigation of Sylvia Robinson, a very good friend of Sheriff Gentry. It seems he had been giving her horseback riding lessons shortly before she was murdered. If you remember, Captain, her brake lines were tampered with, we believe."

"I do remember the case. So it has never been solved?" he asked.

"No, sir. Sergeant Hoover is assigned the case but, quite frankly, it has been on the back burner for lack of evidence regarding Carl Johnson. CJ remains Lynn's only person of interest."

CHAPTER EIGHT

Carl Johnson was born near Layton. His parents were not well educated. His mother, Thelma, graduated from high school, but in his father's words, "I don't much cotton to book learning." Carl's father, David Johnson, was an auto mechanic and seemed to always smell of automotive grease. The family lived in a small wood-framed house with a detached garage which was always occupied with cars that needed fixing, as his father moonlighted privately, working on cars at their home. Their lives were pretty quiet until Carl's younger brother was born.

Lester, they knew very soon, wasn't quite right. This immediately caused arguments between Carl's parents. His father was angry and blamed his mother and her side of the family for Lester's mental problems. Thelma had an uncle who had suffered from some form of mental illness, which his father always brought up in discussions about Lester. This is when Carl's father began drinking very heavily, and he was a mean drunk.

Carl's father explained to him early on, "Lester is your responsibility. You need to watch out for him." As they grew older, the first time Lester came home and had been beaten up, Carl's father, David, beat Carl severely. "You were told to take care of that idiot. Don't let that happen again, or you'll get worse next time." Lester's mental illness seemed to encourage bullies to torment and beat him. Carl couldn't always be around to protect his younger brother, resulting in their father beating Carl, who was seemingly always suffering from broken ribs and severe bruising.

Their mother would not intervene, knowing that would only result in more beatings to her by her drunken husband. Carl watched the beatings of his mother. Often wanting to intervene, however, he knew the beating would then focus on him.

Carl was usually fighting the bullies who had hurt Lester. There was one time a bully had slapped Lester around, resulting in Lester receiving a black eye. Carl was enraged but knew the bully was much bigger and tougher, and Carl would only get himself beaten up. Carl devised a plan. He began following the bully, Oscar Ripone, learning his habits. He nearly caught Carl following him one dark night. Carl had turned back and ran down a dark alley. Oscar finally quit trying to find who had followed him. He probably shouldn't have given up his search so quickly, as Carl was only ten feet away, behind a telephone pole. Soon after, on a moonless night, Carl was waiting to see if Oscar was taking his usual path home. When he turned into the predicted alley, he did not hear the young man wielding a baseball bat come up quietly behind him. Carl swung his best home-run swing directly to Oscar's head. The only sound Oscar made was his large frame hitting the dirt alleyway. Carl swung the bat into Oscar's head and torso many more times. Carl ran toward home, stopping briefly to crawl into a dumpster. He went through several layers of trash before leaving the bat, which he covered with the vile smelling garbage, then ran home. As Carl entered his bedroom, a very warm, pleasurable feeling came over him. He hadn't planned on killing Oscar Ripone; his intent was to hurt him badly, but when he hit Oscar and saw him fall to the ground, he just couldn't stop. Just thinking about what he had done only twenty minutes ago gave Carl an erection. That was about the time that it occurred to him that he might enjoy killing people.

The following day, while Carl was out mowing neighbor's lawns, two police detectives came to the Johnson home. The detectives said they were following up on a homicide of a local boy, Oscar Ripone. They wanted to speak to Lester about the murder of the young man from the neighborhood. A shocked Mrs. Johnson, said, "I know the Ripone family, and we know of Oscar. Somebody killed him?" she said.

"Yes, ma'am, we are afraid so."

"But why are you here and wanting to talk to Lester? I don't think Lester even knows the young man," his mother said. "Lester is a little boy, as well as mentally retarded. He didn't murder anyone," she said, protectively.

They said they were following up on a report that Lester had an altercation with the victim, Oscar Ripone.

"Well," she said, "Oscar was a big bully, and he did hurt my son two days ago. He gave my little boy a black eye." Lester's mother called him into the room. His black eye was even worse. His mother said, "Just look at his eye. Oscar did that to him. I'm not sad that Oscar is dead. I do feel for his parents, though, especially his mother."

The detectives talked briefly with Lester. They found him to be very small, as well as retarded. Lester told them that he thought

Oscar was a mean boy who had hit him and caused his black eye. He further stated, "He's way too big for me to fight with." He was asked if he owned a baseball bat. He said, "No, sir, but I sure hope I might get one for my birthday." After talking with him, the detectives felt no reason to suspect Lester. When they asked him if he knew anyone that might have done this to Oscar, Lester hesitated, then said, "I think he had a fight the other day with Jimmy Roberts." The detectives thanked Lester and Mrs. Johnson and left.

Carl had almost returned home when he noticed the unmarked police car parked in front of his house. He turned around with his lawn mower and pushed the mower back up the street. He waited in a neighbor's driveway until he saw two detective-looking men leave the house. When they were out of sight, he returned home. His mother told him about the detectives being there. He found it interesting that they had come to talk with Lester.

Lester shouted to Carl, "I told them it was probably Jimmy Roberts who killed Oscar. Remember, Carl? Jimmy and Oscar had that fight after school?"

"That's right, Mom. Lester is right, they did have a fight. Jimmy probably did this thing." Carl just hoped the cops wouldn't want to talk to him.

The murder of Oscar Ripone was in the newspaper and on the television news for several days but finally went away. Much to Carl's relief, the cops never returned.

Carl thought again that he might enjoy killing people.

Life went on as usual in the Johnson household. His father was never told about the visit from the detectives. His father continued to drink heavily. Their mother didn't have a chance. Any sort of conflict would result in their father beating their mother. During one of those earlier beatings of his mother, when Lester was four or five, he grabbed his father, trying to protect his mother. His father, who was well over two hundred pounds, with a closed fist, hit little Lester directly in the head. An unconscious Lester fell to the floor. His father started to kick him when his mother screamed, "You can hit me all you want, but if you ever lay another hand on that little boy, I will kill you." For the first time in David Johnson's married life, he was sober enough to be afraid of his wife. Lester remained unconscious for almost three days. David refused to call for medical help for his son. He told his wife and Carl, "If he dies, our story is he came home from school and told us he had fallen from the monkey bars and landed on his head. He seemed fine except for sleeping a lot. Besides, there isn't any head injury that will make him any more retarded, the little son of a bitch." The drinking quickly overtook any fear he had of his wife, so the beatings continued.

Carl asked his mother many times, "Why do you let him beat up on you?"

"I need him to take care of us" was her usual response.

This pattern continued for years. Carl was now in his teens. He'd gotten a part-time job at a local ranch. This gave him the chance to become a cowboy. He was growing tall and lanky. Soon he was bucking hay as well as the older men. The ranch owner liked CJ, as he now called himself. He was given the chance to work with the horses. He thoroughly enjoyed breaking horses, working cattle, and many other ranch jobs.

Things at home, however, had not changed. After his father had brutally beaten their mother, once again, CJ and Lester devised a plan, as well as Lester could. David, their father, seemed to always be working beneath a car up on some pretty unstable jacks. They schemed for the right moment. When that opportunity came, they both ran together and hit the car with their bodies as hard as they could to see it fall upon their screaming father. When they were satisfied he was dead, they ran into the house, shouting, "Mom! Dad is hurt! Call 911!"

Now CJ felt a greater sense of freedom. He also felt something inside himself again, much like the feeling he had gotten when he had killed Oscar Ripone. Killing someone excited him. As he heard his father's dying cries from the weight of the car on his chest, CJ had an almost sexual feeling. It felt good. He knew Lester would keep their secret about their father's death.

CJ was now seventeen and tired of school. He had started to date. Amy was the first one he had sex with. They were going steady, at least according to her. CJ was, however, secretly seeing other girls. After several months, CJ tired of Amy and broke up with her. She was not terribly unhappy with the breakup. However, after a couple of weeks she asked to meet with CJ. When she revealed she was pregnant, the enraged CJ shouted, "It is your fault, you told me it couldn't happen at that time of the month!" They tried to discuss the problem, but CJ could only place blame on her. He also knew, or at least suspected, that Amy had been sleeping around. The last thing the seventeen-year-old CJ wanted was to be blamed for making Amy pregnant.

This is when the dark side of CJ reemerged. He called Amy. He told her he was sorry for the things he had said to her. She seemed to be accepting of his apologies. He suggested they secretly meet at The

Bluff, east of town. It was a spot where kids parked and made out. He and Amy had parked there many times. He said, "Please don't tell anyone, okay? I have a surprise for you." He saw her car and walked up to the top to find her waiting for him.

"What's the surprise?" she asked.

He took her by the hand as they walked to the edge of The Bluff. "I think we need to get married!" he exclaimed as they reached the edge. She excitedly hugged him.

"I'm so happy!" she said as he pushed her away from him. "What's wrong?" she asked.

CJ gave her a hard shove, and she plummeted to her death hundreds of feet below. He hurried home to find his mother holding the phone with the bad news. The news gave CJ that familiar erotic feeling.

The county coroner autopsied Amy's body and found she was pregnant. The county sheriff's investigator looking into Amy's death interviewed several boys who had been dating Amy, including CJ. None of the boys revealed anything which would lead investigators to find something which conflicted with the coroner's finding, which was death by accident or possibly suicide.

This event only furthered the seventeen-year-old CJ to never want to have a child. He dropped out of high school after Amy's death. He was young, strong, and wanted the rodeo as his career. He began with local events, always trying to be the best all-around cowboy. He won some buckles and a little cash but wasn't satisfied. A local former world champion cowboy, Tyler Hopkins, had observed the hard-charging CJ. They talked; advice was offered. Tyler gave the young cowboy some tips, especially steer wrestling and saddle bronc riding; however, he told CJ he was too tall for bull riding. CJ resented hearing this, but was told "A bull will likely kill you." Tyler knew his advice about bull riding had fallen on deaf ears. Like most youngsters, they needed to learn the hard way.

That's the time, at age seventeen, CJ told his mother he was leaving home to follow the rodeos. Despite his mother's protests, she knew there was nothing she could do to persuade him to stay. He told her how important it was that she take good care of Lester. His mother had found a job at a local diner. CJ explained he planned on making good money as a rodeo cowboy and promised he would send home money when he could.

His rodeo career went fairly well, placing and occasionally winning some events. He traveled a great deal, had bought a horse trailer and a couple good roping horses. The times he was injured continued to be the result of riding bulls. He finally realized it was time to discontinue riding bulls. He had good success with the female rodeo *groupies*, but nothing very serious.

The thing about CJ, he came across as a decent, friendly guy. He made friends easily. Among the regular rodeo guys, he was thought well of. He seldom got into the bar brawls his rodeo cowboy colleagues seemed to relish. He never avoided a fight but seemed to control himself. The fact that he had another violent side to him never seemed to be a problem. Certainly no one noticed anything unusual about him. He didn't appear in any way to be a cold-blooded killer.

CHAPTER NINE

━━━━━━━━━━━━━ ● ● ○ ● ● ● ━━━━━━━━━━━━━

CJ constantly traveled the rodeo circuit. He was on his way to Kansas City, hauling his horses, to compete in another rodeo. He left Enid, Oklahoma, where he had done pretty well. He won another buckle but, more importantly, earned over $7000. With this long drive, he was thinking about his rodeo career. He still wanted to ride bulls, but the money he was making was more from roping and saddle bronc riding. The times he was hurt the worst were from riding bulls.

He finally rolled into Kansas City, dropping off his horses at the rodeo grounds and registering for the events in which he planned to complete. After checking into his motel room, he took a shower. He noticed across the street was a bar and restaurant. Outside the bar was a marquis with the words "WELCOME, COWBOYS." Inside, the bar was filled with rowdy cowboys. CJ recognized several of them. Although under age, he was seldom asked for an ID. He ordered a beer and was thinking about dinner. As he ordered his second beer, a loud voice behind him said, "This cowboy's beer is on me." Carl turned to find a tall, lanky man who he recognized as a team roper. "You're Carl Johnson," said the man.

"Yep, but I prefer CJ. You are Brent Marshall. Thanks for the beer."

"That's right." Brent sat next to CJ at the bar.

CJ said, "You and your partner just won the team roping in Enid. You guys are really good."

"Well," said Brent, "thanks for the compliment. I've been watching you rope and think you have some real talent."

"Thank you," said CJ. "Where's your partner?"

"He's not here, he's been having some back problems. What you saw in Enid was Buster's last team roping event for some time. Buster is on his way to El Paso to have major back surgery. Enid might have been his last roping event. This has been going on for a long time. The poor guy has been living on pain pills."

"I'm very sorry to hear that."

"That's why I'm talking to you. You are a natural header, and as you know, I'm a pretty good healer."

"You are one of the best," replied CJ.

"Buster and I were talking about maybe giving you a chance replacing Buster, at least on a temporary basis. You might have the talent to be able to work with me for a while. At least give it a try. Your roping horse is pretty fair. Maybe if I tweak him a bit, he might be able to improve. What do you think here, CJ, want to give it a try?"

"Sure, I'd like to try, but how would it work? We don't have enough time to test it out here in Kansas City. Do we?"

"Maybe. I've got access to a first-class roping facility just a few miles from the fairgrounds, and it's available for us to try out tomorrow morning. If I feel we are up to competing here, we will enter. There are some conditions, however, CJ."

"Such as?"

"If I think we can at least be competitive, you will have to scratch in the saddle bronc and bull riding events here in Kansas City." CJ started to protest when Brent cut him off, "Let me finish, if we can become a team here, even if we don't place, I'll pay you what you earned in Enid, which I believe was about seven thousand dollars."

Now CJ was very interested. It sounded like a win-win for himself. "Wow, that's seems pretty generous, Mr. Marshall."

"CJ, please call me Brent. I'm only thirty-five years old, and Mr. Marshall makes me feel like an old man."

"Okay," replied the younger man.

"Here's the thing, CJ. Buster and me have become pretty darn wealthy from team roping, endorsements, and we even get some guarantees just by entering and competing in rodeos. If you agree, CJ, I'll give you directions to the roping facility. When you pick up your horses, be sure and scratch from the bull and bronc events. I'll see you in the morning at eight o'clock." Brent left with a handshake. CJ went into the café for dinner feeling very good about what had just happened. He was feeling pretty sure that maybe this is a chance for him to send home more money for his mother and Lester.

The following morning, he arrived at the training facility at seven forty-five, finding Brent already there with his horse saddled up. Brent was talking to two men. As CJ got out of his truck, Brent greeted him with a handshake, saying, "I'd like to introduce our hosts, Bernie and Lennie."

CJ watched the two men approach with outstretched hands. CJ immediately thought to himself, *These guys are queers*. He reluctantly offered his hand but felt like he needed to wash his after shaking with these two guys.

Brent could sense CJ's aversion to Bernie and Lennie. "Why don't you go saddle up, partner, we got some work to do." Their hosts had already rounded up some cattle to be used for the first-time team ropers. Both Brent and CJ did some warm-up sprints with their horses. They prepared their ropes. CJ was feeling a little nervous working with Brent. Bernie was timing, and Lennie would do the calf release. The two cowboys indicated they were ready. When Lennie released the frightened calf, CJ hesitated, and by then it was too late, the calf had run to the end of the arena. Brent said, "That's okay, CJ, were going to try again. Tell me when you're ready, okay?"

CJ replied, "I'm sorry, Brent, I just got surprised a bit, I'm ready now." The calf came out, and both Brent and CJ's horses exploded after the release. With their ropes set, CJ roped the head and steadied his horse, while Brent expertly roped the heels, and their horses did the rest.

"Just under eight seconds!" shouted Bernie. "Let's try it again, I think I see something with your horse, CJ, but let me watch again." The next calf burst out and was roped in what seemed to be better time. "Better," proclaimed Bernie, "seven point two seconds." He said, "Brent, we need to talk for a minute."

CJ noticed Bernie and Lennie talking, their heads shaking vigorously. They dismounted and the four men met. "What's up?" inquired Brent. He already could guess what was going on but remained silent.

Lennie began with "We see a problem with your horse, CJ. Before we talk, just let me tell you Bernie and I both saw it. Your horse is a good roping horse, but he has a pause just as the calf is released which causes a very important loss of time. It's a bad habit we often see from horses that have been used in training."

"I saw it too," said Brent.

"This is a good roping horse. I paid twelve hundred dollars for him, and he's won me some money," said CJ. His feelings were obviously hurt.

"Bernie and I have an idea," said Lennie. "If you want to give it a try, we have an outstanding horse you might have some interest in. She is a mare, over fifteen hands tall."

Brent asked, "Is she here?"

Lennie called out to a young man nearby and told him to bring out Ginger. She was a beautiful sorrel, young, and looked spirited. She was walked over to CJ. His first comment was "How much?"

Lennie said, "CJ, why don't you saddle her and do a few warm-up sprints." She felt unlike any other horse he had ever ridden. Soon he and Brent were ready for the next calf. The calf exploded, and so did Ginger, nearly leaving CJ on the ground, but he stayed with her, roped the head, and Brent did the heels.

"Five point nine seconds!" exclaimed Bernie. Brent was obviously pleased. CJ was in a state of disbelief. They did many more tries, each time improving on their time. When Brent said they had done enough, CJ saw Bernie and Lennie conferring.

"How do you like her?" asked Lennie.

"What can I say? She is unbelievable."

"We would like to sell her to you, CJ. She's worth more, but we will take twenty-two thousand dollars."

"I can't afford that much money, even though I'm sure she is worth it."

"Excuse us," they said. "Brent, can we talk?"

Brent joined Bernie and Lennie while CJ was grooming Ginger. She had worked up a big lather. *What a horse,* thought CJ, *if I only had the money.*

After a while, the three returned, and Lennie said, "We have a proposition for you, CJ. Ginger is easily worth, at a minimum, twenty-five to thirty thousand dollars. Since Brent here is a very good friend, we would like you to have Ginger."

"Here is what we can do," said Bernie. "Twenty-two thousand dollars for Ginger. We can give you two thousand for your horse, which will work great in our training programs. Your balance is twenty thousand for a very outstanding roping horse. We take 25 percent of your winnings for the next three years, or until Ginger is paid off, after which our commission is 20 percent as long as you and Brent continue to work together. If, for some reason, you and Brent are no longer a team, or you fail to pay our commission, we will repossess Ginger. We feel you will be making lots of money with Brent and Ginger. We can do the contract right now."

"Sounds like a great deal," said Brent, "although I think you should keep your horse. Roger would be a good backup horse if you should have a problem of some sort with Ginger. I'll give these gentlemen the two thousand dollars as a new partner gift."

CJ said, "I'll take it. Thank you very much, Brent." CJ had momentarily forgotten about these two guys being queer. None of them knew CJ was known for not paying his debts.

They trained together the next morning with even better results. Brent was pretty impressed with his new partner. He was even more impressed when they won the team roping in Kansas City. He convinced young CJ to pay the 25 percent to Lennie and Bernie, as well pay $6,000 toward the purchase of Ginger. CJ felt rich. They had each won over $20,000.

Cherokee County Iowa was their next rodeo stop. As they were loading up, Brent said, "I have something for you." He handed CJ a .22 magnum caliber, chrome-plated, derringer. "This is actually Buster's, but he left it behind. I always carry one and think you might ought to as well. Being on the road the way we are, one never knows. It is registered in Buster's name; you can keep it unless Buster wants it back."

Cherokee had similar results as Kansas City, with them winning first place, but with smaller prize money. CJ was very pleased and felt that he and Brent might get their pictures in some cowboy magazines. CJ, however, began to notice that Brent often had his arm around him. He thought Brent was being his friendly self, but it was starting to make CJ feel embarrassed. If it kept up, he might say something to him. He realized the big break Brent had given him and thought it was probably more of a father-son situation.

Their next stop was Cheyenne, Wyoming. This was a big one, with big prize money. After first registering and paying their entry fees, they left their horses and drove to check in at the motel. The desk clerk could not find a reservation for them. Each mistakenly thought the other had made a reservation. With the rodeo in town, they had only one room left with two beds. They reluctantly took the room.

The competition in Cheyenne was very strong. Even the existing world champion team ropers were entered. After a few tense, hardworking days, Brent and CJ had made it into Sunday's finals. Both of their horses were crazy with energy. Brent and CJ won first prize over the world champs by one-tenth of a second. Both men were exhausted. They drank too many beers at the bar next to their motel. That evening they crawled into their beds, knowing the drive tomorrow to Great Falls, Montana, was a long one. Brent fell asleep quickly and soon began his terrible snoring. CJ said to himself before he drifted off, *Never again am I sharing a room with this snoring bastard.*

CJ was having an erotic dream when he suddenly awoke to find a naked Brent on top of him with his tongue in CJ's mouth. Horrified and sick, CJ pushed Brent off of the bed. Brent was screaming, "I'm sorry, I'm sorry! I must have had a nightmare, CJ! I'm sorry, I'm not like that! I'm not a queer, please believe me!" CJ went into the bathroom and vomited violently. When he came out of the bathroom, he found Brent fully dressed, apologizing over and over.

CJ said, "I accept your word, Brent, that you are not a queer. If anything like that ever happens again, I swear I'll kill you."

"It won't, I promise, I am not that way."

Breakfast was very quiet in the all-night diner when Brent said, "Great Falls is about an eleven-hour drive. There is a spot about half-way which is quiet, lots of parking, grazing, and water. I've stopped there in the past. We can unload and hobble the horses and give them a little break. The café can make us a couple of lunches."

"Sounds good," said CJ. "I know the spot you're talking about. Why don't you get the lunches, I'm going to head out ahead of you. We can have our lunches when you get there." CJ left at six thirty in the morning after picking up his horses.

Several hours later, Brent pulled next to CJ's rig. CJ was very quiet as he helped Brent hobble his horses next to the small lake. Brent said, "I'll get the lunches, and we can eat down by the lake."

"Sounds good, I've already let my horses out and am set to head out after lunch," said CJ.

The road leading to the area was gravel, and anyone driving in could be heard. All was quiet. Brent stood after putting down the food, and CJ shot him in the back of the head, using Buster's derringer. Brent died instantly. CJ removed Brent's wallet and a wad of cash. He pulled out Brent's pockets, making it look like someone had robbed him. CJ picked up both lunches, ran to Brent's truck, and took a great deal of cash from his partner's hiding place inside the vehicle.

CJ drove out to the highway all the while thinking, as he ate both lunches, *You are one dead queer cowboy, partner.* He knew Brent's horses were safe, with plenty of grass and water. Someone would find them soon. He arrived in Great Falls just before dark, drove to the rodeo grounds, checked in, and registered their team saying, "My partner will be along shortly." It finally occurred to CJ there would be no team roping. Once his partner's body was found, he would scratch from team to individual roping using Ginger.

Shortly after checking into the motel, he showered, dressed, and heard a knock at the door. It was two Montana State troopers. Brent Marshall's body had been found. "It appears to have been a robbery," said one of the troopers.

"Where did this happen?" asked a distraught CJ. The trooper explained where and what likely happened. CJ did a great job of apparently sobbing while explaining how he left early after having breakfast with Brent who, CJ explained, had a terrible hangover from the previous night and was going to leave a little later. CJ said he drove straight through from Cheyenne. The troopers seemed to accept CJ's story, however, told him to keep them informed of his whereabouts. They were given Buster's phone number to find out about next of kin and make arrangements for Brent's horses and other property.

The following morning, CJ scratched from team roping to the shock of rodeo officials learning of Brent Marshall's death. He entered individual roping. He didn't even make the finals. He blamed the problem on Ginger, believing she was inexperienced in individual events.

He failed to place at all with Ginger in the next two rodeos. He still had quite a bit of money, in part because he had not been paying the 25 percent to Bernie and Lennie. They had been leaving messages for him, which he disregarded. He was in Missoula, Montana, and had gone to pick up Ginger. He found her stall empty with a repossession notice tacked outside the stall. *Those damn queers!* he cursed to himself.

He called and yelled at Lennie, who just said, "A deal is a deal, CJ. Were very sorry to hear about Brent," and hung up.

CJ had no idea of the downward spiral facing him. He was back struggling, trying to ride bulls and broncs. He won a little money roping with his horse, Roger. He did see a story about his "Riches to Rags" in a Western magazine. The years passed without him being charged with Brent's murder.

He toiled on for the next few years, making enough money to send some home to his mom and Lester. He continued to feel responsible for his younger brother. At times he thought of bringing Lester along on his rodeo circuit, but he knew it would just add another distraction to his very difficult traveling schedule doing rodeos. He bought a new roping horse a few years later and started winning or placing in different events. Then he met Melba.

CHAPTER TEN

I t all started with Melba. CJ was now into his late twenties. His plans for fame and fortune had quickly faded, until the night he met Melba. She had just turned twenty. He was doing pretty well with competing in rodeos, winning lots of belt buckles and a good sum of cash. He decided, one evening, to watch the women's barrel racing. He saw Melba compete and win the barrel racing event. Not only did she win, she was crowned Rodeo Queen. He thought at the time, *I'm going to marry that woman.* Melba was beautiful. He, during that week, began watching where she went. The last night of the rodeo, he followed her into a local rodeo bar and saw she was accompanied by her royal rodeo queen sisters. CJ watched her for a while when suddenly there came an announcement.

"Ladies and gentlemen, it is our pleasure to announce, our rodeo's All-Around Cowboy, Mr. Carl Johnson!" CJ rose and bowed, then heard, "And our Rodeo Queen, Ms. Melba Conner." The applause was deafening.

Things began to again settle down, when Melba said, "Hello, Mr. All-Around Cowboy."

It was then that CJ actually fell in love with Melba. Their courtship was fairly brief. Melba, who was twenty years old, due to being raised a Southern Baptist, proclaimed to CJ she was a virgin and planned on remaining that way until she was married. Despite CJ's efforts, she was determined. They only lived about twenty-five miles apart, so they saw each other quite frequently. One night, CJ popped the question. Melba excitedly accepted his proposal.

When Melba told her family about her engagement, the news was not received very well. "What do you really know about this guy?" asked her father, Jack. "Have you even met his family?" asked her mother. Her two sisters both said they had not even met CJ. Julie, her older sister, asked, "Why haven't any of us met him? Is this some great secret? When did you meet him? Where?" Melba replied, "Carl is kind of shy. I plan to have him come over to meet all of you very soon. By the way, I am twenty years old and can marry anyone I wish."

Jack Conner was a former marine. While in the Marines, he became his battalion's heavyweight boxing champion. In fact, he resembled, both physically and facially, the former late heavyweight champion Rocky Marciano, flattened nose and all.

Jack had worked very hard building his successful construction business. They were not wealthy, but not by any means poor. He was a stern but fair boss. The men and women who worked for him admired him for a number of things. One, he was a very physically powerful man. He would be seen carrying large beams which would normally require two men to carry. He was not someone to pick a fight with.

Jack had fathered three daughters and adored each of them. The two oldest had been relatively easy to raise. They had aspired to become wives and mothers. They married nice young men, both of whom had come to Jack seeking his approval to marry his daughters. This pleased the old-fashioned Jack very much.

The youngest, Melba, was another story. She had an independent streak. She, like many young girls, fell in love with horses. Since they lived on a property of several acres, he had indulged her by buying her a horse. She was told that the horse was entirely her responsibility to take care of. Horses became a great part of her life. In middle school, she began barrel racing. Each daughter, by then, had their own horses, but none had the passion which Melba possessed.

When the older daughters left home, Jack completely indulged Melba and was quite proud of her barrel racing interest and abilities. He was especially pleased that she didn't have much interest in boys. She prevailed as a barrel racing champion to the point of becoming state champion. Then she met Carl Johnson.

"It would have been nice if he had come to me and asked permission to marry you," proclaimed her father. "I guess they don't do that anymore, too old-fashioned," he grouched. "By the way, it happened with both of your sisters. Both of their future husbands came to me and asked permission, like the true gentlemen they are."

CJ did come to Sunday dinner. He met the family. There was a very strange, uncomfortable quietness at the dinner table. As he was leaving, CJ said to Melba, "Just because your family don't like me, I hope you still plan to marry me."

"Of course, I do. It will get better after were married."

A couple of things Melba didn't tell Carl about were past boyfriends. Although there had not been many during her high school years, she had found that Carl could be extremely jealous. On the occasion when they had been out to dinner or having beers, the jealously became evident. If Carl stepped away from the bar for a minute, occasionally another cowboy, seeing her sitting alone, would come over to talk with her, offer to buy her a drink.

The first time this happened, Carl appeared and yelled, "This is my fiancée, you son of a bitch, get away from her!"

The next time any guy approached she would immediately say, "You best get away, my fiancé is over there and he won't understand."

Melba excelled in barrel racing and worked very hard to improve. She steadily improved, winning, or nearly winning, every event in which she competed. She had become very well-known on the rodeo circuit. Carl was very encouraging and seemed to totally support her. CJ, however, was winning fewer events, suffering more injuries.

Melba finally told Carl, "I want to enter in barrel racing at the National Rodeo Finals in Oklahoma City. I just found out I have qualified!" she said, very excitedly.

"Well, let's do it!" he said, seemingly as excited as she was. CJ found his cumulative wins and placing in saddle bronc riding also qualified him to enter the finals.

Off they drove, hauling Melba's horses behind CJ's truck. This turned out to be the only vacation they had taken together. Melba's father financed the trip, reluctantly, as he was not fond of Carl Johnson. Melba was having great success. The final day ended with her winning second place, with prize money of $15,875. CJ did surprisingly well, finishing in fourth place with prize money of over $12,000. That was a sizable amount of money for them, beginning their lives as a married couple.

They were married in a simple Southern Baptist church ceremony. Melba's sisters served as bridesmaids. Lester was CJ's best man, and a couple of Carl's acquaintances were groomsmen. Carl's mother also attended the wedding but felt awkward and a bit inferior to Melba's family. She couldn't wait to leave. CJ could feel the bitterness Jack, Melba's father, was projecting during the marriage ceremony.

CJ was nine years older than Melba, which didn't mean much to her. She continued to barrel race and, in fact, won the state championship several times, even after they were married. CJ, on the other hand, was having trouble competing in cowboy events. One day, after recovering from his latest injuries, he suggested they buy some acreage and raise hay and cattle. They found a place south of Layton with twenty-five acres. It had an existing home and was partially fenced. They still had part of the cash they had earned at the national finals. Melba's father, Jack Conner, also loaned them a great deal of money for the down payment. With the large down payment, their mortgage was not huge. The property had a tractor, baler, rakes, and many other implements. They were ready to begin raising hay. They bought some calves to raise as beef steers.

CHAPTER ELEVEN

T he first year's hay crop did well, and both Melba and CJ, being horse people, developed reliable clients who bought their hay. The years were passing quickly. For the most part, the hay business was pretty good. He supplemented the income by selling cattle. Melba worked part-time at the local community college, teaching equestrian subjects. Life seemed to be going pretty well, except Melba began wanting a child.

CJ continued to tell Melba that he was trying very hard and maybe it was her fault. The one thing he had never revealed to her was, one night, before they met, when he was competing in a rodeo in Southern Texas, he went across the border and had a vasectomy done by a Mexican doctor. CJ knew he never wanted any damn kids;

he was afraid that potential children might be born with Lester's mental illness.

They began to argue, especially over money. CJ felt they should discontinue making payments to Melba's father on their loan for the down payment on the ranch. Melba couldn't believe his saying such a thing. Sure, the hay market was down, but they we're obligated to pay back her father, and she wouldn't hear of it. Her father was generous enough to loan them the money for the down payment, and they needed to pay him back.

Melba continued to teach equestrian classes at the community college. Seeing other college instructors caused her, at times, to wish she had gone farther than high school.

Melba was really getting on CJ's nerves, constantly asking him to go get checked to see if something was wrong with him since she was not getting pregnant. She had been checked and found nothing was wrong with her. CJ told her he had seen a doctor and there was nothing wrong with him. The years passed, no children. Both of Melba's sisters had several kids, which hurt her even more. They had made love so many times when she knew she was likely to get pregnant but was always disappointed. Melba was now forty years old and had accepted the fact they were not going to have children.

Eventually their arguments became volatile, and he began hitting her. He never hit her in the face, but her body bore many deep, long-lasting bruises. CJ was especially brutal when he learned Melba's father set up his will to leave Melba's share in a separate bank account, which CJ couldn't get to unless she was dead. Her father left her $100,000, which CJ eagerly wanted.

Melba's father should have known better than cross his son-in-law. Melba's mother had passed away a few years earlier. He had suspected that CJ was physically abusing his daughter. When he questioned Melba about abuse, she refused to discuss it with him. Her father, Jack, learned from his other daughters they believed CJ was physically hurting Melba. Jack Conner stopped by the ranch one day while Melba was teaching at the local college. He confronted CJ about the suspected abuse. CJ violently denied the accusation. He told his father-in-law to "Get off of my property. If you ever step foot here again, I'll kill you."

Jack, the ex-marine boxer, said, "You'll kill me? You wife-beating, cowardly, worthless piece of garbage!" as he turned to charge after CJ. CJ turned and ran as fast as he could toward the house, barely making it inside the door and locking it in the nick of time, his heart almost pounding out of his chest.

Jack hit the solid door, nearly knocking it off the hinges, yelling, "Come on out and kill me, you miserable coward!"

CJ stayed in the house, peeking through the curtains, until Jack left, growing more courageous when Jack finally was gone. CJ thought, *Something has to be done with Jack.*

Melba never knew of her father's visit or CJ's threats.

Shortly after Jack Conner's visit, he was killed leaving a local tavern. The investigating officer's report determined he had been run off of the road and into the river. His blood alcohol was just below the legal limit, but his alcohol impairment was found to be a contributing factor in the accident. No suspects were ever located.

What was not discovered was the fact that Carl Johnson had followed his father-in-law to the tavern. CJ knew Jack Conner's habits. He had followed Jack to the tavern many times. He knew that Jack was a fairly heavy drinker but would only drive when he felt he was under the legal limit. CJ had waited, very patiently and quietly, in the tavern's parking lot that fateful night. Carl knew his brother, Lester, had a close friend who owned a very beat-up International pickup. Those things were built like a tank and very heavy. Carl arranged for Lester to borrow the International for one night. As instructed, Lester had left his friend's pickup next to his trailer with the keys under the seat. Lester knew that Carl was going to borrow the pickup for the night and would return it to Lester's driveway.

Carl sat at the rear of the tavern's parking lot. He sat there for a couple of hours, and predictably, Jack exited the bar. Jack paused and stretched, looking up at the heavy fog which had rolled in. Jack hesitated for a moment, as though considering returning to the bar. He suddenly seemed to focus on Lester's friend's pickup, staring for what seemed to be several minutes. CJ became very nervous. He knew if Jack came over and discovered him sitting there in a strange pickup, Jack would cause him some serious trouble. CJ had been in his share of fights but knew Jack Conner was way bigger, stronger, and, even despite his age, someone who could and would kick his ass with pleasure. Jack turned away, and CJ began to breathe again, grateful that Jack had not approached him in the pickup.

At last, Jack got into his truck. He drove out into the heavy fog with CJ following at a short distance. As Jack approached the curve, CJ hit his hi-beams and drove hard into Jack's left rear fender. Jack, suddenly blinded by the bright lights and not expecting the collision, lost control of his vehicle and went into the river, where his pickup quickly filled with water. It didn't take long for him to drown. CJ returned his brother's friend's truck and returned home.

Late the next morning, CJ was working in his pasture when he saw a state trooper's car pull into his driveway. In a few minutes, a very distraught Melba called to him. "I need to talk with you," she shouted.

CJ did very little to comfort his wife. He made remarks about how her father had never approved of him. He said he was sorry for her, but only for her. "Your dad was never a good father to you," he repeated many times. "Sometimes, people get what's coming to them. He never had a kind word for me."

According to the state trooper, her father's vehicle had been hit very hard from behind. Whoever hit his vehicle would have sustained damage to their own vehicle. It occurred to Melba that her husband was possibly somehow responsible for the death of her father, but she found no evidence on CJ's pickup, no indication it had been in an accident.

After their father's funeral, Melba's sisters talked with her about leaving CJ. She explained that he would likely kill her if she did, in fact, leave him. All that her sisters could give was advice: "Report him to the police. File for a restraining order." Melba knew taking any legal action against her husband would only result in her being more severely beaten or even killed. Melba again discussed how he had been abusing her with her two sisters who said, "Leave him." The loss of her father was devastating to her. Other than her sisters, she was now alone with an abusive husband. Her sisters were too busy with their own lives to provide much help. She realized whatever action she would take would result in severe consequences to her.

Melba finally decided to leave him when the opportunity occurred, because she was now very afraid of him and what he might do if he found out her plan to leave. She had learned, long ago, how mean he could be. This was a far cry from the gentle cowboy she had met and had fallen in love with. Little did she know he possessed something far more than a mean streak.

CJ's plan didn't happen until one sunny morning. CJ, being in an unusually good mood and being nice to her, said, "Let's go fishing! We will go up to Grand Lake where we haven't been in a while." When they arrived, he noticed there was no one else on the lake. They drove around in the boat until they were over the deepest part of the lake.

As he had planned it, he started an argument with her. It continued with many accusations against each other, many by her about his suspected infidelities, when he suddenly stood up and hit her hard. Melba, who was a large, physical woman herself, struck back for the first time. She connected hard with his jaw.

A surprised and partially stunned CJ was seeing stars. That's when he tried to push her over the side of the boat. She grabbed him and they both went into the water. CJ, trying to get to the surface, knowing they were both going to drown, hit her with everything he had, and she released him. He made it back to the boat, grabbed his fishing pole, hooked her body before she went under, and was able to slowly reel her body to the boat. He pulled her aboard and found she was unconscious but still breathing. He looked in all directions and didn't see anyone else on the lake. CJ knew that this was the very deepest part of Grand Lake. Using a spare anchor, he tied the anchor rope around her torso and pushed her over the side. He watched as she momentarily seemed to float, and then she went under, leaving a trail of bubbles.

The following day he created the kidnapping story.

CHAPTER TWELVE

———————•••○•••———————

M axine Bolton Farrell had grown up in Iowa until the family moved to Center County when she was eleven. Her brother was already in high school when they arrived. She attended local schools, and in high school she became very focused on boys.

Maxine's older brother, Earl, after graduating from high school, joined the army. He had been injured in a jeep accident while stationed in South Korea. His injuries were such that he received an honorable discharge along with a lifetime pension due to his injuries. His pain was almost unbearable. He began drinking very heavily. He moved back to Center County rarely sober. Earl wasn't much of a role model for young Maxine, as he was almost always intoxicated when she looked to him for advice. Earl did, however, teach Maxine to drink.

Her parents spent little time with Maxine. Her father was obsessed with his work in the computer industry. Her mother was usually seeing other men on the sly, which young Maxine knew about. As a result of Maxine keeping the secret of her mother's indiscretions, the young girl was given far too much freedom for a girl her age.

As she grew older, if her mother attempted reign her in, Maxine resorted to blackmailing her mother over their secret. Given her lack of restrictions while in high school, Maxine became quite the manipulator, especially with boys, as well as some male teachers who felt compelled to give her straight A's.

Maxine somehow graduated high school without becoming pregnant. After high school, she enrolled in the local community college, wanting to become a nurse. She found very quickly that, in college, male instructors slept with students without repercussions. She had lost her ability to manipulate the staff and now had to actually study. She began to really enjoy the classes and, with surprising results, graduated at the top of her class.

She became a registered nurse, remained in the community working several assignments at the two local hospitals. That was how she met Glen Farrell. He had been brought to the emergency room, having been injured in an accident while driving a cement truck. He was a handsome young man, only four years older than her. Glen had suffered only minor injuries and wouldn't be admitted to the hospital. As he was being discharged, he asked Maxine to go out with him. She had already established that he wasn't married. Maxine was in a long-term relationship with one of the young men she had dated while in high school, but was becoming very bored with the guy. She had also been cheating on him all along, so what would be wrong going out with Glen?

They slept together on their first date. After that night, Glen was smitten. A few months later, Maxine and Glen became engaged. Her parents liked and approved of this handsome young man, especially her mother, who still looked pretty good. After their marriage, Maxine worked as a registered nurse and Glen drove a cement truck. They had a daughter, Stephanie.

The years passed with monotony eventually settling in. Glen became a terrible alcoholic and had been taken away from driving trucks for fear of him driving drunk. He was reassigned office duty and other odd jobs. He later died at work, ironically being struck by a cement truck at the plant.

Maxine retained her flirtatious ways and, like her mother, had several affairs. She lived in her own home in the city of Bradley. Stephanie moved to Des Moines, Iowa.

Maxine began attending the local senior dance, where she met CJ. He had asked Maxine to dance with him. He tolerated her clumsiness on the dance floor and asked her if she would meet him for coffee the next day.

She insisted on paying for the coffee, which was okay with him. Maxine told CJ she had been widowed for several years. Her late husband, Glen, had been killed in an industrial accident, having been run over by a cement truck at his workplace, she explained. Glen's employer's insurance settled with her for well over a million dollars. She chuckled. "I suspect Glen was most likely very intoxicated, but thank goodness, they did not check him for that." Being a retired registered nurse, her pension, coupled with the one million dollars from Glen's case, made living fairly comfortable for her. She boasted to CJ about being very wealthy. This gave him his chance to move in. He told Maxine he would like to visit with her again and perhaps show her his spread. She told him that she had always been fond of cowboys, and they began dating. Maxine was a little younger than most widows and, against his better judgment, they had been having sex.

Actually, CJ sort of liked Maxine, but especially liked her money. Mostly, he liked the fact she had kept their involvement a secret. She did reveal, however, she had mentioned his name, CJ, to her companions at the senior dance where they met. This bothered him some, but couldn't be helped.

Finally, he told her it had been a bad hay year and he was behind on his property taxes. The upcoming hay year was going to be great, but with taxes and all, he didn't have the cash to plant his crop of hay. "Me and Lester have our grandaddy, back in Tennessee, who is very old, ninety-seven, in bad health, and also very rich. He tells me that when he is gone, he has me and my brother getting all of his money, but not a penny until he dies. Lester barely gets by on SSI and welfare, so he can't help." CJ finally asked Maxine if he could borrow some money in order for him to get hay seed and supplies, and he would repay her when his crop came in.

Maxine had fallen in love with this cowboy by then, despite the age differences, and he was damn good in bed, unlike Glenn, who, when sober, had hopped on and off like a rabbit. She asked, "How much do you need?"

"About twenty-five thousand dollars should cover it," he said.

"I'll see what I can do." They later met in his bed, and afterward she said, "I've got some money for you. I could only get forty-six hundred dollars for the time being." She gave him the cash and, in his rage, he strangled her to death in the bed in which they had just made passionate love.

The stingy bitch, thought CJ.

CJ threw Maxine's body into a garbage dumpster at a condominium complex in the city of Bradley, several miles away. Unfortunately for CJ, some might call it fate, the waste disposal company failed to empty that particular dumpster on its scheduled day due to a substitute crew. Residents complained to the on-site condominium manager about a terrible smell.

A retired police detective who lived near the dumpster was pretty sure he recognized the smell and called the Bradley Police Department. The responding patrol officer then called for a detective to respond. On arrival, Detective Ron Adams took charge. The waste disposal company sent out a team to conduct the search. It wasn't long before they found what appeared to be the body of a decomposing female. The county coroner and pathologist responded, along with the Bradley Police crime scene team.

CHAPTER THIRTEEN

—— • • ○ • • ——

Ron Adams was a local product. He was born and raised in Center County. His father was a letter carrier for the United States Postal Service. His mother worked as a salesperson in women's wear. She had worked for Len Fleetwood, when he owned the shop in the mall. Both of Ron's parents were very proud of their only son.

He grew up having better-than-average grades. Ron did well in high school sports, in particular basketball. As a six-foot-three senior, he was a threat not only with ball handling, but hitting shots from the three-point line. Despite being offered some small sports scholarships, Ron's heart wasn't in basketball. He wanted to join the army as his father had done. His parents told him they were proud of him in whatever he decided to do.

After graduation, he joined the army. The young lady, Jill Douglas, whom he had been seriously dating, said she would wait for him. Shortly before leaving for boot camp, they became engaged. Eighteen months later, while he was on leave, they were married by a local judge. Jill remained in college as Ron was in South Korea. He was an MP and felt law enforcement might be what he wanted.

Jill was not too happy when he told her he wanted to reenlist for another two years but agreed to accept his decision. She, however, wanted to stay in college. The army was pleased to have Ron reenlist and promised him a promotion to sergeant, as well as a continuation of his assignment in the military police.

The separation was difficult for Jill. She was lonely and began seeing a former boyfriend. When Ron came home for a surprise visit, he found Jill and the old boyfriend together in their bed. That ended the short marriage. Ron finished his second tour in Germany. He loved the army and being an MP, but not so much that he wanted to remain as a career. On a leave while visiting his parents, he found the Bradley Police Department had an opening for a police officer. After testing, he was offered the job, which would be held for him after his discharge from the army. With his MP experience, he was transferred to Detectives in short order.

He now found himself investigating the brutal murder of Maxine Farrell. As the detective in charge, Ron Adams attended the autopsy of, as yet, an unidentified adult female. The autopsy revealed the case to be a homicide. Despite the decomposition of the body, the pathologist, Dr. Luke Evans, was able to determine that strangulation was the cause of death. Whether by someone's hands or by ligature, could not be determined, due to the advanced state of decay. There was, however, enough left of several fingers to take fingerprint impressions. Submission of the fingerprints to NCIC and AFIS, the National Automated Fingerprint System, quickly identified the victim as Maxine Farrell, age seventy-one of the city of Bradley. As a nurse, it had been required that she be fingerprinted.

Maxine Farrell had been reported as a missing person two weeks earlier to the Bradley Police Department. Her daughter, Stephanie Farrell Combs, of Des Moines, Iowa, had come to the city of Bradley to file the missing-person report regarding her mother. She filed the report, mostly out of caution, as her mother did occasionally go away with a boyfriend for an extended period of time. Her daughter was concerned since she and her mother spoke on the phone weekly, even if her mother was on a trip with someone.

The daughter was now on her way back to Bradley to help with the homicide investigation.

Meanwhile, Detective Adams interviewed both of Maxine's friends, Louise Blanchard and Thelma Davenport. They repeated the same information they had provided to the police department in the missing-person report. The last time they had seen Maxine was at the senior dance. She had danced for some time with a cowboy-looking guy named CJ. They were both sobbing heavily at the loss of their friend and surely hoped the detective would catch whoever murdered her.

Adams talked with the manager of the dance hall who told him a local cowboy occasionally attended the senior dance. "His name is Carl Johnson, but I believe he goes by CJ. I think he has a ranch south of town."

On the arrival of Stephanie, Maxine's daughter, she was unable to offer anything more than in the missing-person report. The withdrawal of $4,600 was odd. If her mother went on a trip with a man, he would pay all of the expenses. Stephanie searched her mother's home, along with Detective Adams. Other than a few dollars, nothing more in the way of evidence was found, except someone had written in her daily appointment reminder the initials CJ. Her daughter confirmed the initials were in her mother's distinctive handwriting. The lack of further evidence was very frustrating to Detective Adams.

His interview of Carl Johnson, CJ, was equally frustrating. Since CJ lived out in the county, he had stopped to chat with Captain Willis at the sheriff's department. That's when Adams learned of similar frustrations Sheriff's Detectives were having regarding CJ. Captain Willis found Sergeant Hoover and assigned her to accompany Adams on the visit to CJ.

The moment they drove up, an excited CJ immediately confronted them with "What are you here to accuse me of this time?"

Detective Adams introduced himself saying, "I believe you have already met Detective Sergeant Lynn Hoover. We are not here to accuse you of anything."

"I sure don't believe that to be true. Why are you here?" asked CJ.

"We want to talk with you about Maxine Farrell," said Detective Adams.

"Who?" asked a very loud CJ.

"Maxine Farrell," repeated Adams.

"Never heard of her," replied a suddenly pale-looking CJ. He also felt that familiar heartburn. "Who is she?" he asked.

"She is the victim of a vicious murder," said Lynn Hoover.

"Why are you talking to me? I don't even know who she is!" replied CJ in a very high-pitched, angry-sounding voice.

"It is our belief you knew her," replied Adams. "We have several people who saw you dancing with her at the senior dance."

"I dance with many women at that damn dance. One of those women gets murdered, and you come to me? Why?"

"We are talking with people she was associated with. We also have some physical evidence."

"What physical evidence?"

"We are not at liberty to disclose at this time; however, we can tell you the pathologist found semen in her," said Adams, thinking he might bluff CJ a little with this lie.

This brought some immediate relief to CJ who remembered he used a condom every time he had sex with Maxine, since she slept with so many men, he had been afraid of catching something.

CJ, again, expressed anger at the two detectives telling them, "Get off of my property, or you will be hearing from my lawyer."

"Who is your lawyer?" asked Lynn.

"None of your damn business," replied CJ.

As they drove away, Adams expressed his frustration regarding the Farrell case, while also thanking Lynn for the assistance. "How about I buy you lunch?" asked Adams.

Over lunch, they talked a bit about each other's careers. They both agreed to having a passion for their jobs as detectives. After discussing some former cases, Lynn mentioned their cases which involved CJ. As both were unmarried, a little personal chemistry was beginning between them. After lunch, Lynn invited Ron Adams back to her office to share some of the other files in which the initials CJ were mentioned. She shared their cases, as well as the Layton Dottie Lambert case investigated by Sergeant Bill Burris. The Lambert case also included CJ.

"We gave it a shot," replied Lynn. "I have to tell you, I believe he's your guy," she said. "Don't overlook possible DNA from the finger impressions on Maxine's throat. I still have the three-year-old Sylvia Robinson homicide, which we think he is good for."

Before they parted, Ron asked Lynn, "How about dinner and a movie sometime?"

"I would really like that," she said. They exchanged phone numbers.

* * * * *

CJ spent the following days and weeks reading the local papers for a story, but nothing appeared. He felt much relief as Maxine had mentioned to him that, when they met at the dance, she told her friend his name was CJ.

CHAPTER FOURTEEN

---•—•—•—○—•—•—•---

Alice Fleetwood had been born in Center County to Thomas and Francis Burke. Her father was a dairyman, one of the largest farms in Center County. For a farmer he was fairly well to do.

Her mother was a homemaker. She took good care in raising their two daughters. The girls were raised in a loving but fairly severe Catholic environment. Her mother attended Mass on a daily basis and was considerably determined her girls would be devoted to their faith as much as she was.

Alice's older sister had rebelled while in high school and became pregnant before graduating. Her parents disowned Rowena when she refused to marry the boy who had impregnated her. Rowena left the home and was never seen again.

Rowena's behavior had a very severe impact on young Alice. These events happened while Alice was a freshman in high school. Alice began attending daily Mass before school. Her beliefs had an impact on her friends, of which she had many, of course with similar beliefs as Alice. In fact, Alice felt compelled to become a nun. Alice's mother was very supportive of her decision to enter the convent after graduation from high school. Her father, however, wasn't convinced that it was the right thing for his only remaining daughter.

Her plans had a dramatic turn during her senior year in high school. After Mass, she was in the church's social hall when she was introduced, by her father, to a young man named Leonard Fleetwood. Leonard was home visiting his family during Easter break. Leonard was also raised in the same community as Alice. Alice had never met Leonard before, but it didn't seem unusual since he was four years older than her.

They talked for some time while drinking punch and eating doughnuts. Leonard was graduating from college soon and planned touring Europe before joining his father in running the very successful women's wear shop in the Montclaire Village Mall. After Easter break, Alice and Leonard began writing and calling each other. This pleased Alice's father very much. Every chance they got, Alice and

Leonard saw each other. She began thinking that in her heart she had fallen love with Leonard and certainly was not joining the convent.

Alice, after graduating high school, enrolled in the state university nearby. She spent her four years living at home while achieving her bachelor's degree in business. Leonard, who was now Len to all who knew him, was now practically a member of Alice's family. Len asked her father's permission to marry Alice which her father granted with great joy.

Len and Alice had a very good marriage, although they never had children. She and Len were involved in the Catholic Church, Chamber of Commerce, and many civic organizations. They traveled a great deal. The shop was extremely lucrative. Alice put her business degree to work by helping out with the shop's bookkeeping. The years passed, and one day, Len fell dead with a heart attack. Alice had been grieving for several years. Alice Fleetwood was now a very well-dressed, petite widow.

Even today, in the produce section of her local supermarket, she was dressed immaculately when she heard behind her "Excuse me, ma'am" with something of a twang.

She turned to find a slender, sort of tall, middle-aged, cowboy-looking man and said, "Are you talking to me?"

He replied, "I'm so sorry to bother you, ma'am."

Alice asked, "How may I help you?"

"Well, ma'am, I was noticing that you picked out a cantaloupe for yourself."

"Well, yes, I have, why do you ask?" she replied.

"Well, ma'am, my mama's dying very shortly, and she asked me to bring her a fresh cantaloupe because that is her very favorite fruit, and I noticed how much time you took to pick out yours."

"Well, sir, I'm very sorry to hear about your mother. You must care very much about her."

"Well, yes ma'am. Beside me and my mentally retarded brother, we are all the family she has left. She only has a day or two left, and I just want to make her happy. Once she is gone, it will only be me and my brother, Lester," he said.

"I'll tell you what," said Alice, "I know this melon, which I picked out, is not only ripe and fresh, but likely exactly what your mother wants, so please take it for her."

"Ma'am, that is so kind of you. I just know she will be so happy. By the way, my name is Carl Johnson, but people call me CJ."

"Well, CJ, I hope this helps your mother in some small way," said Alice. "It must be difficult for you and your brother. How long has your mother been ill?" she asked.

"It's been for a number of years, but the past couple of weeks she has taken a bad turn, and now it is almost over."

"You have my sympathies," she told him, "and I hope it is for the best."

"It surely is," said CJ, "'cause of her pain and suffering. But still it ain't easy, 'cause I love her so, and since I lost Melba, my wife, it has been really tough. I don't know why I'm telling you all of this, since I don't really know you."

"Well, my name is Alice Fleetwood, and it seems you need someone to talk with."

"Yes, I believe I do, Alice," said CJ. "It has been a while since I have talked with anyone, except maybe for my horses."

"You have horses?" questioned Alice.

"Alice, do you have time to have some coffee with me, a perfect stranger? There is a coffee shop here in this market."

She said, "I am about finished with my shopping. Sure, I'll have a cup with you."

They sat in silence for a few minutes, tasting their coffee.

"CJ, you mentioned you have horses," said Alice.

"Yes, ma'am, my horse is named Junior and Melba's is named Louise."

"You must live in an area where you can have horses?" asked Alice.

"Yes, ma'am."

"Wait," she said, "please call me Alice."

"Sorry, Alice. I actually have a spread south of town where I raise alfalfa hay and raise some cattle too. I hardly break even, but it is about the only thing I know how to do. Right now, with my mama living her last days with me, it is a sad time. I have a woman taking care of Mama at home, but it is terribly expensive, money which I don't have. I guess I'll figure out some way to find the money, but not exactly sure how. Me and Lester have our grandaddy back in Tennessee who is very old, ninety-seven, in bad health, and also very rich. He tells me that when he is gone, he has me and my brother getting all of his money, but not a penny until he dies. In fact, he wants Mama's body shipped back to Tennessee with me paying for it, since he thinks her sons are supposed to pay these costs. Lester barely gets by on SSI and welfare, so he can't help. Wait a minute," he said,

"I shouldn't be telling you my problems. I'm very sorry, I just sometimes need someone to talk to."

"That's all right," she said. "I'm told I'm a pretty good listener."

"Well, thank you, Alice. Do you mind telling me a little about yourself?" he said.

"Okay, I lost my husband, Leonard, several years ago from a heart attack. It happened so suddenly it was hard to accept. Personal loss is a terrible thing," she said. "I think of Len every day," she told him.

"What line of work was Leonard doing?"

"He owned a women's clothing store in the Montclaire Village," Alice said. "It was actually his father's business. Len took over after his father became ill and passed away. It was a very successful business for many years. We sold mostly high-quality dress wear and had a loyal clientele. I managed to sell it when Len passed away. The sale of the store, coupled with Len's life insurance, left me fairly comfortable," she said. "I must tell you, I grew up riding horses. My father was a farmer, a dairyman, so we had lots of cows and a few horses. I guess, like many young girls, I truly loved horses and rode about any time I had the chance."

ROD WELLS

"Well, Alice, after this thing with my mama, maybe you would like to come to my ranch and ride Louise, Melba's horse?"

"CJ, what happened to your wife?"

CJ went on to explain the same story about Melba he had told Dottie and how the detectives hadn't done anything. "The cops seem to think I had something to do with Melba's disappearance. Now it's been five years, five years, since she disappeared."

Alice said, "As to riding with you, I might be a little too old for that, but I might be willing to try sometime. I haven't really done very much physical activity sine Len passed away. There is also a great difference in our ages. However, I certainly believe we can be friends."

"Well," said CJ, "you seem like a young woman to me. I truly think we can be friends. Shucks, I already like your company. What do you like to do when you're not shopping?" he asked her.

"Well, I do like shopping for clothes. I guess, being married to Len and he being in the women's clothing business, I became something of a clothes horse," blushing, she replied. "But since I sold the store, I mostly shop other shops as I no longer buy at cost from our former shop. I am also something of an amateur photographer. I have

126

all sorts of camera equipment and have actually won some ribbons at the county fair. It really keeps my interest and helps pass the time."

CJ said, "I see how nice you are dressed today, you look great. Melba was more of a cowgirl, wore mostly Wrangler jeans and boots, but still looked really good."

"I'm sure she did," she replied.

"I can't tell you how much I miss her," he said. "Alice, after my mama's gone, may I call you? You have been so kind to my mama and me."

"Well, I haven't been giving out my number, but yes, please call me." She gave him her number. "All the best with your mother," she said.

"Golly," said CJ, "we've been talking for over two hours. I better get going, Mama will be very happy with this melon. I'll be sure to call you."

CHAPTER FIFTEEN

• • • ○ • • •

Captain Willis called in Lieutenant Travis. They discussed some current cases and some strategies. The captain said, "I've had a chance to go over the file on this Carl Johnson. It appears he is a pretty avid fisherman."

"Yeah, he spends a lot of time up at Grand Lake. In fact, he claims his wife enjoyed fishing with him," said the lieutenant.

"What is your take on the wife?" asked the captain.

"As far as we found, she was pretty much a cowgirl," said the lieutenant. "They had been married for over twenty years. She worked with him around the property, helping him plant alfalfa hay and keeping the horses in good condition. She also taught equestrian classes at the community college. The neighbors saw her riding around the place on her horse and occasionally riding out on the road. She also took care of the home, cooking, etcetera. Melba was a barrel racer, competing in rodeos, apparently with some success. In fact, they met at a rodeo. CJ worked the rodeos, mostly bull riding, saddle broncs, along with some steer wrestling and roping. He got pretty beaten up in a few years and had to stop. I almost forgot, Melba was crowned Rodeo Queen on several occasions. She was quite the looker."

"You mentioned marital problems?"

"Well, her two sisters don't much care for him," said the lieutenant. "As they tell it, he had been slapping her around and just being very mean to her. That was about all she would share with her sisters."

"What about finances?"

"That's where we see a motive," said the lieutenant. "When he and Melba bought the ranch, they borrowed quite a lot of money from Melba's father with only a verbal contract for the loan, which was nearly a hundred thousand dollars. They made a few payments but claimed the ranch was not providing the income they had expected and stopped making the payments. We were told by Melba's sisters that Melba wanted to get a loan on the property to repay her father, but CJ wouldn't have anything to do with that."

"What did they expect to earn to make the payments?" asked Willis.

"They planted alfalfa hay which, on a good year with twenty-five acres, would produce about four tons of hay per acre. So, at about four tons per acre and about two hundred dollars per bale, it could make them some money. This, however, is not including the seed for the crop or the cutting and harvesting. They did raise and sell steers as well," said Travis. "We were told by Melba's sisters that money was almost an obsession for CJ. Were it not for Melba's jobs at the college, they could not make ends meet despite the fact they were not paying back the loan to her father."

"The last time you spoke with him, what did you determine?" asked Willis.

"He seems more emotional than ever, telling us, as he always does, we have not done enough to find his Melba."

"If he, for example, put her into Grand Lake, it is unlikely we will ever find her. As you know, it is one of the deepest lakes in the state," said the captain.

"That's true," replied the lieutenant. "We did initially have one of our choppers do several flyovers over the lake but saw nothing."

"I think we need to bring him in again, ask him to take a polygraph," replied the captain.

CHAPTER SIXTEEN

— • ● ○ ● • —

A few days later, CJ called Alice.

"Oh, CJ, I have been concerned about you and your mother."

"Well, it so happened, shortly after I served my mama that melon, she said, 'That's the sweetest melon I have ever tasted,' and she just nodded off to sleep and never woke up."

Alice could hear him sobbing in the background. "I'm so sorry, CJ," said Alice.

"I just want to thank you again," he said. "I feel that you were there with my mama when she passed."

"I'm just glad to hear she passed peacefully," said Alice. "Are there any type of services?" she asked.

"Not really, I had her remains shipped back to Tennessee, and she will be buried at our family burial plot. I can't afford to go back for the funeral. I have gone so far in debt over all of this for my mama, but I would do it all over again. My brother, Lester, is in terrible shape since he can't go back for the funeral. I don't know what he is thinking, since he has never even been on an airplane."

"How are you doing?" she asked.

"Better than I thought I would," he replied, seeming to be still sobbing. "I was thinking about how good I felt talking with you the other day, Alice, and wondering if we might get together. I would really like to talk with you again."

"Tomorrow," she said, "I'm planning to go up to my favorite place for some photography. It is a bluff way above the river. I'm wondering if you might want to go with me? It is a dramatic view; I think it might do you some good."

"Sure," he said.

"Can we meet somewhere?" she asked. "I'm not sure we should be seen together so soon. If my friends should see us together, it would probably start a scandal."

"I can surely understand," he said.

They met the next day at a public parking lot in the city. They drove about twenty-five miles east, in her car, to a parking spot near The Bluff she had mentioned. He followed her up a short trail to the top.

"Isn't this just beautiful?" she asked him.

CJ was wondering why he was so out of breath for such a short hike.

Alice said, "I thought this might get your mind off of all of the things you have been going through. The photos, which I mentioned won blue ribbons at the county fair, were taken from this exact spot," she proclaimed very proudly.

CJ's breath was returning to normal when he said, "This is about the most pretty place I've ever been. I can see how you would win those ribbons. Thank you for bringing me up here, it is truly helping me relax a bit."

Alice took a few photographs, then mentioned, "How about I take a few of you?"

"Please don't, at least not now. Maybe next time." She did not press him.

They drove, mostly in silence, back to Layton where CJ had left his pickup truck.

"Thank you so much for this outing, it helped me clear my head a little," he said. "Do you like picnics?"

"I used to love them when Len was alive. We did picnics several times a year."

"Well, how about tomorrow?"

Alice knew she had her weekly ladies luncheon scheduled the next day. She really liked those get-togethers and thought it would be a good time to talk about her new friend. CJ, however, had that hopeful look about a picnic. *I'll go with the ladies next week,* she thought.

"Well, how about tomorrow? There's a park out on the river where Melba and me used to fish and have a picnic," he said. "I'll bring a bucket of KFC and all of the stuff we need."

"Can I bring a bottle of wine?" she asked.

"That would be fine, but I think I'll stick to beer," he replied. After giving her directions to the park, they agreed to meet there the following day.

* * * * *

Alice said, "Sure you don't want a glass of wine?"

"No thanks, us cowboys only drink beer, and sometimes whiskey, and usually too much of it."

"I have to tell you, this is a very nice spot for a picnic," said Alice.

"I just wanted to show this park to you, since it used to be been one of my favorite places to be alone, but not today," he said. "Being here with you is making it very special. I sometimes wish I could be here and not think of Melba, but, Alice, you are helping me so much with taking my mind off of her and my mama."

"I don't think it is my role to take your mind off of Melba and your mother," she said. "I have become very fond of you, CJ," she told him, "but you must understand that my feelings at this point are not romantic, but as a very dear friend. Additionally, we have a great difference in our ages. We have known each other just a short while, but I feel I can talk with you about most anything. I also believe you are the sort of man I can trust."

"I appreciate you saying that," he said. "Maybe after we have known one another longer, you won't think our ages will matter so much."

"Perhaps," she said.

They enjoyed their lunch, and Alice knew she had consumed too much wine but couldn't remember having such a good time since she had lost Len. She found herself showing interest in how far in debt that CJ might be. She blurted out the question "How bad is your debt?"

He replied, "Shucks, I don't want to bother you about that sort of thing."

Alice said, "If it isn't too much, I might be inclined to help you."

He thought for a moment and said, "It is quite a bit. I guess I need to tell you. But first, I am a very proud man and don't want anyone feeling sorry for me. I was actually thinking of trying out for some rodeos, bull riding, and saddle broncs gives a good purse. That is if I don't get killed."

"CJ," scolded Alice, "you know you are too old, and what you are talking about is clear desperation. How much?"

"Okay. I need seed for the alfalfa crop, but mostly I owe for my mama's costs for the past couple of years, plus shipping her body home. I just wish my grandaddy would help. Anyway, about forty-five thousand dollars. It was costing me over three hundred and fifty dollars a day for my mama's caregiver. It took about every cent I had. I know that is a huge amount of money. I am embarrassed,

Alice, and don't expect you to help me out. I just learned my gran-daddy had a heart attack and is not going to be with us much longer. His will has something called a trust, which has me taking care of Lester using his share of the money to take good care of him. My share will be considerable, and if you should loan me something, I would pay you back with interest," he said.

"Nonsense about interest, let me think about this," said Alice. "If I can help you in some way, it is imperative that it remains a secret between us."

"Of course, it will," he replied.

"CJ, I have to look into some financial things," she told him. "I have to tell you, this picnic is just what I've needed for so long. My life, it seems, has become rather boring. I know that my friends are good friends, but they do enjoy gossiping, so I promise that nothing will be said of us."

"That's okay with me," he said, "but why the secret?"

"Because of what I just said, they are terrible gossips. Thank you for the most wonderful day," she said. "I think I'm a little giddy from the wine."

"Are you okay to drive?" asked CJ.

"Yes, I'm sure of it," she replied. "I just feel good."

"Thank you, Alice. It has been five years since I've come back to this park, not since Melba was kidnapped, but I sure am enjoying it today."

They parted, agreeing to meet in two days at an out-of-town coffee shop. Alice went to her home, wishing she could talk to a friend. She was having some consternation about her relationship with CJ. She thought, *I know and believe his intentions are honorable. How am I going to explain to my bankers the sudden withdrawal of that much money? I certainly have plenty of money, but maybe I need to slow down a bit. I think Len would tell me I am being foolish, and perhaps I am. If only I could discuss this with someone.*

She decided to talk with her priest. She met with the father in the rectory and informally explained her dilemma. The priest said, "I think you are being too hasty, Alice. I have known you for many years and have never known you to act so, well, irrationally."

"I'm sure it seems that way, but I feel this man needs my help," said Alice.

"Who suggested this loan be a secret?" he asked.

"I did," she replied, "in fact, he asked me the same question. I explained to him my fear of gossip and perhaps having problems with my reputation."

"Alice, you asked for my advice. I believe you should slow down, learn some more about this man, this CJ, as you call him. You are moving too soon and too fast. Pray on it. Also, is there any romantic interest with either of you? You mentioned he is much younger."

"Well, that I am unsure of. I don't think he feels I am too old, but I can't be sure. Father, I don't understand any of my emotions. Am I just lonely and need a man's attention?"

"Let's put it in God's hands," he said. "Do you wish to go to confession? How long has it been?"

She declined and said, "I'm not ready at the moment. I will pray on it."

"Alice, is all you will reveal to me about this man's name are his initials, CJ?"

"At this time, yes. Thank you, Father."

"Call me if you wish to talk again," he said.

She returned home, not feeling any better about the situation. She and Len had been friends with the Layton Police chief, back before he was promoted. He and Len had been in the Lions Club together. She made the call but found the chief was on vacation. His secretary asked if someone else might help her, but she said, "When he returns, please tell the chief I called."

She called her bankers and made an appointment to meet with both of them. She met Herb McGuire first, who said, "Alice, why on earth do you need fifteen thousand dollars in cash?"

"It is a private matter, Herb, and I do not wish to discuss it. It is my money."

"Of course, it is, but it is so unlike you. Have you been threatened, or are you in some sort of trouble?"

"No, I have not, and am not in any trouble. Make the withdrawal please, Herb."

She essentially went through the same interrogation with her other banker, Ralph Cook, when she withdrew $10,000 in cash. Telling CJ she could only get $25,000 might be a good test to see his reaction. She could always get the rest of the money. She poured a glass of wine and decided she might tell just a little bit of the story to her childhood and best friend, Elaine Caldwell. She called Elaine, who said, "Where have you been, young lady? It's been days since we talked, didn't you get my messages?"

"Yes, I received your messages, but I have been a little busy."

Elaine asked, "What kind of busy? Have you finally met someone?"

"Not exactly," she replied.

"What does that mean?" asked Elaine.

"Okay, I'm going to trust you as my best friend, but you can't reveal a word about this."

"Alice, I am your best friend! If you can't trust me, whom can you trust?"

"Of course, you are."

Alice revealed just a bit about the meeting at the market in the produce section and the introduction to this nice, very much a gentleman cowboy sort of younger man.

"Younger, is that the watchword?" asked Elaine.

"Well, not a kid, if that is what you mean. More like twenty years younger. But, Elaine, this is not yet a romance. This is all I'll tell you."

"Does he have a name?" asked Elaine.

"CJ, and that's all I'm going to say."

"Well, you seem happy," she said. "Please do not do anything really stupid."

Two days later, at coffee, Alice told CJ, "I have good news and bad news."

"Please tell me the bad news," he said.

"Well, if indeed it is bad news, I was only able to get twenty-five thousand dollars."

His heart began beating rapidly, he even had some of the chest heartburn discomfort as he felt on The Bluff.

"I have to explain," she said. "When I went to the banks, I thought withdrawing from two separate bank accounts would alleviate some suspicion. I had forgotten that Len was something of a jealous man. His will stipulated if he died before me, that no other man would get his money. So the bankers told me I can loan money, if I have a valid contract. I told them I had already done the contract and also told them I want to keep it private and want to keep it personal. Because of the will, this is all I can withdraw at this time. Try to understand, CJ, they are businessmen and think they are looking out my best interests."

"Well, I don't think that is bad news," he said. "I can completely understand why Len was concerned, being married to such a beautiful woman and all. I appreciate the amount of money you were able to get for me, Alice."

"CJ, I'm happy to do it. I know you will pay me back."

"Of course, I will," he said.

Alice gave him $25,000 in cash. "Pay me back when you get your grandfather's money," she said.

"Alice, I am so grateful to you," he said. "This will help me so much for the time being. In fact, let me call some folks and arrange to pay some of the bills in the morning. I am so grateful to you, Alice. Why don't we celebrate a little bit?"

"How?" she asked.

"Let's go up to The Bluff and take some pictures of us!" he said.

"I thought you didn't wish to be photographed."

"I know, but I would be proud to have a picture taken with you. Alice, you have made me a very happy man."

Alice thought for a moment and said, "It is a perfect day for some shots from The Bluff." Alice also was thinking, in a little embarrassed way, *How could I have ever distrusted this man?*

They traveled from the coffee shop up to The Bluff in her car. On the way, CJ was carrying on most of the conversation about how she had changed his life. "I know how much you and Len were in love, so was I, with Melba. I do have to say I'm beginning to think that Melba is really dead. That's very difficult for me to say."

Alice responded, "I know it is hard for you to admit this, but it is quite possible that is the case, after all of this time."

They arrived at The Bluff. CJ helped her with the camera equipment up to the viewpoint, arriving at the summit just when he thought he needed to sit. He was strangely so out of breath.

Alice set up her camera on a tree stump so she could set up the timer in order for them to take a picture together. Alice walked to the edge of The Bluff to join CJ. She said, "Our countdown will be five, four, three, two, one. Be sure to smile, dear!" At the count of three, CJ stepped forward.

Alice said, "What are you doing?"

He turned and gave her a hard shove. Her screams seemed very brief as she fell twelve hundred feet to her death.

CJ gathered up her camera, knowing it was worth a lot. He looked around and found no evidence they had ever been there. He strolled down to Alice's car and within five minutes Lester drove up with his truck.

CJ got in and said, "It's done."

CHAPTER SEVENTEEN

●━━●━━●━━○━━●━━●━━●

The next morning, Captain Willis, at his desk, was reading the local newspaper and noted the headlines: Local Woman Falls to her Death at The Bluff, a Popular Site for Photographers. The body of Alice Fleetwood, a prominent figure in many local social circles, was found dead Wednesday at the bottom of The Bluff, a popular spot for photographers. Her car was found nearby. Mrs. Fleetwood was the widow of the late Leonard Fleetwood who previously owned a very popular women's shop in the village. Mrs. Fleetwood was known to be a very avid photographer who has won many ribbons at the county fair, as well as the state fair, mainly for her photos taken from The Bluff. This is being classified as a tragic accident according to the sheriff's department. Arrangements are pending.

Ron Willis knew Len Fleetwood from their association with the Lions Club. He had met Alice socially on a number of occasions. As a Catholic, he knew her from attending Mass. He felt badly by her death. He asked his secretary to get him the reports on the death of Alice Fleetwood.

Lieutenant Travis interrupted his thoughts with a knock on his door. "Have few minutes, Skipper?" he asked.

"What have you got?" asked the chief.

"I'm thinking of bringing Carl Johnson in for an interview."

The captain's secretary knocked on his door. She said, "Captain, you have a call from Pastor O'Brien, he says its urgent."

"I'll take it. Hello, Father, this is Ron Willis."

"Ron, I need to speak with you rather urgently," said the priest.

"Here at my office, or yours?" he replied.

"I will come to yours," said the priest.

"Jeff," said the captain, "can we speak a little later? My priest is coming in regarding something urgent."

Father O'Brien said to Ron, "I'm sure you have heard about Alice Fleetwood's death."

"Yes, I read about it in the morning paper. I've also read the report from our deputies. What is your concern about this, Father?"

"Ron, Alice recently visited me at the rectory. She was rather distraught about a man she had met and was seeking counseling from me. Before I continue, Ron, this conversation was not protected by Canon Laws. I feel her counseling request as only that. Her untimely death requires that I reveal our conversation."

"Okay, Father, what do you have?"

"Alice seemed to have a dilemma. She had met a man who seemed to feel very strongly about her. She seemed to have similar feelings but was concerned that there were at least twenty years difference in their ages. Anyway, this man had encountered some financial difficulties, and Alice seemed somehow compelled to financially help him. Please keep in mind, she barely knew the man, having just met him."

"What advice did you give her, Father?"

"I explained that she was being hasty, to slow down and to pray on it. Ron, you have known both Alice and Len for many years. This is Alice I have known both as a parishioner and a friend. This was so unlike her, I felt she was acting in an irrational manner, making financial decisions very hastily. In this case, to give, or loan, a substantial amount of money to a man she had just met, and a much younger man."

"Father, did Alice give you the name of this man?"

"No name, only the initials CJ."

The color completely drained from the captain's face. "CJ? Alice gave you this name? You are sure of this, Father?"

"Yes, I'm sure."

The captain summoned Lieutenant Travis. The captain made the introductions with the priest and lieutenant. "I think we may have a common denominator, at least with the death of Alice Fleetwood." The captain asked Father O'Brien to relate the story he had just told to Travis. After hearing the story from the father, Lieutenant Travis understood the implications. Captain Willis thanked the priest and asked if he had any ideas, to please get in touch. Father O'Brien left the office.

"So where do we go, Captain?"

"First, we have the missing wife, Melba. Now we have a suspicious case of Alice Fleetwood," said the captain.

"Do you know any of Mrs. Fleetwood's friends?" asked the lieutenant.

"I do know and believe that she and Elaine Caldwell are best friends. I'll give Elaine a call," replied the captain. "I think it's time to bring in Mr. Johnson for a chat. Why don't you take care of that, keeping in mind, an offer to him to submit to a polygraph might be in order."

The captain arrived at Elaine's home. She answered the door chimes. "Hello, Ron." She appeared to have been crying.

"I wanted to be sure that you have heard the sad news."

"Yes, I learned of it in this morning's paper. I just cannot believe that she is gone. I just spoke to her two days ago, she seemed to be so happy. She told me she had met a man, actually, a much younger man. She was being very discreet, only telling me bits and pieces. She would not admit any romantic feelings, but I sensed there was something stronger than friendship."

"Did she reveal the name of this man?"

"Only CJ," she said.

Captain Willis returned to the office. Lieutenant Travis was waiting for him. "I just received a call from Herb McGuire, manager of the Layton Bank. He told me that Alice Fleetwood, a longtime client, was in recently withdrawing a significant amount of money, all in cash. Mr. McGuire, it seems, had lunch yesterday with Ralph Cook, manager of Central Bank, who also had a visit from Mrs. Fleetwood when she withdrew a large amount of cash. She told them, when questioned about the withdrawals, that the money was for a loan to someone whose identity she would not reveal, and it was her money to do with as she pleased."

"How much money are we talking about?" asked Ron.

"Privacy laws prevent them from disclosure. They do, however, welcome subpoenas. Both bankers thought her actions very unlike her."

CHAPTER EIGHTEEN

———— • ● ○ ● • ————

Gloria Rawlings Hansen, age seventy-four, had grown up in Wyoming. Her father worked with the US Forest Service. He was assigned to the ranger station and worked mostly in the largest part of Yellowstone, which is in Wyoming. Her mother was an elementary school teacher. Apart from the, at times, brutally cold weather, Gloria enjoyed living near Yellowstone.

She was a good student and had many friends. Gloria's father's job required a great deal of horseback riding and they owned several horses. At age twelve, she was given a horse as a Christmas gift. This experience of horse ownership taught her the importance of taking care of one's animals. It was hard work taking care of horses. The cold environment of Wyoming could easily kill the horses if they were not tended to and kept out of the elements. Being a caretaker was likely why Gloria decided to become a teacher.

During high school she dated some, but nothing very serious. She could be counted on to study very hard. During those long Wyoming winter evenings, she wrapped herself in a warm blanket reading English literature, especially Shakespeare. Upon graduating high school, Gloria enrolled at The University of Wyoming in Laramie as an English major. After her first year living in the dorms, she was ready, as a sophomore, to move in together with some of her fellow students. All three of her new roommates had attended high school with her.

One cold Saturday night, Gloria and her roommates went out, sort of bar hopping. That was when she met Eric Hansen, a tall, blond Viking. She by then had consumed two beers and was feeling it. Her roommates were ready to move on to another bar. Gloria told them to go ahead, she wanted to continue talking to this Viking. She and Eric continued to talk and drink some more. Eric, she learned, was taking Fire Science classes at UOW and wanted to become a state firefighter. The meeting that night developed into a wonderful romance. She and Eric were inseparable. It was destined to become marriage at some point.

Shortly after Gloria graduated from the university, she accepted a position teaching high school English in Casper, Wyoming. Eric by now had been working as a state firefighter and living in Casper as well. The couple was now engaged. The impending marriage was approved by Gloria's and Eric's parents. The couple married. Both worked very hard. They wanted children, which they later determined could not happen. Rather than feeling down, this only seemed to strengthen their marriage.

There came a time they were both tiring of Wyoming winters and began looking for employment elsewhere. Gloria found a position in Riverview, which was in Center County west of Nevada. Eric followed her out West. Eric was hired as a state firefighter. Gloria went to work teaching English at Riverview High. They both ended up retiring about the same time. Then Eric became ill and died.

* * * * *

Gloria had seen CJ riding a horse on his ranch. She pulled up next to his fence, so he rode over to see her, a well-dressed, older woman. She greeted him with a "Good morning." He asked her if she needed some help. She replied, "I used to ride quite a lot when I was younger, and seeing you on horseback brought back some wonderful memories."

"My name is CJ. I'm about to go to the barn, and from what I can see, you are dressed very nicely, or I'd ask if you would like drive up to the barn and meet my horses."

"Never mind how I'm dressed. I would love to meet your horses." Gloria drove up to the barn. "My name is Gloria Hansen." They shook hands. She noticed him to be a tall, lanky cowboy and kind of handsome, in an outdoors sort of way.

"This fella is Junior," he said, "and he has put in a full working day. I'm about to groom him."

Gloria very excitedly said, "May I groom him, please?" followed by "It's been a while, but I'm sure I am up to it, never mind how I'm dressed, please?"

"Well, that is mighty kindly of you, Gloria. Sure, I've still got some chores to do and appreciate the help. Do you like Mexican food?" he asked her.

"I love it," she replied.

"Well, if you have time tomorrow," he explained the nearby restaurant, "I would like to invite you to lunch."

"Sure, only if it isn't a date, I am far too old for you," she told him.

"I'm not too sure about a date, but I could surely use some company," replied CJ.

That is how it started. At lunch the following day, he told her about Melba and her kidnapping five years ago. She offered her sympathy. At his invitation, Gloria began to visit, helping with some chores, cleaning horse stalls, feeding the horses and cattle, bringing treats such as carrots and apples for the horses. She told him the exercise was good for her and she had actually lost five pounds. She told CJ she was seventy-four years old and had been widowed six years ago. Her late husband, Eric, had been a firefighter for the state and retired with a good pension. Gloria was a retired high school English teacher. Having been a teacher for thirty-eight years, she also had a nice pension and, according to her, she had invested wisely. She and Eric never had children. She and Eric had traveled extensively until he had been stricken with a form of leukemia that took his life very quickly.

CJ didn't mind her hanging around the ranch. She did, on a couple occasions, ride Melba's horse around the ranch. He could tell she had done some riding. For some reason they never left the property but did sit and have long chats. If possible, thought CJ, he kind of liked her. It was also time to work on her.

"Gloria," CJ said one afternoon, "I have an opportunity to invest in very well-known stud horse and a well-known mare. This is a very private matter, but as a friend, I know I can trust you. A good friend went in over his head in buying this stud. He borrowed everything he could to buy the horse. I have been helping him pay back the costs for the horse. Since the stud fees have skyrocketed, he will soon get out of debt. This past year, he bred the stud, resulting in twin foals. My ten-thousand-dollar investment with him earned me seventy-five thousand in fees for the sale of the foals. Gloria, you have helped me a great deal and have become my friend. My friend's stud is going to breed again with another mare"—he spoke her name in her ear—"and, as I remember, you're an investor. This stud's fees have more than doubled. If you wish, I'll give you an opportunity to invest in this next one with me. This will be the last time I will be able to do this, as he will pay all of his debts with this next breeding."

"Well, CJ, thank you for thinking of me," she replied. "When will this breeding take place?"

"In about two weeks," he replied.

"Will I be able to see the horses?" she asked.

"I guess that you will have to trust me on that. You see, the horses are both being boarded in Kentucky. I can probably get you some pictures of them; that is, if you don't trust me," replied CJ.

"Of course, I trust you."

"Maybe I shouldn't involve you in this," he said.

"Don't be foolish. I'm very appreciative and hope I haven't hurt your feelings. I really want to invest in this opportunity. How much will I need?"

"Can you come up with twenty to twenty-five thousand dollars?" he asked. "How about twenty-five? Even if it's only one foal, it is an almost guaranteed hundred-thousand-dollar profit," he said. "But it has to be in cash, and our secret."

"Okay, I'll do it."

"You're a smart woman, Gloria. Bring me the cash as soon as you can."

"Tomorrow afternoon," she said.

"Great" was his reply.

CJ had mentioned his wealthy, very elderly grandaddy in Tennessee. He mentioned his brother, Lester, and Lester's mental issues. He told her about his grandaddy leaving his wealth to him and his brother. Gloria just didn't seem at all interested in him, which sort of hurt his feelings. When he told her about Melba's kidnapping, she appeared concerned about him and why the police always seemed to think he had something to do with his wife's disappearance.

"Now, I was wondering if you would like to load up Junior and Louise and take a little trail ride tomorrow?" asked CJ.

"That sounds like fun, but do you think this old woman is up to it?" asked Gloria.

"Oh sure, I've seen you ride here and believe you will do just fine. It is, for the most part, pretty easy. I won't let you get hurt. We will make a real day of it."

"May I make a picnic lunch?" she asked.

"That would be great. There are some very pretty spots along the river," he told her. "I do have to ask if you have told anyone about you helping me here at the ranch?"

"Only April, my sister who lives on the East Coast. I have only told her that I have met a nice man who is a real cowboy and you let me help out with ranch chores. She fully understands, having been an avid horse lover as well. I've also mentioned that you are much younger and there isn't any romantic relationship between us, okay? Why do you ask?" replied Gloria.

"It's just I'd rather not have any rumors or gossip get out that I'm seeing a woman, even though we know we are just friends. You know how rumors start," he said. "Gloria, due to what happened to Melba and the detectives having trouble with my kidnapping story, I just try to keep to myself. That's why I want your investment, and us being friends, kept as a secret. I hope you understand."

"I think I do and am looking forward to our trail ride and picnic tomorrow," she said.

"See you here in the morning," replied CJ.

Gloria encountered similar problems with her bankers as had the other women. That's why she went to her bank and Credit Union taking $10,000 from one and $15,000 from the other. She had created some emergency cash needs but was still very scrutinized by the two bank managers. At one point, she began to question herself and hoped she was not being foolish. How well did she know CJ?

She called her sister, April, who lived in Vermont, and told her what she was planning. April seemed surprised about what her sister was going to do, which April described as rash behavior. Gloria admitted that something was bothering her, but this man seemed so sincere, and she really thought he was doing her a favor by making some easy money.

April asked the man's name.

Gloria said, "His initials are CJ, but that's all I can reveal, it is supposed to be a secret." Gloria said she was more concerned about this investment being illegal or some type of insider trading than she was worried about the man.

"Twenty-five thousand dollars is a substantial amount of money," said April. "Come on, sis, I know you have always been something of a risk taker, but this doesn't sound like a good idea." Before ending the call, April said, "I think you are being rash."

CHAPTER NINETEEN

⸻ • ● ● ○ ● ● • ⸻

After a pretty restless night, Gloria returned the following morning with $25,000 in cash.

CJ reassured her of making the right decision. He said, taking the money, "In just about a year from now, you will be at least a hundred thousand dollars richer. By the way, so will I, I invested the same amount as you."

"That's right, the gestation period for a horse is close to a year," said Gloria.

She watched CJ effortlessly load the horses into the trailer. He suggested she leave her car keys in the tack room, as he explained, "The one thing people lose on trail rides are their car keys."

Shortly after CJ and Gloria left with the horses, Lester drove up to the ranch and retrieved Gloria's car keys from the tack room. He had been instructed by his brother that, when driving Gloria's car, to obey traffic laws, as it would be a problem if he got pulled over. He gave them a twenty-minute head start, then started to take the same route, following his brother.

They drove up to the foothills, some twenty-five miles east to a very remote site, where he parked his truck and horse trailer on a grassy area next to the river. After unloading the horses, he made sure they were alone. When he was certain there wasn't anyone else around, he said, "We're pretty much ready to go," as they had saddled the horses before loading them at the ranch. He gave her a quick lesson on unloading the horses. Gloria was told, "Next time you get to do it," trying to gain her trust for what was about to come.

CJ stowed the picnic lunch in a saddle bag, and off they rode. Gloria carried on about the beauty of the river and how smooth the trail was. As they rode, Gloria asked, "What is that roaring noise?"

"That's your surprise, it's called Equinox Falls. Don't ask me what that means, but I hear it was named by early Indian tribes."

Gloria was feeling pretty comfortable riding Louise and thoroughly enjoying herself, thinking about just a short while ago her major activity was the ladies book club. She felt that CJ, despite him being younger, was putting some spirit back into her life. She was losing weight, becoming stronger, and loving life, thanks to this cowboy.

They dismounted. CJ motioned to a very large pine tree which had fallen across the top of the roaring falls. "This is truly beautiful," said Gloria.

"And we are going to picnic on the other side," he replied.

"No, CJ," she replied. "No way I'm going to go over on that tree."

"There is nothing to it, even little children cross over here all the time," he responded.

"But I'm afraid."

"Nothing to be afraid of," he said, "I'll hold your hand. We will have the best picnic ever. You have to trust me."

"Okay," she replied, "I trust you completely."

CJ removed the picnic lunch from the saddlebag and went first. Gloria extended her hand and, about halfway across, CJ smiled at her and said, "I am holding your hand so I can shove you!"

Gloria screamed as she fell into the horrible turbulence.

As he got off the log, a surprised CJ saw Gloria surface momentarily with outstretched arms screaming, "CJ! Please help me!" He just stood and watched as she was pulled under again. This time she did not resurface. She was gone.

CJ very calmly walked back to the horses. He was joined shortly by Lester, who appeared from the brush. "You did it, why did it take so long?" asked Lester.

"Sometimes we just have to work a little harder."

"Well, you hit it big time!" Lester told his brother. CJ, again, felt both indigestion, along with some sexual arousal.

They rode the horses back to the parking area during which Lester was questioned about how thoroughly he had cleaned up Gloria's car. Satisfied it didn't contain any evidence of Lester being in her car, they returned to the spot where Lester had parked Gloria's car.

CJ moved the truck and trailer away, and his brother parked Gloria's car in the now vacant spot. CJ made sure his brother was wearing gloves. The spot was grass, and no tire prints would be left from his rig. CJ took Gloria's car keys and casually threw them into the river.

"How much did I make?" questioned Lester.

"Eight hundred dollars," replied CJ, "but first, we need to get back to the ranch."

"Wow," replied Lester, "that's a lot of money. Thank you, CJ."

On the drive, they shared the delicious picnic lunch Gloria had prepared. CJ thought this was a good time to talk with his brother. "Lester," he said while driving back to the ranch, "we need to talk about how you have been helping me."

"Okay," he replied.

"You need to know I was questioned again by those mean detectives about Melba's kidnapping."

"They shouldn't be mean to you," replied Lester.

"I know, but that's the way they are. You need to know they may try to talk with you."

"They scare me," he said.

"Don't let them scare you," replied CJ. "Please listen very carefully, Lester. If the cops, any cops, try to talk to you, you tell them, 'I won't talk to you, I want a lawyer.' Do you understand what I just told you? What do you say if the cops want to talk to you?"

"I won't talk to you; I want a lawyer."

"Very good," he told his brother.

CHAPTER TWENTY

G loria's body was discovered by two fishermen who had been trolling from their boat. Her body had been badly bloated and pounded from river rocks. The bloated body had snagged on some willow branches which reached out into the river. One of the men was dropped ashore to try and get help in notifying the sheriff's office.

The sheriff's deputy, Harold Drummond, who responded to the river, picked up the waiting fisherman who directed him to the location of the body. With help from the fisherman who was still in the running boat, they tied off the body as well as they could with some extra anchor rope from the boat. Deputy Drummond hoped the rope would hold until the search and recovery staff arrived. At this point, he had no idea who the deceased might be. As a fairly new deputy, this was his first dead body, and being cautious, he called for a detective. He recalled a white car parked on a grassy area when he picked up the reporting fisherman who had been waiting for him.

Meanwhile, the deputy radioed dispatch seeking any information on any recent missing persons, as he was unable to determine the sex of the deceased. The body was dressed in jeans, a partially intact blue shirt, and had a Western boot visible on the right foot. The other leg and foot were still submerged. He quickly returned to the unoccupied white car, ran the license plate, and returned to the body. The vehicle was registered to a Gloria Hansen, near Riverview.

The search and recovery team arrived at the same time as the crime scene investigators. Detective Sergeants Lynn Hoover and Bill Morris arrived shortly after and took charge of the investigation. They had returned from Allen County the previous day, following up on the Alice Fleetwood case.

They first interviewed Deputy Drummond. He informed them that the registration of the white vehicle was for a Gloria Hansen. The car was unlocked and appeared to have been there for a period of days. The deputy described being dispatched to the scene regarding a deceased person. He went on about meeting one of the fishermen who was waiting for him. He recounted, "According to the fisherman, he left the boat and found a nearby home from which he called the sheriff's department."

Two divers from the recovery team went into the swiftly running river. They found the deceased's other leg caught in parts of the submerged willow tree. They carefully tied off the body and removed it to the riverbank. The detectives interviewed, thanked, and released the shaken fishermen, who both proclaimed they were finished fishing for the day. The crime scene team took a number of photographs of the body, which was missing the left boot and sock.

Both Hoover and Morris determined the deceased to be an adult female. Morris carefully searched the body. He found the back pocket of the jeans had a closed zipper. He opened the zipper and found a DMV driver's license for Gloria Hansen, with an address in Center County, near the city of Riverview.

Deputy Drummond was thanked and complimented on doing a very thorough job. "That information will be passed onto your supervisor," Sergeant Morris told him.

He asked if they wanted him to make the death notification at the woman's residence. "No, thanks," said Sergeant Lynn Hoover, "we will take care of it. We are not even sure of what we have at this point." She told the deputy he could return to duty. She did mention, however, "Please make your report a priority and have a copy directed to Sergeant Morris and me."

"You got it," he replied, as he returned to his beat.

In checking with dispatch, they found nothing as to her being missing.

The county coroner took over with the remains. He told Morris and Hoover, "The autopsy will be conducted in the morning by Dr. Luke Evans, unless you find this to be something more than an accident or suicide."

The crime scene team searched all the way to the falls, looking for any type of evidence. The terrain was mostly grassy. All that was found was what appeared to be fairly fresh horse manure. The unit supervisor, Sergeant Mark Conrad, said, "Take all of the horse shit. Take lots of photos first. I hope this is not all of the evidence we find, or we will be the brunt of many jokes." Gloria's unlocked vehicle was processed and photographed. A county tow truck removed the vehicle to the sheriff's impound for further processing.

After they cleared the scene, Morris and Hoover discussed what they had just seen. Morris said, "What do you think, suicide or accident?"

"It could be either," said Lynn. "I do know, if she went into the Equinox Falls, or if anyone else did for that matter, she was likely doomed."

The sergeants arrived at the address listed for Gloria Hansen. The door was answered by an adult female. After identifying themselves, Lynn asked if this is the home of a Gloria Hansen. The woman immediately said, "Something's happened to her?" she asked anxiously. "I just know it."

"May we come in?" asked Sergeant Morris.

"Yes, please," answered the woman.

"Are you related to Ms. Hansen?" asked Sergeant Hoover.

"She is my older sister. Please tell me, has something happened to her? I just arrived here this afternoon from Vermont. My name is April Beaumont. I flew out because I have been terribly worried about her. My calls have been going to her answering machine."

As previously discussed, Lynn would deliver the bad news. "Ms. Beaumont, it is our sad duty to inform you that a body has been found in the river. We believe there's a good chance it is your sister, Gloria Hansen. We can't be completely certain; however, her car was parked nearby, and her driver's license was found in a pocket of the jeans the deceased was wearing. We are very sorry for your loss."

The detectives waited patiently and compassionately until the grief and crying subsided. "Oh my god, not my sis! Why can't you tell me if it's her?"

"Sadly, Ms. Beaumont, the body has been in the water and been dragged over many rocks in swiftly moving current. We will know for certain shortly after her fingerprint information comes back. That is, if her fingerprints are on file."

"I'm sure they are," said April, "she taught high school for many years." As she had somewhat regained her composure, she said, "I told her it was a bad idea. She shouldn't have trusted that guy. She planned on making lots of money from that scheme."

"What scheme?" asked Sergeant Morris.

"She met a guy who had talked her into investing money in a stud horse, as she described. Apparently, the guy had loaned the horse's owner a considerable amount of money to purchase the horse. The stud horse's owner was paying back the loan by letting this guy sell the foals when they were born. Anyway, something like that, it sounded fishy. Gloria told me that she completely trusted this guy. I told her she was being rash."

"How much money did she give this guy?" asked Morris.

"Twenty-five thousand dollars," April replied, "which Gloria claimed would net her at least a hundred thousand dollars when the foal, or foals, were born."

"Do you have a name for this guy?" asked Morris.

"Gloria would only give me his initials, CJ."

Lynn gasped. "CJ?"

April, hearing Lynn's reaction, asked, "Do you know who this CJ might be?"

Sergeant Morris promptly said, "Those initials have come up in another investigation we have been working. That's all we can tell you right now."

Sergeant Morris received a page to call the office. He was told the coroner had confirmed the deceased's remains to be Gloria Hansen. April was immediately given the confirmation information. She again began sobbing.

"Ms. Beaumont, if you feel up to it, may we talk a bit more about your sister's relationship with this CJ?"

"Okay," April replied, "she told me she had met this cowboy, sort of by accident. Incidentally, Gloria and I were brought up riding horses. She spoke to him after she saw him riding around his ranch on horseback. After a bit, she ended up grooming his horse. This led to her hanging around the ranch, helping with chores. She cleaned the horse's stalls, fed the animals, etcetera. This was all voluntary on her part. Gloria was feeling better, lost weight, and just enjoyed being in the outdoors and riding his horse, Louise, which she described as belonging to his kidnapped wife. She and CJ became friendly, Gloria told me; however, not romantically. He was younger, and she was not ready for a romance with any man. This had been going on for a while, when she told me about the investment, which she called it. She had complete trust in this man, CJ. Again, I tried to get her to reconsider but knew she was going forward with the deal. That's about it," said April. "Being in Vermont, it was very frustrating for me."

"Thank you, Ms. Beaumont," said Lynn.

Since they were already in Ms. Hansen's home, they asked for April's permission to have the crime scene people search and process the house. She gave her permission. The search only found a daily calendar listing a number of days with CJ as an apparent reminder to do something, along with his telephone number. No fingerprints were found other than those which were later to be determined as Gloria's.

Lynn mentioned to April she needed to go to the coroner's office to make arrangement for her sister's remains after the autopsy, when the body is ready for release.

"Oh my god!" said April. "I'm not sure I can do that."

"Tell you what," said Lynn, "no need to go there today. Does Gloria have a will or burial instructions?"

"Yes, we both do. I actually have all of my sister's information. I am administrator of her estate."

"Do you know where she banked?"

"Yes, Layton Bank and Mid-Valley Credit Union. I am going there this afternoon to get into her accounts."

"Will you do us a favor?" asked Sergeant Morris.

"Certainly" was the reply.

"The bank manager is Herb McGuire, and Phillip Wilson manages Mid-Valley. You can save us a subpoena by inquiring about the recent large cash withdrawals by Gloria and the amount. It will be helpful to know her explanation for getting that much cash. We will interview Herb and Phil at a later time."

"Sure," said April.

Sergeant Hoover and April seemed to have bonded to some degree. She told April, "If you wish, I'll meet you at the coroner's office tomorrow to try and help you get through this tough time. I can't begin to imagine how difficult this will be for you."

April began sobbing and wrapped her arms around Lynn. "Thank you so much for such kindness."

CHAPTER TWENTY-ONE

———— • ● ● ○ ● ● • ————

The crime scene team had finished with Gloria's home and had already departed. The sergeants departed. Their anxious conversation was focused on CJ. How to proceed? They called for a meeting the following morning with Lieutenant Travis, Captain Willis, and Chief Deputy District Attorney Karen Miller.

Karen Miller was thirty-five years old. She was still single, only by her choice. She was about five feet, eight inches tall and had blond shoulder-length hair. She was born and raised in Southern California.

Her mother, Elaine, was retired as a prosecutor for the Los Angeles County District Attorney's Office. She had enjoyed her career as a prosecutor, retiring after over thirty years. Karen's father had also been a prosecutor in Los Angeles. He was respected by the defense bar, as well as the law enforcement agencies in Los Angeles

County. When Karen was in seventh grade, her father, John, was appointed by the governor to the superior court bench. Until retirement, John ran successfully, unopposed, and remained on the bench for thirty years. He retired just last year. Growing up in such an environment had a great influence on Karen. She became nearly obsessed with the law.

During middle school and high school summer breaks, she would spend the day sitting in her father's courtroom, observing cases. She impressed her father many times by researching both California and California Appellate cases. Judge Miller complimented and thanked her for making his job easier with her case research.

In high school, Karen participated and competed in public speaking, including debate. She did so well in those events, she competed successfully all over the United States. Along with academics, she was popular with classmates. She graduated high school with many honors, including valedictorian of her class.

There was no doubt about what Karen wanted to do with her life. If her background was not enough, Karen's best friend, Rachel Epperson, had been kidnapped, raped, and murdered. When Rachel's murderer went to trial, Karen sat unemotionally throughout the trial.

When the defendant was convicted of Rachel's murder, only then did Karen burst out and cry.

She went to UCLA and completed her undergraduate BA degree in three years, while still living at home. Prior to entering UCLA Law School, she became engaged to a young man she had known since she was in first grade. Benjamin Thomas was a year older than her.

Ben had been a first-year law student at UCLA when his National Guard unit was deployed to the crisis in the Mid-East. Second Lieutenant Benjamin Thomas had been killed in action within three weeks of his arrival. The loss of Ben was stunning to Karen, along with her family and their many friends. Karen was offered counseling but refused, saying, "I'm determined to carry on."

She entered UCLA Law School and never looked back. She took, and easily passed, the California bar and went to work as a deputy district attorney for the county of Los Angeles. Family and friends admired the way she continued on after the loss of Ben. Karen seemed to make it look easy. That was not the case. Nothing was easy for her when it came to Ben. As far as it went with dating, or men at all, Karen had no spirit. She was permanently scarred.

After a stellar career in Los Angeles, she was tired of the big city. She found a recruitment for a deputy district attorney in Center

County, applied, and was hired. She loved the feel of a smaller community. She advanced quickly and, in a few years, was appointed chief deputy district attorney.

Karen was known both locally and statewide as a brilliant but hardnosed prosecutor. She had taken only the most difficult criminal cases. Local judges admired her, not only for her abilities, but because she was always prepared. The local defense attorneys typically cringed when learning Karen would be prosecuting his or her client.

Also attending the meeting were Detective Sergeant Bill Burris, Layton Police Department, and Detective Ron Adams, Riverview Police Department. At the meeting, Sergeant Bill Morris briefed everyone there about Gloria Hansen, who they believed to be another homicide committed by Carl Johnson. Sergeant Hoover, meanwhile, was attending the autopsy.

"Well," said Karen Miller, "I know what I have to say will not make you happy."

"Go ahead, we have thick skin," said Captain Willis.

"Let's begin with who and what we have. First, we have our suspect, Carl Johnson, a.k.a. CJ," said Chief Deputy District Attorney Miller. "He is suspected in the murders of several women, beginning with his wife, Melba, five years ago. Next, Sylvia Robinson, three years ago. Dottie Lambert, Maxine Farrell, Alice Fleetwood, and now, Gloria Hansen. There is a chance there might be others we are not even aware of."

A knock on the door interrupted the meeting. "Captain Willis, Sergeant Hoover is on the line."

He put her on speaker phone. "Hi, Lynn, we're all assembled. What have you got?"

"The autopsy on Gloria Hansen has been completed by Dr. Luke Evans. Her body was in bad shape; however, the cause of death will be listed as drowning. I will be back soon," she said. "I am helping the sister, April Beaumont, trying to get through with all the stuff involved in this difficult situation."

"Thanks, Lynn, we'll see you soon. You will be briefed on our meeting," said the captain.

"We all have the greatest respect for our pathologist, Dr. Evans," said Lieutenant Travis. "I'm sure if he could find anything else in the way of physical evidence, he would have found it."

Karen Miller said, "This is another example illustrating the lack of evidence regarding CJ. We know, or at least believe, he had a relationship of some sort with Gloria Hansen. But she died from drowning. Her car was left nearby. Did she accidentally slip and fall into the water, or commit suicide jumping into the falls, or was she pushed? If we combine the information from all of these cases, we might be able to obtain a search warrant for CJ's property. If I remember correctly, he, at one time, said you could search his place," said Miller.

"That's true," said Morris. "I am not so certain that is still the case."

* * * * *

CJ, under cover of darkness, had removed the cash from his underground safe located at the southwest corner of his ranch. The safe was well built, waterproof, and well hidden. He had concealed it by placing a concrete irrigation cover over the top. Unless he hired someone to help with irrigation, it shouldn't be discovered. It fit well with the surroundings.

The stacks of $100 bills made him very happy. He knew, however, he needed a great deal more cash if he was going to move to Argentina and live the life of a rich cowboy. He wondered if the women down there were called *señoritas*. He was sure they were beautiful. He really needed a big score if this was going to happen. A really big score.

His daydreaming was suddenly interrupted when he heard a vehicle going by on the road, very slowly. This gave him immediate indigestion, and he planned on taking some Tums soon. He waited for about ten minutes, but the vehicle didn't return. He took the Tums and quickly returned the cash to the safe, vowing to not open it until his next score. Maybe it was time to start working on the rich doctor.

* * * * *

"Hello, Mr. Johnson, this is Lieutenant Travis with the sheriff's department."

"What can I do for you?" replied CJ.

"I was wondering if you might come into the office to speak a bit about your missing wife?"

"Do you have news about my Melba?"

"Perhaps a little. Will you come in tomorrow morning, let's say, ten o'clock?"

"Okay," replied CJ.

* * * * *

The following morning, CJ appeared at the Sheriff's Detective Bureau.

"Lieutenant, there is a Mr. Johnson here to see you."

"Thank you, please seat him in interview room one."

Upon entering the interview room, Lieutenant Travis said, "Good morning, Mr. Johnson, I'm sure you remember Detective Sergeant Bill Morris." They offered their hands, but CJ ignored the handshake. "Before we begin, I just want you to know that our interview will be videoed and recorded, just standard procedure. You do understand?"

"Yes, I do. What news do you have?" CJ asked. "Have you found Melba?"

"We will get to that," said the sergeant.

"We are working on some new information," said Morris.

"What new information?" said CJ.

"Is it okay to call you CJ?" asked Morris.

"Yeah, but what is this new information?"

"To begin with, we want to talk with you about Alice Fleetwood."

"I don't know anyone named Alice. Who is she?" he asked.

"You didn't meet a lady named Alice?" asked Sergeant Morris.

"Not that I remember," he replied.

"Odd that you can't remember Alice Fleetwood who you spent a couple hours with, drinking coffee."

The heartburn suddenly hit CJ again. "Oh, now I remember, her name was Alice," he said. "I just plumb forgot. I made her acquaintance at the market, in produce. She asked me to help pick a ripe melon. For some reason that happens all the time. Women must think that I'm a farmer or something."

"How did you end up having coffee with her?" asked Lieutenant Travis.

"It was her, she asked to treat me to coffee there in the market."

"You two must have had an awful lot to talk about."

"We discussed her being a widow and stuff like that. She seemed a little lonely. She was much older than me," he said. "Come to think of it, I told her about what happened to my wife, Melba. She seemed like a nice lady, and I liked talking with her."

"When did you next see her?" asked the sergeant.

"I never seen her again," he said. "Why are you asking me about this woman Alice?"

"CJ, this woman gave you a large amount of cash. Don't you think that's a little unusual since you hardly knew her, just having a cup of coffee together?"

"What the hell are you talking about?" a visibly shaken CJ shouted. "She didn't give me any money, why would she? I barely knew her!"

"Because her body was found in the river at The Bluff."

"That woman I met, Alice, is dead? How did that happen, and why are asking me about it?"

"Mr. Johnson, CJ, we have a question."

"What about?"

"What if we leave here right now, accompany you to your home. Will you let us search your home and property?"

"Hell yes, I don't have anything to hide. Let's go," said CJ, *who suddenly remembered Alice's camera was sitting on a dresser in his bedroom.* "Oh, wait a minute I have some errands to do. How about tomorrow?"

"We will see if that works," said Lieutenant Travis.

"We have few more things to discuss," said Sergeant Morris.

"Okay," replied CJ, whose heart was still racing, and the familiar indigestion had returned.

"We received a call that you were seen recently at Grand Lake in your boat, with a woman in the boat with you."

The color in his face seemed to fade for a moment. CJ then jumped up and angrily shouted, "That's a lie! The last time I was in my boat on that lake with a woman, it was fishing with Melba before she was kidnapped. Who is making up such a terrible lie?"

"Our source at this time will remain confidential," said the sergeant.

"Confidential, my ass," replied CJ. "Okay, from the time I lost my Melba, you guys have done nothing to find her. All you do is accuse me and treat me with suspicion."

"CJ, you must understand our position. We only have a statement from a witness who reported you were at Grand Lake with a woman in your boat," said Lieutenant Travis. "You know, maybe you can clear up some of these points, including Alice Fleetwood, by taking a polygraph."

"What's that?" asked CJ.

"A lie detector," said Lieutenant Travis.

"A lie detector? I'm finished here. You guys can't do your job, you have to blame someone, so you blame me. I'll tell you what, just leave me alone. I don't know about a woman in my boat, and I didn't get no twenty-five thousand dollars from that woman, Alice. I am going to get me a lawyer and sue your assess." CJ stormed out of the office.

"Okay, someone stop the video and recording," said Captain Willis. "His blurting out twenty-five thousand dollars tells us we have our man."

* * * * *

CJ was nervously driving home. *What the hell's wrong with me?* he thought. *Did they say $25,000 or did I say $25,000? I must be getting very careless. And her camera, I must be losing it!* he thought to himself. *I should have gotten rid of that camera, even though it's worth lots of money.* He called Lester to have him get rid of the camera. *Those damned detectives trying to trick me.*

CJ really needed a big score. Those cops were starting to get too close. He was almost frantic, trying to remember what kind of evidence he may have at his house. *Should I get me a lawyer?* CJ thought. He just really wanted to get more cash, *fast*, and get to South America. He was pretty sure those detectives could find out he had got himself a passport. He had gotten a passport for Lester too, because he couldn't leave him behind. He realized Lester must remain out of sight, unless he needed him for something. He knew that Lester would fold if those detectives brought him in for an interview. It occurred to CJ that he might have to eliminate Lester after his big score. He knew they were not through with him.

CHAPTER TWENTY-TWO

C aptain Willis called Chief Deputy District Attorney Karen Miller and arranged a meeting in the detective conference room. Ms. Miller joined Captain Willis, Lieutenant Travis, along with Sergeants Morris and Lynn Hoover who had recently been promoted to detective sergeant. Lieutenant Travis set the stage about the death of Alice Fleetwood, including CJ's blurting out the $25,000.

"Aside from them having coffee, the priest being told by Alice she had met a man named CJ, and him, as you say, blurting out 'twenty-five thousand dollars' is hardly enough to obtain a search warrant, let alone getting an arrest warrant. If we go for a search warrant, what are we looking for?" asked Karen Miller.

"Any evidence we have involving Alice Fleetwood, and especially her camera which was not found at the crime scene," replied Lieutenant Travis.

"I appreciate your belief that this CJ is a murder suspect. Any reasonably good defense attorney will explain away the money. He heard someone mention it somewhere could and would be entirely believable. We need a great deal more evidence," said the prosecutor, "including sudden cash withdrawals. Let's focus on the past couple of years to begin with. Especially any cases mentioning CJ."

"Excuse me, Captain Willis, you have a Detective Dave Dorsey on the line. He is from Allen County." Allen County was two counties north of Center County.

"Hello, Dave, I think the last time we spoke was at last year's sheriffs' convention," said Captain Willis. "How are things?" asked the captain.

"Going pretty well. It has been the same old story here, although we did have the riots a few months ago. I have to tell you, Ron, that was enough excitement to last me until retirement next year." said Detective Dorsey.

"Well, you have certainly more than earned your pension, Dave. What's up?"

"I had a little free time this morning, so I went through some pawn tickets, and guess what?"

"I have no idea," said Captain Willis.

"A camera your office listed on NCIC as stolen during a homicide. The victim is an Alice Fleetwood. It must have just been entered as stolen. Because of the camera's value, the pawn shop's owner checked with my office after it came in and found no record of it being stolen."

"You are right, Dave; it took us some time to obtain the serial number. But thank God you checked the pawn tickets." The captain's heart was pounding with excitement. "God bless you, Dave," he said. "Who pawned it?" asked an excited Ron Willis.

"A guy by the name of John Smith, if you can believe it," said Dorsey.

"Where is the camera now?" which drew some interested looks from all of the people in the room.

"Sitting right here on my desk," Dorsey replied. "I have been very careful and have bagged it. Thought you guys would most likely want to process it."

"Good thinking Dave," said Willis. "This camera is evidence from a homicide case we're working. It will hopefully be very helpful to our investigation." This comment now had the attention of everyone in the room. "I'm going to send up two of the detectives who are working this case," said the captain. "They will bring a photo lineup of our suspect."

"Sort of bad news there," said Dorsey. "The employee who took in the camera quit his job and reportedly moved to Florida. The shop owner, Oscar Garner, is trying to find him. Oscar, by the way, is a pretty good guy and will try his best to find this guy. Incidentally, Oscar is going to be out three hundred and fifty dollars, the amount he paid out to the person who pawned the camera. So his shop did take it in good faith because it had not yet been listed on NCIC."

"We appreciate his situation, Dave, but I don't know how to reimburse him," said Ron Willis. "He could try to file an action to recover his money, probably through our county claims program. I'll send you the forms."

"Thanks, I'll mention that to him," said Dave.

"What is the name of the former employee?" asked the captain.

"Russell Whitcomb. He's forty-eight years old, about five ten, a hundred and seventy-five pounds," said Dave. "I checked the apartment complex where he had been living. His apartment neighbors only knew him to say hello. He lived there a few months, and other than working for Oscar a short while, he was pretty much a stranger around here. He formerly lived in Portland, Oregon. I figured your investigators would want to follow up on Whitcomb," said Dorsey.

"That's correct," said Ron Willis. "Detective Sergeants Bill Morris and Lynn Hoover will be coming up as soon as possible. On this end, we will do what we can to find this Whitcomb guy in Florida. Thanks again, Dave, we really appreciate the good news."

The captain briefed his detectives on the news about the camera. This was met with great enthusiasm. "Finally, a break," said Lynn Hoover. "I'll put together a photo lineup to take along, just in case we find someone who might remember this John Smith along with the former pawn shop employee, Russell Whitcomb."

Detective Ralph Doyle was given the assignment to try and find the key witness, Russell Whitcomb. He sent out a Be on the Lookout (BOL) for Whitcomb, his focus being Florida.

Sergeants Morris and Hoover left for Allen County. Other than recovering the camera, the trip was uneventful. Russell Whitcomb was described as a pretty quiet person, according to Oscar Garner, the owner of the pawn shop. Mr. Garner told them he had given Russell Whitcomb a hard time for accepting *John Smith* as the name of the person who pawned the camera. He explained that all the identification that John Smith had was a fishing license bearing that name. Their interviews with acquaintances of Whitcomb only revealed him to be a quiet guy, who remained pretty much to himself.

They returned home with Alice Fleetwood's camera, which they turned over to their crime scene technicians for processing. Discouraged after many interviews in Allen County, they were no closer to finding the witness, Russell Whitcomb, nor the John Smith who pawned the camera.

On their return to the Detective Bureau, they were met by Detective Doyle. He said, "While you were gone, I located Russell Whitcomb. He is living in Miami and just went to work at a pawn shop there. Miami-Dade detectives do preliminary backgrounds on pawn shop employees. During the background check, they discovered our BOL for Whitcomb. We are working with a Detective Perez. I explained to him about our homicide case and faxed him a photo lineup, which includes CJ's driver's license photo. Detective Perez interviewed this Russell Whitcomb. He remembers taking in the camera and gave them a description of the person pawning it. The description is similar to CJ; however, Mr. Whitcomb told them, with absolute certainty, the person pawning the camera is not in the photo lineup. Whitcomb did tell Detective Perez that the person who pawned the camera seemed sort of slow, mentally. He added, "Perez told me Whitcomb was very cooperative and told Perez he would help in any way he can."

The disappointed Morris said, "Who, beside CJ, could have pawned that camera?"

Suddenly, Sergeant Hoover exclaimed, "What about CJ's younger brother? The slow one!"

CHAPTER TWENTY-THREE

Sergeants Hoover and Morris went to Lester Johnson's mobile home. He lived in a very broken-down mobile home park. There was an older rusting pickup parked in front of his trailer. Alongside, and in back, were two torn-up cars and two rusting automobile engines. The door was answered by a tall, thin man probably close to fifty years old. He was dressed in jeans, a Western shirt, and cowboy boots.

They identified themselves and asked, "Are you Lester Johnson?"

Lester said, "I won't talk to you, I want a lawyer." Both detectives were momentarily shocked and were at a loss for words.

Bill Morris said, "We have only asked if you are Lester Johnson."

"I won't talk to you. I want a lawyer."

"How do you know what we want to talk about?" asked Sergeant Hoover.

Lester repeated the same mantra.

"Quite frankly, Mr. Johnson, if in fact you are Lester Johnson, you are not in any trouble," said Morris. "We cannot understand why you will not talk with us."

This was met with the same mantra by Lester

"Okay," said Lynn, "we are going to go and get you a lawyer and bring him back here so you can talk with us."

This seemed to unbalance Lester. He suddenly was looking from side to side in what they perceived as some sort of panic.

"Let's go get that lawyer," Hoover said to Morris. They got into their car and left the startled Lester Johnson standing in his doorway. The two sergeants drove out of the park, stopping a short distance away. They parked out of sight and watched the entrance. In a matter of sixty seconds, they watched Lester Johnson drive hurriedly from the trailer park. They tailed him, although they had a pretty good idea where he was going.

Soon, Lester drove into CJ's driveway. He jumped from his pickup, leaving the door open, ran to the house, and pounded on the door. He was screaming, "CJ! CJ! CJ!" almost hysterically. There was no answer at the door, but soon they saw CJ coming out of the barn. Lester saw his brother and ran to him. CJ quickly grabbed his brother by the shoulders and walked him into the house.

Bill and Lynn remained parked nearby. They heard what seemed to be shouting, but muffled, coming from CJ's home. The muffled voices continued for some time; however, it seemed to gradually quiet down. After the shouting had stopped, they saw Lester leave CJ's home. He returned to his pickup and drove back the same direction they had followed him. Lester didn't seem to notice them as they turned and followed him back to the trailer park. Both sergeants were now in agreement, Lester might be their best bet. But how to approach him again?

While they had waited, a violent argument went on inside CJ's home. CJ, still holding Lester by the shoulders, yelled at him, "What are you talking about?"

Lester, still in a panic, shouted, "I did what you told me, CJ!"

"What are you talking about?" he asked Lester again. "Settle down, everything is okay. Just tell me what has happened."

This seemed to help Lester calm down a little. He said to CJ, "Those mean detectives came to my trailer. One of them was a girl. Are there girl detectives, CJ?" he asked.

"Yes, yes," he replied, "there are girl detectives. What were the detectives' names?" he asked Lester.

"I don't know their names" was his reply. "One was a man and the other was a girl." Lester giggled. "She was kind of pretty."

"Lester!" shouted CJ. "For God's sakes, tell me what happened! Start again from when they first came to your trailer."

"Okay. I heard a knock on my door. I was eating some corn flakes."

"Go on, Lester," said an impatient CJ. He knew, however, it was necessary to be patient with his retarded brother.

"Well, I opened the door, and they showed me some badges. I think it was the man that said, 'Are you Lester Johnson?'"

"What did you say?" asked CJ.

"I said, 'I won't talk to you. I want a lawyer.'"

"Oh my god!" shouted his brother. "You didn't even tell them your name?"

Lester started crying. "I said, 'I won't talk to you, I want a lawyer.' That's what you told me to say, Carl." CJ knew his brother only called him Carl at times when he was afraid of him.

"All right, all right, don't cry. What else happened?"

"They told me all they wanted to know is, am I Lester Johnson."

"What did you say to them?" asked CJ.

"I won't talk to you. I want a lawyer."

"You didn't even tell them your name?"

"Carl, I did what you told me to do," said Lester, sort of sheepishly.

"Okay. Please try to remember exactly what they said."

"Okay, that's easy," said a relieved Lester. "They said they were going to get a lawyer and bring him to me. They seemed kind of nice when they told me that."

"Lester," asked CJ, "what would you have done if they came back with another person and said to you, 'This is your lawyer.' Would you then have talked to them?"

Lester was not sure how to answer, but he guessed and said, "I guess I would have talked to them since I had me a lawyer. Is that right?" he asked CJ.

"Wrong answer!" screamed CJ. "I told you what to say!"

Lester began sobbing violently. He said, "When Rachel got killed, I think I wasn't myself."

Rachel Smart was his longtime girlfriend, who also worked with Lester at the training center. Rachel had been struck and killed by a hit-and-run driver. Her death really upset his brother. CJ often wondered, *A retarded person with a last name of Smart.*

"What did you do after the mean detectives left?" asked CJ.

"I got in my truck and drove over here to tell you."

"Did they follow you?"

"I don't know," replied Lester, who was becoming nervous again.

"What do you mean, you don't know? How could you not know if you were being followed?"

"Carl, I need to go to the bathroom."

"No, not until you tell me if they followed you."

"Carl, I have to go, *now*," he said, stepping side to side.

"No, not until—" he began to say, when he noticed a growing puddle of urine on the floor.

Lester began crying again, saying, "I'm sorry, Carl, I just couldn't hold it no longer. I don't know if they followed me."

An angry CJ said, "Go get some paper towels and cleaner and clean up this damn mess you made. Then, get the hell out of here, Lester, go home. If these mean detectives come back to your trailer, do *not* answer the door, do you understand me? Don't answer the door. Say it again," said CJ.

"Don't answer the door if those mean detectives come back."

"Very good," said CJ, which seemed to calm Lester down a bit. "In fact, gather some of your stuff and come back, you're going to stay with me for a while. Maybe we'll go up to Grand Lake and go fishing."

This news made Lester very happy. CJ knew how much he liked fishing. "Can I bring my magazines?" he asked CJ.

"Only if you promise to not be jerking off and messing up the sheets with those porn magazines."

"I promise," replied a hurt Lester.

Lester returned shortly with his bag full of his stuff, along with his magazines. He was happy there were no detectives at his trailer.

CHAPTER TWENTY-FOUR

C J told Lester to feed and water the livestock, and if he did a good job, they would go fishing in the morning. Lester very carefully did what he was told. He was excited to be going fishing the next day, because his brother would sometimes change his mind and cancel a fishing trip. He sure hoped that his brother was not still mad at him for pissing his pants. He was very sad that happened, but he told CJ that he really had to pee. Lester slept very well, awakening a few times though, from dreams about the different times he had helped his brother when CJ did some bad things to women. He awakened just before daylight to feed the livestock. He would try to be quiet so he wouldn't wake his brother. He sure hoped CJ had some corn flakes.

Something was still bothering him about all of those women. He sure hoped his brother hadn't hurt his wife, Melba. Lester had really liked Melba. He often wished she could have been his wife; she was really pretty.

CJ had a terrible night, awakening several times trying to figure out what he should do with his brother. He knew it was just a matter of time before those damn detectives broke down Lester. His brother knew too much, and the more they contacted him, the greater the likelihood they would succeed. He couldn't let that happen.

Lester fed and watered the stock. He moved the cattle into another fenced area so they would have fresh grazing while he and CJ were fishing. When Lester had finished the chores, he returned to the house. CJ was sitting in the kitchen, drinking coffee.

"I've finished all the chores," he told CJ.

"Did you move the steers?" CJ asked Lester.

"Sure did, and filled the water tub. Does that mean we can still go fishing?"

"Absolutely," replied CJ. "We are going up to Grand Lake. I hear they are really biting."

Lester said, "I can't wait!"

"Then let's get going, but we need to take both trucks."

"Why?" asked Lester.

"Because my truck has been cutting out lately, and I don't want us stranded in case it breaks down."

"Okay," said Lester, "but I have to get some gas."

"Here's twenty bucks for gas. Do not tell anyone you're going fishing. Promise me."

"I promise," said Lester. "You got any corn flakes?"

"They are in the cupboard, but hurry up with them. We need to get going," said CJ. Lester hurriedly downed a bowl of cereal.

They hooked up the boat and loaded it with fishing gear. CJ placed a heavy hand-sized rock in the rear, below the outboard motor.

A relieved CJ found the lake to be deserted. He launched the boat with an excited Lester already waiting for him to get them underway. Lester was talking nonstop about how he loved fishing with his big brother. CJ, starting the motor, felt a twinge of anxiety for what he was about to do to his brother. Raising Lester had been a challenge for him. Strangely, he thought, Lester had never once mentioned how they had murdered their dad. Well, he knew now, if the cops keep trying to talk with Lester, he would probably tell them, in some way, what had been going on. CJ could not take that chance. He stopped the boat near his usual disposal spot.

Lester, sitting in front of him, said, "CJ, this place is too deep, we can't catch no fish here."

"That's the way it used to be, but they're catching more fish here than any spot on the lake," he told Lester. They baited up their hooks and cast them over the side. Lester kept his bail open, as his brother had instructed. "With the bail open," he told Lester, "they can run for a bit in the deeper water and most likely swallow the hook." As CJ was looking all around to be sure it was clear, Lester was absently staring across the lake. *There is too much at stake,* thought CJ, *I have to do this.*

Suddenly, CJ said, "Look, Lester, you have a bite!" Lester quickly reached down to grab his fishing pole, as his trusted older brother grabbed the rock and violently hit him in the back of the head. CJ quickly grabbed his bleeding unconscious younger brother. He was sure that Lester was dead. He tied him to a heavy foot-long piece of railroad track, which had been on the ranch property for many years. CJ had hidden it beneath the outboard motor. Lester's unconscious body was pushed over the side.

A disturbed CJ saw that, before he went under, Lester began choking and sputtering from inhaling water. His natural reflexes kicked in as he tried to stay afloat. "Carl, Carl, help me!" he gasped.

CJ just stood in the boat watching his brother struggle. When Lester finally went under, bubbles were forming, similar to the bubbles left by Dottie's body.

CJ now knew Lester had been alive when he entered the water. He was fighting tears when he exclaimed, "Lester, I'm sorry, I didn't want you to drown! I'm sorry, I'm sorry!" as he broke into big sobs, thinking, *Well, he is now with Melba. Lester always really liked Melba.* CJ felt that familiar heartburn-like tightening in his chest.

Some memories of his raising Lester flashed before his eyes. Memories that were mostly good. He thought, however, there was too much at stake, and his brother could no longer be trusted to keep quiet. With Lester out of the way, he could now go after Dr. Christine Lawrence.

When he arrived home, he unhooked the boat. CJ began scrubbing down the boat to get rid of Lester's blood. He was alarmed on seeing the rock he had used on his brother. He ran the hose over the rock and tossed it a pretty good distance from his boat.

Two days passed and CJ heard nothing. He thought someone would have discovered Lester's abandoned pickup. Instead, he was paid a visit by Sergeants Hoover and Morris.

"Hello Mr. Johnson, we are trying to find your brother. He is not at his trailer and neither is his pickup."

"Why are you asking me?" he said. "You dirty bastards are the ones who nearly scared him to death. He came over here crying after you two threatened to arrest him."

"Wait a minute, Mr. Johnson."

"Wait a minute my ass," replied a visibly angry CJ. "You take a mentally retarded person like my brother, scare the living shit out of him, and tell me now you can't find him? Well, if something's happened to him, you two are to blame. He is not only retarded, he is suicidal and quite likely killed himself because of your threats. Telling him that he would be going to prison if he didn't tell you things about me, that is just plain cruelty," said CJ.

"Mr. Johnson—"

"Don't Mr. Johnson me. My brother just lost his girlfriend. They worked together at that training center for retarded people. She got hit by a car, walking to work. Lester loved her and was grieving her something terrible." CJ began crying. "And you two most likely killed him. How can you live with yourselves? Lester has never gone away before, that is until the two of you harassed him. Besides, my little brother wouldn't hurt anyone. If something has happened to

Lester, you two are going to be sued for harassing a mentally retarded person."

As Hoover and Morris left, Lynn said, "That didn't go very well."

"What now?" said Morris,

"CJ has a great way of throwing distractions at us," she said. "You know, I've been thinking, there is quite a resemblance between Lester and CJ, that is except for their facial features. Maybe, just maybe, Lester pawned that camera. He dresses just like CJ, with the Western wear and all. I admit, their facial features are dissimilar, but they *are* brothers."

They returned to the office. Sergeant Hoover asked Detective Doyle to resend a new photo lineup, which included Lester Johnson's driver's license photo. Doyle called Detective Perez in Miami and alerted him to expect the new lineup. He asked Perez to please expedite contacting the witness, Whitcomb, with the new lineup. Perez understood the urgency. Unfortunately, Whitcomb was not working that day and not at home. Two days later, as Doyle was returning to the bureau carrying his daily café mocha, the receptionist called to him, "There is a call for you, Ralph, a Detective Perez calling from Miami."

Doyle hurriedly returned to his desk. "Hello, this is Detective Doyle."

Perez said, "Hey, man, you owe me drinks and dinner. We have a positive ID on Lester Johnson. Whitcomb at the pawn shop, without any hesitation, said that was the guy, John Smith, who pawned the camera. Again, you owe me big time. I'm faxing the report today. What's your fax number?" Doyle gave him the number. "By the way, this Whitcomb seems to be a straight shooter. He agreed to come out and testify if and when the time comes."

"Thanks, my friend," Doyle said to Perez, "we really appreciate your help."

"Any time, I'm glad to be able to help. I sure hope you get this guy. Just kidding about dinner, but drinks sound good."

"You never know, it may turn out you may have to come out for the trial, if we ever have one," said Doyle. After hanging up, Doyle found Hoover and Morris in the evidence room, examining the camera. The crime scene technician had found a partial fingerprint, inside the camera. The print was not identifiable in the AFIS system. Doyle shared the good news from Miami. The sergeants were elated.

Sergeant Morris said, "We need to find Lester Johnson and get his fingerprints."

Sergeant Hoover replied, "I'll contact Karen Miller for a court order requiring Carl Johnson to give us his prints. That might sweat him some."

Sergeants Morris and Hoover then briefed Lieutenant Travis. Another round table meeting was scheduled with the same group, including Karen Miller from the DA's office.

Prior to the round table, a deputy sheriff on patrol found Lester's pickup at Grand Lake. It was unoccupied and parked near the boat launch ramp. He radioed the information to dispatch. There had been a BOL for Lester and his pickup. Sergeants Morris and Hoover were at their desks. "Lynn or Bill, dispatch is on the line," said the receptionist. Sergeant Morris was on the phone; Lynn took the call.

"Ask the deputy if the engine is warm or if there is any evidence of how long the pickup has been there."

The reply was, engine not warm, pickup could have been there for at least two days, as that was last time the deputy had patrolled the lake. Sergeant Hoover told the dispatcher, "Have the deputy stand by." She contacted Sergeant Mark Conrad, crime scene supervisor. She explained how she wanted Lester's pickup to be processed and also informed him a deputy is standing by at the pickup.

Bill Morris overheard the conversation Lynn had regarding Lester's pickup. He jokingly said to his partner, "Lynn, maybe after the pickup's processed, we should ask a patrol deputy to tell CJ where he can get his brother's pickup."

"Excellent idea, partner," she replied.

With the help of Chief Deputy District Attorney Karen Miller, Sergeants Hoover and Morris obtained a search warrant. The warrant ordered Carl and Lester Johnson to provide a complete set of fingerprints.

Bill Morris called CJ who immediately started raving about Lester being missing. He told them he had no idea where Lester might be, but feared the worst after "You two threatened to arrest him. Imagine, a retarded person being threatened with prison by detectives. Lester had already threatened suicide, and after the two of you, he probably went through with it."

Morris interrupted CJ, telling him, "We have a court order for you and Lester to be fingerprinted." Did he want them to come to his ranch, or would he come into the office?

CJ said he would come in and "get this bullshit over with." He was fairly certain nothing would be found from his fingerprints. He wasn't sure about Lester's. CJ again had another outburst when asked for the whereabouts of his brother. "I'll tell you again, I don't know where to find my brother. I do know he hasn't showed up at his job. He has never missed a day's work, and now he's missing because of you, cowardly bastards."

Sergeant Morris told CJ to report to the Technical Services Bureau that afternoon. He also reminded him to not give the fingerprint technician a hard time, or there would be consequences. "I'll be there," said CJ. He came in that afternoon, gave his name, had his prints taken, and left without a word. As expected, the print from the camera did not match Carl Johnson's prints.

CJ had given Lester the camera with instructions to dispose of it in a way that it will never be found. For the first time in his life, Lester had disobeyed his brother. Pawning the camera up in Allen County while using his John Smith fishing license made him think, *CJ will never find out.* Best of all, he got $350 from the pawn shop.

On a hunch, Lynn Hoover had contacted the non-profit organization where Lester had been employed. She thought, as a federally funded business, they might have required Lester's fingerprints. *Bingo!* she thought. They were not the best in quality, having been taken by a Human Service employee, but it was all they had. She returned to the office, where Sergeant Morris congratulated her for getting Lester's prints.

The two sergeants took the prints to Technical Services, where they requested Sergeant Mark Conrad personally try comparing a print from Lester Johnson to the print found inside Alice Fleetwood's camera. After what seemed an eternity, Sergeant Conrad asked Morris and Hoover to come to his office.

"Okay," said Conrad, "we have a tentative match of Lester Johnson's left middle finger with the print from the inside camera."

The jubilant sergeants high-fived Conrad. Lynn asked, "Why tentative?"

"As we know, twelve points of fingerprint identification will usually be accepted in court. In our case, Lester's left middle finger is a tented arch with what is probably a horizontal scar across the arch. I can confidently count nine points, and with further enhancing, probably get ten to eleven points. I'm positive it's him," said Conrad. "When you bring him in, we will take a professional set."

"Now, where is Lester?" asked Hoover.

A meeting was held with Chief Assistant District Attorney Karen Miller regarding Lester Johnson. In attendance were Sergeants

Hoover and Morris, Lieutenant Travis and Captain Willis. Morris presented the fingerprint evidence as to Lester.

"Well," said Karen Miller, "we have at least a sale and possession of stolen property charge. I am prepared to issue an arrest warrant for him for those charges. It is a far cry from a case of murdering Alice Fleetwood, although when he is arrested, who knows what he might reveal about CJ. Does anyone in this room believe Lester murdered her?"

"He could certainly, and most likely did, help his brother, CJ," said Lynn Hoover. "The question is, where is Lester? We have been by his trailer several times, but he seems to have vanished."

"How about we do a stake out at Lester's and CJ's homes?" asked Jeff Travis.

"Sure, we should try that for a while," said Sergeant Morris. "Lester's trailer is pretty easy, but CJ's place sits out in the open and, quite frankly, he would be suspicious of any unknown vehicles."

"Perhaps one of CJ's neighbors might let us use their property for a while," said Captain Willis.

"Thanks, everyone, for being here," said Lieutenant Jeff Travis. He told Morris and Hoover to set up the surveillance. "Let's see what we get from the stakeout, I don't want to deplete our overtime budget," he said. "Give it four or five days and keep me posted. I also want to set up another round table in the near future."

"Lieutenant," said Hoover, "I wonder how Lester is getting around, since he doesn't have his pickup." Shrugs all around.

The following day, "Good news," said Bill Morris at the morning briefing with the homicide team. "CJ has a neighbor who is not too happy with the guy. They have had words over the years. Anyway, he has a barn overlooking CJ's home. The barn is fully equipped with electricity and plumbing, including a bathroom. It's ours for surveillance as long as we want."

"Great," said Lieutenant Travis, "you and Hoover set it up, two shifts, 6:00 a.m. till 10: 00 p.m. Same for Lester's trailer. Be sure you have a plan in case Lester shows."

"Understood," said Morris. "We want to take down Lester away from his brother's house and keep his arrest from CJ as long as we can, giving us a chance to work him against CJ. Hopefully, Lester will return to his trailer and we can grab him there."

Morris put out the BOL nationwide, which instructed the arresting officer to immediately call Hoover or Morris. Several days later, Lester had not been seen. CJ seemed unaware of any surveillance. He carried on daily activities around the ranch, including loading bales of hay and leaving the ranch for up to one hour, returning with an empty truck and trailer.

Lieutenant Travis called off the stake outs. "We aren't getting anywhere," he said. "I know it's frustrating, but we haven't gotten anything to justify continuing to watch their homes."

CHAPTER TWENTY-FIVE

"Hello, Dr. Lawrence?"

"Yes, who's calling?"

"Hi, it's CJ."

"Hi, CJ, what can I do for you?"

"Well, I have some primo hay and am wondering if you want first choice, knowing how well you treat and feed your horses."

"Of course, CJ, and thank you for thinking of me."

"Well, Doctor, I actually think of you a lot," he said.

After a pause, she said, "I will take that as a compliment. Can you make your usual delivery tomorrow?"

"Sure, I'll come by tomorrow morning with your hay. See you then."

CJ was now trying to hatch his newest scheme. *I know she is a widow,* he thought. Someone had mentioned that her late husband was a well-known doctor of some type. *He had been killed,* he thought, *by a hit-and-run driver.* CJ couldn't quite recall. It didn't really matter to him.

All the rumors about her gambling habits, he thought, *were most likely true.* She was very wealthy according to the stories in the papers. She had recently broken up with a popular politician. How is a poor cowboy going to stand a chance with her and her money?

Christine Lawrence, MD, was sixty-seven years old but certainly looked much younger. She had retired at sixty-five, planning on the continued large income from her very successful cardiologist husband. Six months after her retirement, her husband, Bernard, Ben to many, while jogging, was struck and killed by a hit-and-run driver. Ben had left her with considerable money, and she at first felt it was plenty, until her compulsive gambling habits took over.

Her gambling started with sports betting. She and Ben loved to fly to Las Vegas to take in fine dining and the shows. She began playing Black Jack and became pretty good at the game. They attended many medical conferences in Las Vegas, which allowed for countless visits to the casinos. She began studying different systems and became more aggressive in the amounts she wagered. She had her own money from her practice, and Ben had no idea how much she won or lost. Deep down, she knew she might have a gambling problem. After Ben's death, she began going over to the casinos all too often. The casinos treated her as the high roller she was. She enjoyed the attention given to her, everything being complimentary including hotel rooms and meals.

Christine had her ranch. She had her horses, which she rode competitively in certain easier types of riding competition. All of which kept her fit, trim, and, she believed, reasonably youthful.

She had grown up in Arizona and was popular in high school. She was an outstanding student, became a cheerleader, was student body president. While in college she was an avid tennis player and had been ranked in the top ten in the country in both women's singles and doubles. In fact, she had strongly considered becoming a professional tennis player.

Both of her parents were medical doctors and pushed her to follow them as a physician. She reluctantly acquiesced to their wishes. She was accepted into the University of California and completed her BA degree in three years. She was accepted into Colombia Medical School, did her residencies and internships at USC, moved to Layton, and joined a well-established practice. Within two years, her mentor, Zach Holland, decided to take an early retirement. Zach's wife was suffering from early dementia, and he felt compelled to take care of her. Dr. Holland believed Christine was, despite her lack of experience, a very capable physician. In fact, he offered to sell his practice to her. With help from her parents, she bought the practice from him. It was a great decision on her part. Her practice became even more successful under her leadership. She had easily paid back the money she had borrowed from her parents.

During her successful practice, she met Dr. Bernard Lawrence, a local cardiologist. They married and had three children, all of whom were out of the home and into their own careers. She seldom saw her children, and now her grandchildren. All three of her children had been well educated, but none of the three was interested in studying medicine. Her daughter, the oldest, was a university professor of English literature. Both of her sons had been business majors, one now a stock broker, the other an investment banker. All three lived on the East Coast. As the years passed, their visits together became less frequent.

Her recent break up with Congressman Hunter had caused a great deal of family distress. All three of her children had adored Ed Hunter.

After Ben's untimely death, she focused on her work, becoming nearly a workaholic. Aside from gambling, she returned to snow skiing during the ski season. The ski areas were only about seventy-five minutes from her home. As part of skiing, she volunteered to work ski patrol. She was happy to provide medical services on the ski runs, since the ski resort paid her malpractice insurance. Ski patrol also provided some perks, such as season ski lift passes. The casinos were an additional bonus for such an active gambler. She often skied with some female friends, and they would frequently stay at the casino hotels. The casinos also offered live musical entertainment, which they enjoyed. It was a fun time for them. As they were all professionals, they could let off some stress with nice dining, seeing a show, and an occasional spa treatment as part of a nice weekend. Most important to Christine was saying good night to her friends, and then she would head to the Black Jack tables.

It was during a day of ski patrol she was summoned to an injured man. The injured skier had been hit from behind by an out-of-control snowboarder. As it turned out, the man's injuries were not too serious. Most probably he had overstretched his calf. Trying to keep his balance, he fell forward and his ski binding did not release. Out of caution, he was transported by the ski patrol on a sled to the medical facility. There, he was turned over to Dr. Christine Lawrence, whom he observed to be a very attractive woman, about his age he guessed. After her examination, she ordered a walking splint, which he could pick up in the village pharmacy.

Christine, when first meeting the man, observed he was about her age and quite handsome. When learning his name, Ed Hunter, she knew he was a United States Congressman from a city about twenty-five miles from her home—a very senior, powerful congressman.

After treating him, they had a cup of coffee together. He was impressed she was on the ski patrol which he knew required a high level of skiing. They engaged in some small talk, which revealed they were staying in the same hotel. He asked her to dinner that night. Christine had not been out with another man since Ben had died. Ed could see some doubt in her demeanor, which led him to say, "I lost my wife to cancer, nearly four years ago." Knowing they had both lost their spouses, she agreed to dinner that night. The dinner evolved into a very serious romance.

Christine found herself suddenly on what she thought of as a world stage. Traveling with Ed was something of a delicate balance for both of them. Sitting at the head table with a well-known, well-liked, and very powerful politician felt quite natural to her. The fact that he was extremely handsome didn't hurt either. It didn't take long for her to understand his presidential quest. His outstanding chances of becoming the President of the United States were very real.

She and Ed became engaged. Prior to proposing marriage, the congressman had a complete background investigation done on Christine Lawrence. If nominated for the presidency, he did not want any surprises. Her background, as he suspected, was spotless. There was a brief note which suggested she enjoyed playing Black Jack occasionally. She, it seemed, had the great qualities necessary to become the First Lady.

Christine's thoughts returned to the explosive breakup with Ed Hunter. She remembered vividly that terrible day and how all they had planned for went up in smoke.

She and her fiancé of now nearly two years, Edward Hunter, a US congressman, made a popular couple in political and social circles. Edward was very well thought of in Congress and was on many select committees. Edward, being a widower who lost his wife several years ago due to breast cancer, had garnered a great deal of sympathetic support from constituents who had also lost their spouses in a similar way.

They got along quite well and planned on marrying. Edward revealed to her that he was going to become President of the United States. He believed she would be the perfect First Lady. Christine did believe she was in love with Edward and enjoyed the prospects of a political life.

That is, until the past weekend. They had traveled to Nevada for a political convention. Christine did very well as his astute, loyal companion, until she could no longer avoid the gambling casino where they were staying. She left Edward while he was in meetings. The casino managers were always happy to see her, where she played in the somewhat private high-stakes games. She was extended a large amount of money, meaning she could play with almost unlimited credit. She felt very lucky and knew she had at least a couple of hours before she had to meet up with Edward. She was playing Black Jack, commonly known as 21, a card game. At one point, she was ahead by nearly $100,000 and was watched very closely by an anxious pit boss. She knew she should stop and cash in, but the gambler in her said, *You are on a streak!* so she continued in a blind gambling haze when she realized she had lost a $150,000. In disbelief she wondered, *What have I done?*

Suddenly, Edward came in and saw a tearful Christine sitting in disbelief. "I thought you promised to stop gambling."

"I'm sorry," she told him.

"I have been looking all over the place for you!" he said. "How much have you lost?" One of the dealers was already on the phone to one of his newspaper contacts. Christine told him of her loss. He screamed at her, "You have just destroyed my career!"

He was right. In the following days, newspapers and television reports shouted, "Congressman Edward Hunter's Fiancée Loses $150,000 Gambling While Many in Our Country Go Hungry." Christine now knew what her compulsion had cost.

She promised Edward she would stop gambling. His reply: "Your promises are empty. When we were talking of marriage, you promised. I feel sick right now. Everything I have worked for is finished. I was going to take you with me to the top, but you and your crazy insane habit have finished it." They began packing for their trip home when he announced, "I just arranged a ride home with a colleague. As for you, we came here in your car, so drive home on your own. I don't care if I ever see you again. You have ruined me. Goodbye."

They broke up. She was still in something of a haze but knew it was over between them.

These memories brought her back to the present. She still had plenty of money, she thought. Unknown to anyone, she had over a quarter million dollars cash in her safe at home. She thought of it as her mad money.

* * * * *

Christine heard a truck driving up to her barns. She looked out and saw CJ with a load of hay. She checked herself in the mirror, wondering, *Why am I doing this? It's only a cowboy delivering hay for my horses.*

"Hi, Dr. Lawrence," he said. She greeted him and thanked him for the special hay. "Well, it's my pleasure. You have been a great customer, and I appreciate it."

She paused, looked him over, and saw a tall, slender, real cowboy that she had really never noticed before. *He must be at least ten years younger than me,* she thought. She knew the reports about his wife's kidnapping several years ago. She said, "CJ, I haven't had lunch yet, may I treat you to lunch?"

"That is rightly kind of you, Dr. Lawrence, sure!" he said.

"How about Mexican?" she asked.

"I love Mexican," he replied.

CJ was now trying to focus on his big and final score. In his mind, he needed enough cash to take him to South America where he could live in comfort for the rest of his life. CJ knew that Dr. Lawrence had the money to take him on his grand trip.

They went to lunch. He played it pretty much as an employee being taken to lunch by an employer. While they dined at lunch, CJ was thinking she is no longer just a client. He had read the stories about her breakup with the politician but would deny knowing anything about it if asked. He wasn't sure of anything about her, except he thought she looked pretty good, even if she was a good deal older than him; plus, she reeked of money.

They talked a while when she inquired of the story about his wife. He went into his usual Melba story and how the detectives had just called him again. Instead of any news of Melba, they again were questioning him more as a suspect, rather than looking for his kidnapped wife. Christine noticed how distraught he had become.

Christine felt compassion for this cowboy and his alleged mistreatment by law enforcement. She asked, "Has there ever been any type of results?"

"No," said CJ, "all they ever do is suspect me of doing something to my precious Melba."

"How would they suspect you in her disappearance?"

"That's the problem. From the day Melba was kidnapped, they, for some reason, somehow thought that I had something to do with it. It truly hurts me. I loved my wife with all of my heart, it just seemed that when I called, I immediately became a suspect."

"Have they ever given you any reason for suspecting you?"

"As far as I know, her two sisters made up some vicious lies about us."

"Such as?"

"Well, I'm not sure, but that Lieutenant Travis told me Melba's sisters told him that I was hitting her. Sure, we argued sometimes, but what married people don't have disagreements? I loved her far more than I care about myself, and I would never hurt her. I have to tell you, Dr. Lawrence, it hurts me so much that they can even think that I had something to do with her kidnapping."

"Christine please, CJ," she said.

"Well, I'm pleased I can call you something besides Doctor."

She responded with open arms and pulled him into a friendly hug.

"Thank you for treating me to lunch," he told her.

Christine was having some strange thoughts about this cowboy. He was likable in that sort of charming, cowboy way. He was also pretty handsome, tall and strong. Could she really fall for the hillbilly sort of guy standing in front of her?

CHAPTER TWENTY-SIX

T he investigators assembled in the Center County Sheriff's squad room.

"We thank all of you of you for being here today," said Captain Willis. "What we discuss here, I hope, will remain within this room, at least until we capture this guy. You have been asked to bring some files pertaining to missing women. Most of these cases seem to involve elderly women. For your information, our sheriff has spoken to each of your chiefs, some of whom are here today. My boss, Sheriff Gentry, has proposed that we proceed as the lead agency, and we are prepared to do so. If anyone objects, please state your objection now." The room was silent. "We also have with us today Chief Deputy District Attorney Karen Miller. Thank you for being with us,

Karen. Okay, we have coffee and Danish if anyone is interested. Oh, and I forgot, doughnuts as well," which drew some chuckles.

"Ladies and gentlemen," explained Captain Willis, "we have what we believe is a monster preying on older women in our communities, somehow becoming friendly with ladies in different ways, but whose sole purpose is to get money from them, then murder them. He probably murdered his own wife. He is an authentic former professional rodeo cowboy, which some people seem to think of as glamorous. We believe older widowed women find him to be sort of charming, certainly charming enough to withdraw large amounts of cash shortly before they disappear or are found murdered. We have found no trace of the cash which they had withdrawn. Carl Johnson, a.k.a. CJ, is our prime suspect. He has a ranch south of Layton where he raises cattle and grows hay. He seems to begin his quest for some of his victims by meeting and dancing with them at the senior dance in Layton.

"We do know from some of our investigators that Johnson doesn't seem to be particularly bright, but quite likely pretty clever. Add that cowboy charm and a bit of luck, we have a difficult guy to deal with. Working together and combining our resources might just give us the edge we need. Let's begin with Chief Deputy District Attorney Karen Miller."

"We hope that by describing each other's cases, we might have enough, collectively, to go after Carl Johnson, a.k.a. CJ," said Karen. "Many of our cases are difficult enough to even prove they are anything more than accidental death. One of these cases tend to suggest a fall from The Bluff. Another appears to be a drowning. The bottom line is, we just need more evidence in these cases."

Sergeant Bill Morris went first, describing the five-year-old report made by Carl Johnson, alleging that his wife Melba had been kidnapped.

"I, and my partner at the time, interviewed the patrol deputy who took the alleged kidnapping report from CJ. He felt CJ was not being truthful. It was only a cop's intuition, he told us, but Johnson seemed nervous, with his lack of eye contact, glancing all around except not looking at the deputy. Our deputy did all the right things, immediately issuing APB's, checking with neighbors, speaking with the duty sergeant, etcetera. He told us, 'There is just something wrong here, but I can't put my finger on it.' We interviewed Johnson the next morning and could see why the deputy did not believe his story. CJ seemed evasive and had already began accusing us of not doing enough to find his wife.

"We interviewed Melba's sisters. They both learned from their sister that CJ had been beating her. They saw the injuries to her body, but he never hit her in the face, which would make her injuries obvious. The sisters pleaded with Melba to report the beatings, but she refused, fearing he would kill her if she made the reports. Melba told them she was going to leave him, but she was waiting for the right opportunity. Apparently, that opportunity never happened. That was the last time they saw their sister.

"Over the years, nothing has developed as to the wife's disappearance. We have interviewed him a number of times, only hear that we are not doing anything to find his Melba.

"According to the sisters, their father had loaned CJ and Melba a sizable chunk of money for the down payment on their ranch, which they agreed to pay back with interest. According to them, CJ did everything he could to convince Melba they should discontinue paying back the loan. The father disliked his son-in-law so much that he arranged that the hundred thousand dollars he was leaving her in his will could not be touched by CJ. She never received it since she is missing. CJ will surely go after that money when the wife is declared dead under the law, which is two years away.

"CJ is fifty-four. His younger brother, Lester, is mentally retarded. Lester lives on SSI; plus, he also works at the training center. He lives in an older mobile home. You have been provided with some material along with driver's license photos of CJ and Lester."

Sergeant Lynn Hoover next discussed the Sylvia Robinson homicide. She pointed out the fact the victim had been taking riding lessons from CJ shortly before she was murdered. She described that the brake lines on Mrs. Robinson's vehicle were believed to have been cut. "Mrs. Robinson withdrew thirty-five thousand dollars just before her murder. We will see this pattern all along with our friend CJ. This case happened three years ago."

Bill Burris, Layton Police Department, next discussed the missing-person case regarding Dottie Lambert. "I know this one has only been established as Mrs. Lambert being missing. Her son, however, told me his mother was a very solid, stable woman. She appears to have danced with CJ at the senior dance. They left the dance in separate cars to go have dessert. That was the last time she was seen by her friends. Shortly after that, she withdrew twenty-eight thousand dollars. Dottie disappeared without a trace. Again, we have a substantial withdrawal of money. Again, CJ.

"We took a missing-person report on her some time ago. She was seventy-nine years old. I interviewed two of her friends after being contacted by her son, who lives in Memphis. He came out for an interview and to file the missing-person report. He is the administrator of Dottie's estate. Dottie was a widow. She often attended the senior dance, but never danced. One night at the dance, this cowboy-looking guy came over and asked her to dance. Dottie's friends were surprised when she accepted the offer to dance; in fact, they danced for some while, and when she returned from dancing, she announced, 'We are going to meet for coffee and pie.' This was very unlike her, but she did mention, 'It will be okay, we both have our own cars, so I should be safe.' The friends had trouble with the cowboy's name, but it was initials, something like CK or something like that. They felt Dottie was having a very good time. This was the first time she had danced since her husband, Harvey, had passed away. They knew she had been lonely, and her adult children all lived out of state. They felt she was financially pretty well-off.

"Her son is Harvey Lambert Junior. Lambert found that shortly before she disappeared, she had withdrawn twenty-eight thousand dollars. Her banker thought the withdrawal very unusual. She told the banker she had a relative who was ill and she was going to try to help her. The son didn't know of any sick family members. The banker felt caution was in order and had one of the clerks make copies of about half of the bills. This woman was usually very responsible, according to family and friends.

"As you can imagine, this has been very difficult for the family. This lady taught elementary school for over forty years, and to just up and disappear, along with her car, is quite a mystery. The family continues to call, but we have very little information for them.

"Now it appears Carl Johnson, CJ, is our suspect. But where is Dottie? The friends have come to believe that their friend has met with some foul play. Anyway, the last time they saw Dottie was at the senior dance."

"We all need to share all of our cases. It goes without saying, we need to move on this as quickly as possible. I believe the next case is about one Alice Fleetwood. Lieutenant Travis, will you brief us on this case, please?"

Lieutenant Travis began, "Alice Fleetwood was a very well-respected member of our community. She was active in many charitable causes, as well as the Catholic Church. Her late husband, Len, owned a very successful women's wear shop in the mall. She was very well-off financially.

"Her body was found at the bottom of The Bluff. It, at first, was handled as an accident; however, new information points to a homicide."

"CJ, we believe, struck up a conversation with her in the produce section of a market. His MO [method of operation] is becoming very apparent. He must be very smooth in meeting older women and having the ability to acquire large sums of money from them. In the case of Alice Fleetwood, twenty-five thousand dollars.

"The whole key to our case regarding Mrs. Fleetwood is from a few days ago when we brought him in for another interview, this time regarding his association with Alice Fleetwood. At one point, CJ blurted out, 'I don't know anything about twenty-five thousand dollars.'

"We believe CJ is responsible for the murder of Alice Fleetwood," said Sergeant Hoover. "Sergeant Morris and I have been working this case. Again, our evidence is slim, but everything we have points to him, including a large cash withdrawal by Mrs. Fleetwood just before her body was found."

Detective Ron Adams, Bradley Police Department, discussed the murder of Maxine Farrell. "I'm Detective Ron Adams representing the Bradley Police Department. We are handling the homicide case of one Maxine Farrell, age seventy-one. She had been reported to the Riverview Police as a missing person. I have already discussed this case with many of you already. Maxine's decomposing body was found in a dumpster near Riverview. She had been strangled to death. We found she had been seen dancing with CJ at the senior dance. She told her friends she had been sitting with that she was dancing with a cowboy named CJ. Keep in mind, she was actively dating several different men. It was not uncommon for Maxine to meet and 'pick up' men at the senior dance. They did not see anything unusual about her dancing with a stranger. They noticed nothing more about it. As they told it, she had a compulsion for men. They did note, however, Maxine seemed to have a real interest in this man, CJ.

"As we know, these types of cases can take many twists and turns. This case began as a missing person and turned into a homicide. Usually, missing-person cases are a low priority. This case, like yours, Lynn, only has CJ mentioned in some vague way. Maxine did withdraw forty-six hundred dollars from her bank shortly before she was murdered. Much less than has been reported in other cases.

"Maxine didn't have any local family. She had no real local friends. I spoke with a daughter who lives in Des Moines, Iowa. She usually talked by phone with her mother about once a week. When she could not reach her, she checked with as neighbor of her mother, who said she had not seen her in a couple of weeks, which was not entirely uncommon. The daughter revealed her mother, occasionally, would take off with a man, sometimes for ten days or more.

"Her daughter, as per Maxine's will, was appointed as administrator of Maxine's estate. One of the odd aspects of this case is, according to the daughter, her mother withdrew the forty-six hundred dollars from her banking account shortly before her disappearance. I suppose, had we really gotten into this case earlier with fresh information, we might now be in a better place.

"So, in preparing for today's meeting, I've gone back to the beginning when Maxine went missing. I have spoken to, as far as I know, all of the men she had been seeing. None of the men seem suspicious and readily admit to what could be described as short-term relationships. None of them have any criminal history. They, for the most part, met at the senior dance. They enjoyed each other's company, no longer than a couple of weeks, and no arguments when they stopped seeing each other. Each of the men were mid-sixties to early seventies, all widowed, and all resided within our county. They all have good reputations. Based on what I've found, it seems the senior dance is well attended and a good source to relieve loneliness for many of our widowed older citizens. A couple of Maxine's friends did comment that they saw a cowboy-looking man attending the dances on several occasions. Then, Maxine disappeared. Nothing else."

Sergeant Lynn Hoover presented the Gloria Hansen case and her helping CJ at his ranch. Her body was found in the river, below the popular Equinox Falls. She explained the ruse by CJ convincing Gloria to invest $25,000 for a phony stud horse scheme.

"Okay, thank you," said Captain Willis. "I would like to introduce Ethel Harrison from our Technical Services Unit. Ethel is going to prepare a matrix, we will begin the names of our victims, at least that we are aware of today. Okay, Ethel, will you please begin our matrix:

"Melba Johnson first, five years ago. Sheriff's case.

"Sylvia Robinson, three years ago. Sheriff's case.

"Maxine Farrell, seventy-one years old, Detective Ron Adams, Bradley Police Department.

"Dottie Lambert, seventy-nine years old, Sergeant Bill Burris, Layton Police Department.

"Gloria Hansen, seventy-four years old, sheriff's case.

"Alice Fleetwood, seventy-four years old, sheriff's case. We believe we might have as the most compelling evidence of all, regarding CJ.

"Okay, it seems we have had a productive meeting. We all have a similar investment into getting CJ off of the streets as soon as possible. If anyone comes with any leads into these cases, please share them.

"I suggest future meetings be in roundtable sessions, including those of you actively investigating these cases. Karen, we would appreciate it if you will join in with the investigators as you are very necessary for legal advice."

"Of course," she replied.

CHAPTER TWENTY-SEVEN

D r. Christine Lawrence answered the phone.

"Hi, this CJ."

"Hello, CJ, what can I do for you?"

"I'm wondering if I can return the favor and buy you supper?"

"When and where?" she asked.

"There is an Indian casino just over the county line."

"You mean the Princess Casino?"

"Yes, that's it, they have an all-you-can-eat buffet, and I was thinking about going tonight."

"I'll have to call you back in a little while," she replied.

"I sure hope you can make it."

"I will call you in a bit," she said. They ended the call.

Dr. Lawrence was chuckling to herself. *That's about as close to fine dining one would expect from this cowboy,* she pondered. *Do I really want to go out with this guy? What can it hurt?* she thought.

"Hi, CJ, this is Christine. Tonight works, but let's take separate cars."

"That works for me," he replied. "See you there."

CJ thought separate cars was perfect and fit with his plans for Dr. Lawrence. Christine knew how tempted she will be at this casino to play some Black Jack. They met in the parking lot. They sat in the lounge. Christine had a dry martini with two green olives, and CJ had a bottle of beer, no glass. They made some small talk with CJ talking about the hay business. He complained about the low prices being paid for beef.

Christine was becoming bored very quickly. Her thoughts were of the world political discussions she had with her former fiancé, Ed Hunter. As CJ rambled on, she remembered she and Ed, quite conceivably, may have made it to the White House. She wondered how Ed was doing. Now, she found herself preparing for "fine" dining with this cowboy sitting across from her. She ordered another martini.

She had to admit, the meal wasn't bad. With all-you-can-eat, CJ easily finished off two servings of prime rib, plus a lobster tail and a couple pieces of fried chicken. Where did he put it? After dinner they talked pretty easily, mostly about her horses and her ranch, her losing her husband, and loneliness at times. She briefly went into her former relationship with the congressman and the abrupt breakup. She did not mention gambling, although she was very aware of the ringing slot machines.

She asked CJ to give her more details about his wife and her kidnapping. He described Melba, her great abilities at barrel racing, the fact she was state champion, and what a great wife and companion she was. He regretted they were unable to have children, as Melba was unable to conceive. In fact, they were considering adopting some kids when she was taken. He became pretty emotional. "I always wanted to have children."

When asked of his future plans, CJ said, "Just to keep growing hay and raising cattle, and always hoping to see my wife again. You are the first lady I've been out with since I lost her."

"You must realize I'm older than you, and I'm not sure this an actual date, but thank you for dinner," said Christine.

"You are welcome. I don't usually eat at nice places like this."

They left the restaurant and entered the gambling area. "Do you mind if I play a little poker?" he asked.

"Go right ahead, I think I will walk around a bit and walk off some of that great dinner," replied Christine. "Thank you again for dinner, CJ."

She watched some Black Jack games and felt that compulsion to try her luck. She could see CJ across the floor at a poker table. She suddenly sat at a Black Jack table, removing some $100 bills from her purse and placed a $200 bet. The dealer said, "I'm sorry ma'am, but there is a twenty-five-dollar limit."

Christine said, "May I speak to the pit boss?"

The pit boss, who immediately came over, asked, "Is there a problem?"

She said, "I rarely come here and thought you might make an exception on the limit." Unknown to her, the pit boss recognized her.

"Okay." Turning to the dealer, "Two-hundred-dollar limit for the lady please, Rachael." Christine quickly won $2,000 when she saw CJ leaving the poker game. She quickly picked up her chips, tipped the dealer, and went to cash in her winnings. She felt that familiar exhilaration winning gave her.

CJ approached her with "How did you do?"

"Okay, played a few hands of Black Jack. How about you?" she asked him.

"I won enough to cover dinner. You brought me some luck," he told her.

* * * * *

CJ felt he needed to know more about the doctor, especially her gambling habits. It was hay delivery time.

Christine said when CJ called, "Isn't it a little early for your delivery?"

"Well, truthfully, I really am more interested in seeing you."

"That's nice to hear," she said. "But tomorrow works better."

"I'll be there tomorrow," he said cheerfully.

Christine began calling fellow female horse owners who were customers of CJ and reasonably attractive. "Hi, Sally"—as Sally Harris picked up—"this is Christine Lawrence."

"Hi, Doctor."

"Christine, please."

"Okay, what's on your mind? Don't tell me you have agreed to breed Lulu with that renown stud of yours," said Sally.

"That's certainly a possibility. We can discuss that later."

"That is good news," said Sally. "What's up then?"

"I have a question, are you still getting your hay from Carl Johnson?"

"You mean CJ? Yes, I am. Are you having a problem?"

"Not really," said Christine. "I just wanted to compare what we are paying him per ton." Sally told her the price, and Christine found CJ was charging her less than he was charging Sally. She said to Sally, "I guess I am being overly suspicious. Perhaps we can further discuss breeding Lulu when it approaches the time."

"Sounds really good. By the way, Christine, I was saddened to hear of your breakup with the congressman. You two made a great couple."

"Thank you, Sally. It has been a rough time. We were nearly married. I hope you haven't given to much credence to the vicious media circus."

"Well Christine, all I know is, you are a friend and were a great physician. Let the pieces fall where they may is my attitude. There are two sides to every story."

"That is very kind of you, Sally. Let me treat you to lunch soon. We can discuss terms for the breeding." They ended the call. She felt better after talking with Sally. Christine was thinking CJ was giving her a better price on hay, that rascal.

She next called Barbara Ryan, another horse rancher, actually on a much larger scale than Christine.

"Christine, so good to hear from you."

"It has been a while, as you know I have been pretty wrapped up in some things," said Christine.

Barbara said, "I have been meaning to call you but wasn't sure when would be appropriate, so you have saved me the call. What's up?"

"Thanks for thinking of me."

"Certainly, you are a good friend."

"I do want to catch up, is this a good time?" asked Christine.

"Sure, I was truly surprised that you and Edward broke up. You two seemed like the ideal couple; in fact, I saw you being in the White House. Edward is a very popular politician. When the two of you attended my outdoor party a few months ago, you seemed to be glowing. Not to mention Edward being Mr. Prince Charming." This statement immediately brought Christine to tears. Barbara exclaimed, "I'm so sorry, dear, that was insensitive of me!"

"No, don't blame yourself. It is not your fault, Barbara. It has been so recent, and I was, and still am, in love with him. He accused me of preventing him from becoming President of the United States."

"That's purely conjecture on his part," said Barbara. "I know it has to have been a very difficult time for you, but I do have something of a sensitive question for you."

"Okay, ask it."

"Is it true about your gambling loss, as has been reported just about everywhere? I am asking as your friend, and as you know, I do not gossip."

"Barbara, you are the only person I have spoken with about this tragedy. Yes, it is true. I have lived with this problem for many years and am not certain I'm over it. I just can't help myself. There is a certain excitement; in my case, it is Black Jack. It can almost be sexual. I have to admit, I gambled a great deal when Ben was alive. Since I made my own money as a physician, it never became a problem between us. Anytime I attended conferences which had gambling casinos nearby, I would play Black Jack. Many medical conferences are held in Las Vegas, thus the unlimited gambling opportunities. Ben and I both attended many events. Sometime we traveled together, particularly when Ben lectured. I have almost always won; rarely, if

I lost, it was never much. It is not unusual for me to play high-stake games, such as the one which led to our breakup. I completely lost control and lost a great deal of money which, as you know, created a media frenzy. That was very unlike me. I can't believe I let myself not only get so carried away, but careless with my money."

"Have you considered getting some help, with therapy perhaps?"

"It has certainly occurred to me, but I feel I can now keep it under control."

"Well, if you want to talk further, give me a call," said Barbara.

"Thanks so much. Actually, I called to see if you buy your hay from Carl Johnson?" she asked.

"I did at one time, but after we expanded, he just couldn't keep up. That adjacent property which I bought has been dedicated to growing my own hay. Why do you ask?"

"Just curious, I guess. Mostly to compare what he charges me versus other ranchers."

"You could check with Sally Harris; I know she buys from him."

"Thanks, but I just spoke with Sally. I'll make some more comparisons. We all just want to be treated equally," she said.

"Okay, please stay in touch. Things have a way of working out. Remember I'm here for you. Let's talk soon."

She pondered Barbara's wisdom and knew very well she was not a gossip. Christine noticed neither of the women had mentioned CJ paying any particular attention to them. *This is sort of good news,* she thought.

She next called Marylynn Brown. She felt this would give a different perspective of CJ, as Marylynn was a horse trainer and leased her training facilities. She learned that CJ sells hay to Marylynn. She reported nothing derogatory about him. She had been doing business with him since before Melba had disappeared and learned she was paying him the same rate as Sally Harris.

CHAPTER TWENTY-EIGHT

The following morning, CJ arrived late, unloaded the hay bales, and stacked them nicely, something he didn't usually do for other customers. As he approached Christine's home, she came out of the front door.

"Good morning," they greeted each other. Christine came up to him, gave him a warm hug. She thanked him for stacking her hay and wrote his check. CJ found she smelled really good. He commented about her fragrance. She replied, "Just plain old Chanel."

CJ asked, "I was wondering if I could take you to supper again?"

"When and where?" she asked.

"I was thinking about Denny's this time. That casino was kind of expensive."

"Okay," she said. "However, let's go back to the casino, and it is my treat. I feel like playing a little Black Jack."

"I don't know," he replied, "I feel a little embarrassed by not being able to afford to take you to a nice place like that casino."

"Nothing to be embarrassed about," she said. "Women treat men to fine dining all of the time nowadays."

"Well, okay," he said. "I guess, since I haven't had any dates since Melba, it is probably all right. I don't know about these things. Except for our date, of course."

"Of course," replied an amused Christine. "Let's take separate cars again."

"Great!" said CJ.

* * * * *

They met again in the casino parking lot. Christine was wearing matching black cashmere sweater and slacks. She looked terrific, thought CJ. He was wearing his usual pearl-buttoned Western shirt, Wrangler jeans, a big rodeo belt buckle, and freshly polished cowboy boots.

Christine asked, "Can we sit in the lounge and have a drink first?"

"Sure," he said. She ordered a martini again, and so did CJ. Their drinks arrived. CJ had never before tasted a martini and started choking after a sip. "That tastes more like jet fuel!" he gasped.

"When have you tasted jet fuel?" she asked, chuckling. "I'm sorry," she said, "I thought you must have ordered them before."

"No, that's my first and last," he replied. "I'm going to stick with beer," which he ordered, and again drank out of the bottle. Christine ordered a second martini, which made CJ shudder. "How can you drink those things?" he asked.

"I've always liked them, including my very first one," she responded.

"Do you want to sit at the same table as last time?" he asked. "It's open right now." They sat down at the table, which had a reserved sign on it.

"Welcome back, folks," said the host. "Are you the people who reserved this table?"

"No, actually, we sat here last time," said Christine, "and we're hopeful we could dine here at this table again," she said very politely. *And handed him something that looked like money,* thought CJ.

"Well, we are so happy to have you back again, and hope you enjoy your special table."

CJ asked, "Did you tip that man?"

"Yes, I did," she replied. "It's customary when a table is already reserved, but it isn't any big deal since we wanted to sit here. Watch what happens when the people who reserved this table show up."

"Does that mean we will have to move?" he asked.

Just then, a man and woman were talking to the host in what seemed to be a bit of a heated tone and pointing at Christine and CJ. They watched as the host quietly calmed them down. "We appreciate that very much," said the man.

"I'm very sorry for the confusion," said the host, as he led them to another table.

"What just happened?" asked CJ. "They seemed pretty upset."

"Well, we got their table, and they were not happy about that. The host got a nice tip from us. The host, in turn, comped them in some way which made them happy. Now everybody's happy. The host came out ahead, since the comps come from the casino."

"I sure am learning an awful lot from you," said CJ.

Christine asked, "Are you ready for dinner?" She felt good from CJ's compliment. *He does have a lot to learn,* she was thinking.

CJ ate his usual gargantuan portions, while Christine was thinking of playing Black Jack and how compelling was her urgency to gamble. As they left the dining room, she announced, "I am going to play a little Black Jack."

CJ said, "I'm going over to the poker table." As he strolled, he was thinking, *I could sure use Lester's help right about now,* but Lester was gone. He was now on his own for the big score with Dr. Christine Lawrence. She was his ticket to South America.

Christine sat at the same Black Jack table as her last visit to this casino. She noticed a different dealer, as well as a different pit boss. She had brought $5,000 in $100 bills. She observed again, the table limit was $25 a hand. The three other players seemed to be doing well. She quietly asked to speak with the pit boss, who was an exceptionally attractive woman; however, her eyes revealed a great deal of life experience. Christine explained that on her last visit, the pit boss raised the limit to $200 per hand. Again the limit was raised, which caused some looks from the other players.

The cards were dealt and everybody was winning, including Christine who noticed CJ had come over and was watching her as she played. He even held his breath when seeing her playing two hands of $200 each, and winning. She had several thousand dollars in chips in front of her, and the other players were applauding her. "You brought good luck to this table, ma'am," said one of the players.

That's when she observed CJ. "Okay, I'm good," she said, standing, and handed a $500 tip to the dealer. "How did you do?" she asked CJ as they walked to the cashier's window.

"Nothing like you did," he responded.

He overheard the cashier counting out $9,800 in $100 bills. "Congratulations, ma'am, that's quite a win."

The pit boss approached her and said, "Nice playing. If you ever have an interest in higher-stakes games, we play much higher stakes at our sister casino across the state line. Here's my card." The pit boss said further, "I'm sorry to tell you, but we can no longer allow you to play at any higher limits, you have hit us pretty hard on your two visits. I have done some research on you and learned about your first visit. Please don't be offended, you are welcome at any time, however, playing at our established limits."

"I am not offended, and thank you for being candid," replied Christine. "Perhaps I might take you up on your suggestion about the Nevada casino next time."

As they left the building, CJ thought that this might be the time to begin his plan. They walked to their separate cars. CJ thanked her for dinner and congratulated her on the huge winnings. He then took her into his arms and tried to kiss her, but she quickly pushed him back. She said, "This is way too early, if, in fact, it ever happens. I'm still in love with Ed Hunter. I'm sorry, CJ, but there is also a difference in our ages. It isn't that it might not happen, but not right now."

He backed away and said, "That's okay, can we at least be friends?"

"Of course, we can. I really do enjoy your company," she said.

"Well then, it's my turn to treat for dinner, okay?"

"Sure," she replied, "I would like that."

CJ said, "Can we sit in your car for a minute? I have an idea about something."

"Okay."

They climbed into Christine's luxurious. Mercedes sedan "What is your idea?" she asked.

"Well, it might be a little on the wrong side of the law, but not as far as you're concerned. Please at least listen to me."

"All right, but I'm not interested in any illegal activity."

"Understood, but here goes. I think I know how much you like to play Black Jack. My cousin is a dealer at that Nevada casino that lady just told you about. My cousin deals in the very high-stakes Black Jack games. Him and me have been very close for most of our lives. He was dealing Black Jack on the East Coast, in Atlantic City. He has become an expert at what I think is called a 'slip card.' He's told me stories about working with players, where he allowed them to win fortunes. One time, however, he got caught by what he calls an amateur mistake. He did prison time, during which he worked on the slip card and told me it's now foolproof."

"Just a minute," said Christine, "if he went to prison, how is it he is dealing again in Nevada?"

"It is quite a long story," said CJ.

"Well, this is enough for tonight," said Christine. "Maybe we can discuss it later; however, it doesn't sound like a good idea to me."

"Okay," he said. "I do hope you will think about it. After I tell you the whole story, you might change your mind."

"I will give it some thought, and I will listen to what you have to say."

Driving home, Christine thought, *CJ is full of so many ideas.*

That night at home, Christine Lawrence thought about how she had lost her fiancé, Ed Hunter, due to some out-of-control gambling issues. She had another thought, about her $150,000 loss after losing complete control gambling. What if CJ's idea might actually have some merit? She fantasied about going to Nevada and winning back the $150,000 and donating it; plus some more, to charity. She was still deeply in love with Ed and had hope he might still be in love with her; they had been so perfect together. It was hard to accept that it ended so quickly. She thought about calling him; however, she thought it was probably a bad idea. Unless she could make something happen which might get them back together again. She needed to hear more about CJ's plan, foolhardy as it seemed.

Driving home, CJ felt he might possibly have laid the trap. He felt she had enough interest in his plan to at least call him. He had seen how she looked at the casino after winning.

The next few days were uneventful for CJ. He made his regular hay deliveries and took care of his cattle. He often thought about his brother, Lester. He knew he had done the right thing, as it was just a matter of time until they picked him up. Lester would have been easily broken down by those detectives, he was sure of it. He had been patiently waiting for a call from Dr. Lawrence, when she finally called.

"CJ," she said, "I have been wanting to hear more about your cousin's foolproof Black Jack plan. Can we meet for coffee?"

"Sure," he said, "how about Denny's at three this afternoon, it will not be busy."

They drank coffee while discussing her winning streak at the casino and the price of beef and hay. He mentioned that his brother had disappeared and how worried he was about him.

Christine interrupted him with "Tell me about your cousin." They both observed they were alone in a booth and could speak freely with each other.

"Okay," he said, "he works at the Nevada casino the pit boss mentioned to you last week. There isn't anything illegal on your part. If you want, I'll go over to Nevada and talk to him. He will most likely give us instructions, such as to how much cash to bring and what his cut will be. It also has to be the right timing. He works at the high-stakes table on a regular basis. He told me he has made some people very wealthy, and again his part is foolproof."

"I'm not sure about any of this," she said, "I only want to know how it works. I have plenty of cash but want some assurances I'm going to win. I cannot afford any more embarrassment."

"Well," said CJ, "I need to drive over to Nevada. First, I need to get someone to take care of my stock while I'm gone. Usually my brother, Lester, takes care of things for me. Boy, I sure wish I knew where he went."

"I'll tell you what," said Christine, "I will have my hand, Roberto, come over and do your chores. He's very reliable, and I'll compensate him for the work."

"Thank you. Have him come by tomorrow morning, and I'll show him what to do. I think I can be back the following day after I go over the plans with my cousin. I'm not going to give you his name so you won't have to be involved much at all."

The next day, CJ gave Roberto instructions on taking care of his ranch and stock. He told him to plan on two days. He told Roberto to be sure and move the cattle to the other fenced-off section and be sure to give them water. Roberto seemed a little bit offended. "Remember, señor, I am a caballero, so I know what to do. Gracias." This backed CJ off some, as Roberto was a very big caballero.

"Okay, I'll see you in a day or two," he told Roberto.

He left later that morning after packing overnight camping gear, fishing gear, and supplies. He traveled into the mountains to one of his favorite camping and fishing spots. It was very unlikely that he'd meet anyone he knew, especially this time of the year. There wasn't any need to travel to Nevada, since he didn't have a cousin working high-stakes games over there. Camping overnight gave him time to work on his plan for Dr. Christine Lawrence.

It occurred to him that maybe he shouldn't be in any rush to contact Christine and give her a chance to stew, which would indicate to him just how serious she might be. He further was thinking about another woman who could probably come up with some money. Did he have the time and opportunity to pull off another scheme, especially without Lester?

CHAPTER TWENTY-NINE

C hristine Lawrence was indeed anxiously waiting to hear from CJ. He had been gone for two days, and Roberto had told her Señor CJ had returned. *So, what was going on with him?* she asked herself. When the phone rang, she tried not to show her eagerness to talk with this cowboy.

"Hello?" she answered.

"Hi, Chris."

Her jaw dropped, she couldn't process the words, but finally, "Hi, Ed." *This,* she thought, *is the man I am hopelessly in love with, but I am unable to even speak.*

Finally, "How are you, Chris?"

"Uh, okay, Ed, how are you?"

"I'm still pretty miserable. I thought I should at least offer you an apology. Things happened so abruptly, and I know I should have handled the entire matter differently, rather than exploding. You certainly deserved better. Anyway, I truly hope you are doing well, Chris."

"I am getting by," she said. "I do have my ranch, which keeps me pretty busy. Having good friends, I have found, is very important during difficult times." Another awkward pause, until she asked Ed, "How is Congress going?"

"Quite well, actually, based on what happened."

"Really, Ed, what did happen? What happened in a matter of a few moments?" she asked, now becoming very emotional. "You did indeed explode, leaving me without a chance to respond. Leaving me, when we were so much in love. Leaving me with all of our hopes and with all of our plans. You left it up to me to try and explain to our friends what happened. You left me alone to handle what happened. What kind of a man does that?"

"Chris, please—"

"Ed, I am not finished!" shouted Christine. "Hear me out! When I lost Ben, I felt as though my world had ended. Ben was everything I could ever want in a man. For whatever reason, after

Ben died, I felt no compelling need for a man in my life. I was keeping busy with competitive riding, generally having a ball. Attending
theater events, fine dining, sporting events, even playing some tennis
again. Actually, having a good time. Then we met and fell in love.
We shared the most precious of times together. Ed, you asked me
to marry you, and I said yes. You began telling me about the great
chances of my becoming First Lady of the United States. Did you
really mean all of those things, Ed? Did you?"

"I—" he tried again.

"So, Ed, you are a well-thought-of and respected senior congressman. Quite likely your party's nominee to run for the presidency. It meant that I would accompany you on this adventure. That
is, until my fiasco happened and you told me that I had ruined you
and your presidential plans. You mentioned nothing about our love
for each other, only that I had ruined you. You didn't even consider
how I felt at the time. No, as always, it has been, and will always be,
all about you."

"Yes, yes," he said, "but there is a great deal which you have left
out of your summary. The parts where we fell in love had nothing
to do with Congress. I also lost my wife to a hideous disease. I have
been reflecting a great deal about our falling in love, the wonderful

times we've had, and the many places we traveled together. I'll have, and will, cherish those memories forever. I guess what I'm trying to say is, my friends in politics continue to urge me to get back in the race. They also agree that we made a mistake, breaking up over what should have been a trivial matter."

"What are you saying, Ed?"

"I am not sure, but I think I would like to try it again. Maybe we could try to start it all over?" he asked.

"I'm not sure of anything yet," she said. "Give me a few days to think this all over. Where are you, by the way?"

"That is certainly okay with me; after all, I sprung this on you very suddenly. I'm in Washington. We go into ten days of budget appropriations tomorrow. Incidentally, the president has appointed me as chair of the Defense Budget Committee. This means I'm still pretty much in good standing. Will it be all right if I call you when we finish with these sessions? I, at least, would like to talk some more about us."

"Thank you for the call, Ed," she said. "It means so very much to me. Please call me when you have finished with the budget."

A confused Christine asked herself, *What just happened?* It was such a surprise to hear from Ed, she thought. *Has he really missed me? Is he truly sorry for the breakup?* What had she learned from his call? Her inner turmoil was taking over, clouding her thoughts. She needed to take a couple of steps back and try to remember Ed's exact words. *Were they truthful? Is something else going on in his personal or public life?* Christine began to attempt to analyze their conversation. *Do I still love him? Of course, I do. Does he still love me? It sounds as though he does. Are we still in love?* she asked herself. *He did sound contrite,* she thought. She couldn't think of any other motives he might have other than wanting forgiveness and truly is still in love with her, which certainly made sense.

Christine was actually proud of the way she sort of told him off. He certainly did need that type of response from her. She had ten full days to consider the manner in which she would respond to his next call. The timing could not be more perfect for her to win back her gambling loss, which had started this whole mess. If CJ's plan is safe, legal, and guarantees big winnings, she would impress not only Ed, but his constituents as well. Making a very large donation to a charitable cause could, quite possibly, minimize the damage she had done by her prior Black Jack loss of $150,000. Now, where the hell was CJ? She was tempted to call, when her phone rang.

"Hi, Christine. It's CJ. Sorry it has taken me so long to get back to you. I do have some good news for you."

"Hi, CJ, what is the good news?"

He said, "We need to meet in private to go over this plan. It's a little more difficult than I thought it might be. Don't get nervous, it will work even better than I thought it would."

"Where and when do you want to meet?" she asked.

"How about that coffee shop you like?" he asked. "Tomorrow morning at ten, okay?"

Christine said ten sounded fine. She wondered what he meant by it is a little more difficult than he thought. Since Ed's call, she had become more nervous about CJ's plan. *Will it work? Can she trust CJ? Why*, she thought, *am I even getting worked up over something which I know nothing about?*

* * * * *

After a restless night, Christine, the next morning, arrived at the coffee shop. She found CJ sitting in the last booth, next to a window. He arose to greet her.

"What has taken so long?" she asked, appearing visibly upset.

"These kinds of things take time. If you are no longer interested, we can just forget it," CJ retorted.

"No, no, I am still interested," she replied. "I just know from Roberto that you have been back for several days from your trip to Nevada. Couldn't you at least have the courtesy to call me?"

CJ now knew he had her. "I'm sorry, Christine. Yes, I did get back a few days ago, but I have also been busy trying to find out what happened to my brother, Lester. I'm worried sick about him. I've always felt responsible for him, he's all the family I have." CJ paused for a few seconds, seemingly expressing some grief. "Now, if you want, we can discuss what I've learned from my cousin.

"Isn't your cousin family?" replied Christine.

"Not really, just by marriage. He's my second cousin, I guess. We are more friends than family. I mean, the very best of friends. We both trust each other. He has never even met you, Christine, so he has a bunch of rules. He told me to tell you that either you accept the rules or we don't do business."

"My first question, CJ, is whether or not this is legal?"

"As far as you are concerned, it is completely legal. You just happen to be a very high-stakes player who suddenly has an outstanding piece of luck. In fact, the whole thing will require that early on, you are going to have to lose a very large amount of money."

"I'm not sure I like the sound of that," she said. "I thought I was there to win a lot of money."

"Christine, if you are not interested, just tell me, we can just forget it," he said. "I've told you before that there isn't any risk to you, either legally or money-wise. It is entirely up to you. Shall we just forget it? I, at least, need your answer soon. I haven't even told you the details."

"Okay, tell me how it works," she said.

"This is what I have written down from what my cousin told me." CJ withdrew a sheet of paper from his jeans pocket. "First, we have to travel to Nevada the day before. By the way, you will have to arrange for Roberto to take care of my place."

"Okay."

"Next on my list, you'll need to bring one of those fancy-looking briefcases made out of metal, I forget what they're called," he said.

"Attaché cases," said Christine. "I actually have a new one. My former fiancé, Ed Hunter, gave it to me as a gift."

"Is it big enough to carry two-hundred and fifty thousand dollars?" asked CJ.

"Yes, I believe so, but why do you ask?"

"Now don't get excited. My cousin requires that you bring that much cash with you. It is good faith money, he calls it. He said that those really rich Arab oil guys always bring at least that much cash, usually a lot more. Sometimes they have two or three of those cases full of cash."

"I just don't know about this, CJ. That is a lot of money."

"Christine, it takes a lot of money to make a lot of money gambling. Just let me finish."

"Okay."

"My cousin will meet with us the day before, once he gets his assignment for the next day or night. You will be told what time and which no-limit, high-stakes table."

"No limit?" she asked. "I have seen them before. Huge amounts of money are bet."

"That's what you are wanting to do, right?"

"Of course," she said, "continue."

"This is what he told me. You sit down with your case full of cash. Sit where he told you to sit. He will be working at a table which cannot be monitored as well from upstairs behind the mirrors on the ceiling. Make some large bets until you lose seventy-five thousand dollars. Now remember, he will go over all of this with you the day before. Anyway, after you lose the seventy-five thousand, you bet another seventy-five thousand. You will win that hand, leaving a hundred and fifty in front of you, which makes you even. You win the next hand leaving you with three hundred thousand dollars. You drag a hundred and fifty and let the other hundred and fifty ride and win one last time for three hundred thousand, that's it. By now, the pit boss will be nearby watching. That's all my cousin will let you win. He will explain it to you. He gets fifty thousand, leaving you with two hundred and fifty thousand. Pretty simple, right?"

"This seems so easy," replied Christine. "Is it really that easy and legal for me?"

"Yep," he said, "remember, he only does this two or three times a year, which earns a great deal of money for him. He guarantees me that this slip card system of his can be watched by experts and never discovered. Besides, some other high roller will be playing at another table. He told me that, quite often, some of these Arabs lose millions of dollars at one sitting. He is also very trusted by the casino staff. He easily spots cheaters and reports them to the pit bosses. In fact, they pay him more than other dealers because he can spot the cheaters."

"What about you, CJ? How much do you get out of this?"

"That is completely up to you, Christine. I'm sure you'll treat me fairly."

"Let me make sure of what I have to do," she said.

"Just what I told you. We go over in separate vehicles. I'll stay at a local motel; you stay at the casino hotel. We can't be seen together."

"This seems hard to believe I can make a quarter million dollars so easily. I really appreciate what you're doing, CJ. Please let me go home and think about it. I'll let you know tomorrow."

"Please don't take too long, Christine. I understand that the casino is going to quit the no-limit Black Jack games very soon. That's why my cousin has agreed to do this one last time."

"You will have my answer in the morning," she told him.

CHAPTER THIRTY

Congressman Edward Hunter was reflecting on his call and apology to Dr. Christine Lawrence. His apology to her was, for the most part, sincere. He failed to mention the other reason for the call. Shortly after their highly publicized breakup, his campaign manager, Stewart Hamilton, asked for a private meeting away from Ed's office. They met at a lounge near Capitol Hill which they knew would afford some privacy. After their customary drinks, vodka martini with lots of olives for Ed, vintage single malt scotch for Stewart, they began to talk business.

Stewart began with condolences, again, for the romantic breakup. He knew he could be straightforward with Edward. Next came, "You are one stupid son of a bitch, though, letting Christine go. You want to be President of the United States, and you let your major ticket to the presidency go?"

"Wait a minute, Stewart," said Ed.

"Wait a minute my ass, Ed Hunter. You have no idea what that woman meant to your campaign. Sure, she lost some money gambling. Ed, the American people loved that woman, they didn't and don't give a damn about her mistake at a casino Black Jack table. The two of you represent the ideal couple people in this country care about. Damn it to hell, Ed, her gambling didn't cost you a chance at becoming president; your sheer idiocy has nearly done it. You have to remember; the American voters are very forgiving. Remember Betty Ford? She was seriously in trouble with alcoholism and addicted to medications. She explained her problem rather than denying it. The American public not only forgave her, but embraced her with offers to help. We now have a very famous Betty Ford Clinic. Christine's gambling problem only tells us that people have character flaws. Accept that, Ed.

"Think about it, both of you represent a symbolism of America. The Camelot which JFK and Jackie possessed. Only now, a mature Camelot with you as King Arthur. You have both been widowed. You both loved your first spouses. Despite those losses, you both found love again. These traits are essential to provide that Camelot charisma, which American voters love."

"You have lost a large percentage in all of the polls; I believe because you no longer have Dr. Christine Lawrence at your side. Bring her back and watch your numbers climb too, better than ever. I'm only your campaign manager who reads you like a book. If you still want to become our president, you need that woman. If you don't want to get back together, you can find another campaign manager because I'm not interested representing a loser."

Having been a long-term US congressman, Ed was used to being criticized; however, those condemnations by his campaign manager really stung. He was sure that Stewart knew what he was talking about. Stewart still believed Ed could become president but needed the presence of Christine at his side.

Those powerful words were echoing in Ed Hunter's head, like bass drums and cymbals. Could he get Christine back without groveling? He knew Stewart was probably right. He knew and trusted his advice. They had been together for many years. Stewart had threatened to quit before, but he had never heard him threaten as seriously as now. *How do I approach her about reconciling?* he thought. *She likes flowers, I'll send her some roses, her favorite,* he mused.

He wished the budget hearings were over. He knew the importance of the president appointing him as the chair of the Defense Budget. Politically, this appointment would help him in his campaign speeches. These hearings were taking away precious time in which he could be trying to make amends with Christine. He really did love Christine. She had been a great companion and had been good enough in bed. When she wasn't available, he never worried about his sexual needs in Washington; there were plenty of ladies to take care of those things. Christine never suspected any infidelity by him. When he recently called her, he thought she seemed a little cool toward him. He could be mistaken; it may have only been her surprise at receiving his call. He was sure she would be receptive to him wishing to reconcile.

After the budget meetings, he was planning a trip to Russia and some of the former Soviet countries. Christine loved that part of the world. Perhaps, a carrot to entice her, it would put them together again on the world stage. Ed was desperately wanting to become the next president. Shortly before their breakup, he had been reelected and was now in his sixth term. This would allow him time for the rigorous campaign ahead.

He still had to deal with her gambling. Ed had one of his interns do research on gambling or, specifically, out-of-control gambling. He learned that gambling addiction can be a disease, and in fact, a part of the brain is involved. He found that a number of programs are available, any of which Christine could easily afford. Could he convince her to participate in one of these programs? It would have to be discreet, of course, or would it? It might just be possible he could use it. There were some very strong possibilities it could be used as an advantage in his campaign to become president. He couldn't wait until after the budget hearings were over to speak with her again.

"Hi, Chris," he said, calling during a recess.

"Hi, Ed," replied a surprised Christine.

After an unusually long pause, he said, "I miss you very much, Chris. It has been absolutely crazy here with these budget hearings. We hardly have time for lunch and dinner. We worked until one o'clock this morning and back at eight thirty this morning." Another long pause. "I'm sorry, Chris, how are you doing?"

"I'm doing all right, Ed," she said. "Certainly not as busy as you have been, it sounds. Do you know when the hearings will be finished?"

"Most likely on Sunday, being optimistic as hell. As chair of the Defense Appropriation Budget Committee, it can almost always be an uphill battle. We are making some progress, it seems. But that is not what I'm calling about."

"Why are you calling? You said you miss me. What does that mean, Ed?"

"It means just that. I cannot get you off of my mind. I know now our breakup was ridiculously wrong. I should have been supporting you, rather than blowing up and leaving. I behaved very childishly and am ashamed of my conduct. I want to be with you again, so much it almost hurts. I do not want to continue without you, Christine. I know this is difficult over the phone," he told her. "It is the best that I can do right now, but I am being completely honest with you. Chris, I want us back together, and I want to marry you."

"Oh, Ed," said a sobbing Christine, "I still love you so much it hurts!" Another very long pause when she finally said, "You have really caught me off guard. You do remember I have a gambling problem, are you ready to forgive this problem?"

Ed said, "It can be straightened out with therapy. There are so many therapeutic programs available, Chris. We can work out this problem together. Incidentally, I plan to run for the presidency. In doing so, I truly need you at my side. You bring out the best in me."

"That is great news, Ed," she said in a serious tone, her sobbing now gone. "I have a question for you."

"Yes, what is it?"

"What if I do not want to stop gambling?"

An astounded Ed Hunter, for about the first time in his political career, was at a loss for words. Finally, he said, "Are you really serious, Chris?"

"I've never been any more serious. I find gambling therapeutic at times. I've never hurt anyone playing Black Jack, except for the problem I had, that one time which led to our breakup. I, in fact, did lose a significant amount of money that day. But, Ed, it did not hurt anyone seriously, except your ego and presidential aspirations. Do you still want me with you, knowing I may gamble, even if I become First Lady? I am not asking for your answer right now, Ed. When you finish the budget hearings, give me a call and we will discuss this further, okay?"

An exasperated Ed Hunter merely said, "Okay, Chris." They hung up their phones. Christine knew she had given Ed a hard time. They needed to get this gambling stuff out in the open.

Now, she needed to call CJ and let him know that she was ready for the trip to Nevada. With an easy net of $250,000, she could make the huge charitable donation, which would put her in good graces with the voting public. She would then tell Ed she was through with gambling forever. Just thinking of being with him on the campaign trail and helping him win the presidency made her feel happy inside. She called CJ, but surprisingly, there was no answer.

CHAPTER THIRTY-ONE

———— • • ◦ • • • ————

Christine called CJ again. CJ answered on the first ring.

She immediately said, "Why don't you get an answering machine? I called you yesterday."

"I'm sorry," he said, "I guess I should get one of those machines, but am not sure I would be able to operate one. I know people like me who bought one of those things and have never been able to figure out how to make it work. It's just gathering dust in their house."

"Okay, okay," snapped an irritated Christine.

"Something wrong with you?" asked CJ. "You don't sound like your usual happy self. Have I done something wrong to make you upset? I'm sorry I didn't answer the phone."

"Dammit, CJ, I am dealing with some personal issues. Which issues, by the way, are none of your damn business. I would appreciate it if you will let me take care of my problems, okay?"

"Okay, Christine. Let's just plan our trip over to Nevada. Can we begin with what day we are going to leave? My cousin tells me that Wednesday is the best time to do this plan. He told me the really rich, high-stakes players favor playing on that day because there aren't as many gawkers."

"All right," she said, "let's pick the day."

"How about this coming Wednesday, as the sooner we do this thing, the better."

"I'll call you in a little while," she told him. She hung up.

Christine, again, had some reservations. Since Ed's call, she was troubled by his reaction to her question about her continuing to gamble. She had been testing him when asking "What if I continue with gambling, even in the White House?" That caused him to react with silence. She let him off of the hook by telling him they would discuss the matter after the Congressional Budget Hearings.

Now, she really had to focus on this Black Jack trip with CJ. She certainly didn't want him knowing she had a quarter million dollars in her personal safe at home. She went over the plan again in her mind. It seemed so simple. She knew and, in fact, had observed on many occasions, men who appeared to be from the Mid-East betting huge amounts of money at high-stakes tables.

Christine wondered if she could retain her composure while being part of this scheme. She recalled that she occasionally must have appeared nervous at the Black Jack tables, especially when betting a very large amount. That's when it occurred to her that, when scheduling an MRI for a claustrophobic patient, she would prescribe Valium to control their anxiety. She always received much gratitude from her patients who felt the Valium had made the procedure much easier. She hesitated to prescribe Valium for herself, that would be frowned upon by the DEA. She did, however, have a couple MD friends, and either of them would be more than happy to write her prescription. She could always tell them she was having an MRI and suffered from mild claustrophobia. *Five milligrams should do the trick,* she thought.

Postponing this trip to Nevada would likely only result in another delay. CJ had told her the casinos were soon going stop the no-limit games. He also mentioned his cousin was only going to do the slip card thing one more time. Christine knew she was excited about the plan. Again, she reflected on how her winning that much money could impact her life by making a huge charitable donation. She had to continue to believe this would be very helpful to Ed's campaign for the presidency. There should be no reason for anyone, including Ed, to know the donation came as a result of her playing Black Jack. *Despite all of the positives, why am I so concerned?* she asked herself.

She had gone over the process time and time again. It seemed so simple. She had always heard the adage, "If it seems too good to be true, then it is." Then again, it seemed to be viable and made sense to her. She would have reached $300,000 at the Black Jack table after only a few bets. The fact she would initially be down $75,000 should establish some credibility for her; $300,000 minus the $50,000 for the dealer, would leave her with $250,000. She had to give CJ something for his work in setting up this scam. She had in mind around $20,000. She was pretty sure he would believe that amount to be fair.

Christine called an anxious-sounding CJ. "I thought you were going to call me right away," he said, "you know, it isn't easy just standing by this damned phone."

A just as testy Christine said, "If you had a damned answering machine, you wouldn't have to wait around the damned phone."

"I'm sorry," said a subdued CJ, "it's just seeming to take so much time. I just want to get this thing over with, and we might be running out of time."

"Well, I'm thinking it might be a bad idea anyway. It's not something I wish to hurry up, especially when I already have reservations. Don't forget, CJ, I am the one fronting all that money. I'm the one who is taking all of the chances. Other than you having the connection, you have very little invested."

CJ was seeing the possibility of his plan falling apart.

Christine interrupted his thoughts with "I know it is taking a while, CJ, but I still need some more time. Please don't try and talk me out of it, understood?" she asked.

"Okay," he said. "Please call me soon."

CJ was beginning to think his scheme wasn't going to work. Christine seemed to be worrying too much. It occurred to him, maybe he should change the plan. If he could just get her to show him the $250,000, he could kill her on the spot, maybe take her body to another dumpster, or take her up to the lake.

Christine, on one hand, wanted to talk with Ed, while on the other, it didn't seem like a good idea. She decided to call him. After all, he had made both of the recent calls to her. In her mind, she owed

Ed a call. His office number was one she remembered with a happy feeling, a feeling of joy from their former romance, the romance she hoped was still alive and well.

Ed's secretary answered, "Congressman Ed Hunter's office, Vicki speaking."

"Hi, Vicki, this is Christine Lawrence. How are you? It's been a while since we have spoken."

"I'm fine, thanks," she replied. "I'm sure you're calling for Ed? He is still in those budget sessions. Frankly, He told me they are deadlocked on a couple of issues, and he believes it will take longer than his party had at first believed. May I take a message?"

"Sure," said Christine, "please tell him that I called, and I wish to speak to him as soon as possible. It isn't urgent, however."

"I'll get the message to him right away."

Christine had met Vicki a number of times and found her to be efficient, reliable, and gorgeous. In fact, after she and Ed had begun their romance, she had suspected that Ed and Vicki had an ongoing affair. She had, at no time, seen any evidence, but it did nag at her. She had observed early on what she perceived as a personal intimacy between them. She had convinced herself it was just her woman's intuition kicking in. In any event, after Christine and Ed announced their engagement, she noticed a change in the way Vicki treated her boss. The boss and secretary relationship appeared to be just more professional, much to Christine's liking.

Christine knew that Ed most probably had been with any number of other women after his wife had passed away. Women, it seemed, were drawn to politically powerful men, and Ed certainly fit that bill. This thought brought her back to their recent breakup. It wasn't over other women, but because of her addiction to gambling. This plan of CJ's would not leave her mind. If something went wrong, if she was found out, it would surely expose another gambling scandal about her and Ed. Another one, as bad or worse than the first, would be the kiss of death for Ed's hopes of becoming president.

A couple of hours later, Ed called. "Hi, Chris, sorry I missed your call, these damned meeting are beginning to wear me out. I was in hopes we would be finished by now. I should know better by now after all of these terms in office. Sorry, Chris, how are you doing?"

"I'm doing okay, Ed. Our last conversation ended with an unanswered question, if you remember."

"Yes, I certainly remember, Chris," he said. "I was hopeful that we might address that question in person. Our sessions are almost over, and I planned on one of us flying to meet and discuss this on a private, in person level."

"There you are, Ed, the man I am so in love with, evading this question as a politician. Ed, I want to address this right now. If we marry and you become elected to the presidency, will you accept my gambling as the First Lady?"

"Okay, Christine, if you insist, we will handle this over the phone right now. I have to tell you that I've given this question a great deal of thought. I am going to preface my answer with some very serious comments which have been made to me by my inner circle and staff advisers. The first comment from Stewart Hamilton, my very longtime campaign manager was 'Ed, you cannot be elected to the presidency without Christine Lawrence at your side.' He was most sincere in his comment. He rehashed how you and I are per-ceived by the voting public: a perfect couple; mature, with both of us suffering great personnel loss. Since our breakup, my popularity in the polls has dropped dramatically. Stewart predicts that with us together, my rise in the polls will be to a position of better than ever. Chris, I'm told by advisers that our becoming engaged again will ensure that I will be my party's nominee for the presidency."

"Now apart from all of that, Chris, I want us to be married. I don't give a damn if you want to play Black Jack while even possibly occupying the White House. It could prove to be awkward to have you gambling in a casino with Secret Service Protection surrounding you, but if it is necessary to you, we will make it work. Chris, apart from the presidency, I want to be with you more than anything in my life, whether I'm elected or not."

"Oh, Ed, thank you, thank you! You have made me very happy. Please let's not discuss any more gambling. Let's focus on our upcoming wedding and marriage."

They discussed how and when they could get together and ended the call on a happy note.

CHAPTER THIRTY-TWO

• • ○ • •

A furious CJ thought, *How else can I pull off getting that much money from Christine?* The thought crossed his mind again that maybe once she told him she had the $250,000 he could just kill her at her ranch and make her body disappear. She would have to have agreed on the Black Jack scheme in order to get that much cash.

He was getting desperate. He felt the cops could arrest him at any time, and that would be the end of his plan. It would mean no Argentina. It would mean that killing his brother wasn't even necessary. He had worked so hard to pull this thing off.

Well, he decided to let Christine have some more time. He'd say he needed another trip to Nevada to talk further with his cousin. He would be gone a couple days like before. Roberto could take care of his ranch again. Yes, this sounded like the best way to go. He called

Christine and told her he was making another trip to Nevada and asked he she would lend him Roberto again for a couple of days.

Christine asked, "Do you really need to travel to Nevada again? I thought everything was set."

"So did I, Christine, you seem to wobble back and forth so much it's making me nervous. Besides, I have another person in mind to do our plan, if you decide to back out."

"CJ, I haven't told you that I'm backing out. I have said nothing of the kind."

CJ felt, *I have her again.* He told Christine, "I have to look after myself in this. Are you going to do this thing or not? I can't wait much longer."

"Okay," she said, "let me start getting the cash together."

"That's more like it!" he said, excitedly.

Christine Lawrence was now making her list for her travel to Nevada. First, she emptied what few papers she had in her attaché case. She did a rehearsal by removing $250,000 from her safe and transferring it into the case. She was pleased it just fit. She assumed that CJ's cousin would be able to tell without actually counting that her case contained one quarter of a million dollars. She planned her wardrobe being somewhat on the conservative side, probably rather subdued for dinner the evening before.

She went over the process again in her mind. After a few hands of Black Jack, she would have, in addition to her own $250,000, another $300,000, over a half million dollars. When she suddenly realized, after giving the dealer $50,000, she would be left alone to deal with Carl Johnson. Is she that trusting of this cowboy? Especially with her having a half million dollars, which could conceivably have been his plan all along. To rob her.

Christine's head was spinning. She interrupted her packing to call CJ. As usual, he didn't answer. Christine returned to her packing. She made a reservation at the Nevada casino hotel as she had been instructed by CJ. She asked the desk person to make a dinner reservation for one. She was really beginning to feel all alone. Her thoughts were interrupted by the ringing phone.

"Hi, Christine, I was in the barn and heard the phone ringing. Was it you?" CJ asked.

"Yes, I just called you."

"What's up?" CJ asked. "Is something wrong?" That old familiar indigestion was back. He chewed a handful of Tums.

A nervous edgy Christine said, "I'm just having a nervous breakdown is all."

"A nervous breakdown?" asked a frantic CJ. "How did that happen?"

"I'm just kidding, Carl!" she replied. "I'm just nervous about this entire thing. You must understand. I have made my room reservation. Do you know when we will meet your cousin?"

"The plan is, we arrive there on Tuesday, late afternoon. I will talk to him and call your room about the details for the next day, Wednesday. I will have every detail down. You go to the no-limit table, make the bets which we have gone over, and you're suddenly holding a great deal of money. My cousin, the dealer, suggests that you have the casino make a wire transfer with the cash to your bank account. That's for your protection, because that's a lot of money just to be carrying around."

A greatly relieved Christine thought she could kiss him if he were here. Her fears of CJ setting her up were now quelled. She breathed a sigh of relief. "That sounds like an excellent idea. That was an issue which has been bothering me. It seems you have everything under control," she told CJ.

"Well, I keep telling you there is nothing to worry about, we are almost there. We will leave tomorrow. I do have one request of you, now don't call me silly."

"Whatever request do you have that I would find foolish?" she asked.

"Well, just about halfway over to the casino and hotel, there is a turnout marked as a viewpoint. It is just about the prettiest view on earth. I think you can see three states from there. Can we pull over there for a couple of minutes?"

"I have to say, I'm a little surprised at you, Carl Johnson. I never thought of you as the sentimental type."

"Well, that was also one of Melba's favorite spots to stop. In fact, we stopped there on our first trip to Nevada together. We were entered in some rodeo events in Carson City. Melba won the barrel racing, and I won in the saddle bronc competition. She always said that viewpoint brought good luck to both of us."

"Of course, we can stop, CJ. I'll take some pictures. I also want you to know, this will be my final time to gamble. My former fiancé, Congressman Ed Hunter, and I are getting back together. I will quite probably move to the East Coast after we are married and Ed becomes our next President of the United States."

"Wow, that's some really great news, Christine. Imagine, you being married to the president." Actually, thought CJ, *After tomorrow, you won't be anything but dead, and I'll be a quarter million dollars richer and on my way to Argentina.*

After they hung up, CJ was making a list of what would need to be done with his property. He needed to see that lawyer again and sign whatever papers that were needed for the lawyer to sell his ranch. He was also thinking these Tums don't help much with the heartburn, which was happening far more frequently, like right now, he thought. It seemed to come on mostly when he was under pressure, like when he killed his brother Lester.

CJ took a walk around his ranch and thought about which of his tack he should take to Argentina. The horses would have to be sold, along with all of his farm equipment. Maybe everything could be sold as a complete ranch, including all of the necessary equipment. He really liked living here. If it wasn't for those damn cops, he could continue to live here. He knew, however, they would never give up on him. *So Argentina here I come.* After showing the good Dr. Lawrence the great view at the lookout, he would be pretty damn rich.

CHAPTER THIRTY-THREE

The detectives gathered at the sheriff's conference room. The usual group was in attendance, including Chief Deputy District Attorney Karen Miller. Lieutenant Jeff Travis had everyone gathered in another roundtable discussion. "I guess by now," he said, "we should probably be calling ourselves 'The Carl Johnson Task Force'; anyway, it's an idea."

This time, Lynn Hoover gave an update on the Alice Fleetwood murder. She explained, for the benefit of those who had not heard, Lester Johnson's fingerprint had matched the latent fingerprint recovered from Mrs. Fleetwood's camera. An arrest warrant had been issued for Lester Johnson. She reported that Lester had disappeared. She also explained the previous stakeouts of both Lester's and CJ's homes, without results. The fact that Lester's pickup had been abandoned at Grand Lake had made them uneasy as to what may have happened to him.

Each detective gave a report, and all said nothing of consequence had occurred. The victims' families continued to ask for any new evidence or developments regarding their loved ones.

Layton Detective Sergeant Bill Burris gave an update on the disappearance of Dottie Lambert. He reported that he had reinterviewed Dottie Lambert's friends. Gladys Fremont was at the senior dance, sitting with her friend Dottie. They attended the dance on a regular basis. It was, for the most part, nothing more than an opportunity to watch their friends dance. The friends that danced still had their spouses to dance with. Gladys, Dottie, and their friend Betty, were all widows. When this far younger, cowboy-looking man approached them, he asked Dottie to dance. She said that Dottie looked at her and Betty, seemingly seeking their approval. All three were very surprised, as this had not happened before to any of the three. Gladys said that she and Betty gave tacit approval.

"Gladys, if you remember from my initial report to this group, wasn't quite sure of the cowboy's name. She now says, for certain, his name was initials CJ. She described his walking toward them as sort of sauntering, dressed with a pearl-buttoned Western shirt, jeans, boots, and carrying a Stetson-type hat, which he left on Dottie's chair as they begin dancing. What seemed so remarkable to her and her friend Betty was how long they remained on the dance floor. When they returned, Dottie announced they were going out for coffee and pie. This alarmed Gladys and Betty, until Dottie said 'We have our own cars and will meet there at Denny's.' This was the last time she ever saw her friend, Dottie.

"By the way, I ran a photo lineup with CJ's driver's license photo. Without hesitation, she picked our friend CJ. 'That's him,' she said. Betty and Gladys felt he must have been quite the charmer.

"A similar reinterview with Betty DeAngelo didn't reveal anything much more than I already had. She couldn't identify CJ from the lineup with certainty, but said, 'That could be him,' referring to CJ's photo. She is still unsure of his name but sticks with her original story that his name was something like CK. That is as far as I've gotten."

Karen Miller said, "Good to hear we have an ID on him by one of Dottie's friends."

Ron Adams had nothing new on the Maxine Farrell homicide. Ron did announce that he had recently been promoted to sergeant. He would continue to work detectives, however was now Detective

Sergeant Adams. This announcement brought many offers of congratulations and best wishes. What Ron did not mention was that he and Sergeant Lynn Hoover had been seeing each other on a very regular basis. Outside of this group, only Sergeant Bill Morris, Lynn's detective partner, knew about the blossoming romance. As he and Lynn were partners, they shared just about everything. He thought Lynn and Ron were a good fit for each other. Both Lynn Hoover and Ron Adams had prior short-term marriages. Neither marriage resulted in children. They were truly falling in love, and they both were very happy.

Detective Sergeant Bill Morris said, "Either CJ knows we are watching him or really doesn't care. I know how frustrating this case is, so if anyone comes up with an idea, no matter how ridiculous it may seem, please bring it forward. No need to remind you of the importance of finding Lester Johnson. He probably holds the key to closing all of these cases."

The roundtable meeting was adjourned.

Lynn and Ron met for lunch. They briefly discussed the roundtable meeting, both sharing their frustrations with the lack of evidence in any of the cases which were discussed.

"If only we could find Lester," said Lynn.

"I don't have a good feeling about him," replied Ron.

* * * *

The following morning, Jesse Logsdon went fishing at Grand Lake. It had been a frustrating morning bait fishing. He caught a couple of small Rainbow Trout. He was surprised because the fishing reports had been promising. He continued until past lunchtime with no further fish being caught.

He tried his luck at trolling which was also uneventful. He decided to cross the lake to some other shallows. Unlike Jesse, he decided to troll all the way across the lake. When he was crossing the deepest part, his fish finder began its frantic beeping showing something at about thirty-five feet. Thinking it might be a sturgeon, Jesse quickly reeled in his lightweight line.

Trying to remain over the same spot, he grabbed his heavy-weight rod and reel. With shaking hands, he nervously tried several times to tie an appropriate flasher on the heavy line. He finally was successful and, after placing what he thought to be the correct weighting on the line, cast it behind the boat. He made a pass over the object, but he was too high and passed right over it by ten feet.

Meanwhile, the fish finder again was beeping. The fish, if indeed it was a fish, paid no attention to the flasher.

Jesse reeled in the line and placed some more weight to troll deeper. He again cast the line behind the boat and made another pass. This time, he thought he saw the fish's head move slightly toward the flasher. Jesse knew he was at the right depth, so he reeled in and cast out again. This time, the flasher hooked into the object, which moved. He now realized he had probably hooked into a water-soaked log. A disappointed Jesse certainly did not wish to lose his favorite flasher, so he decided to try and reel it to the surface.

As he reeled, he thought a log would be heavier than this object. Nonetheless, the object was moving toward the surface slowly. He just hoped the line would not break. As the object was nearly at the lake's surface, it suddenly broke free. It did not, however, immediately sink, rather seemed to remain in place. Jesse couldn't see exactly what it might be in the murky water.

He decided to remove his expensive flasher. He replaced the flasher with a large plain treble hook, which he tossed over the side. He missed on the first and second tries, then hooked into the object. He slowly raised the thing to the side of his boat, and as the badly bloated body broke the surface, Jesse nearly fell backward out of the boat; his shock was so great. Jesse regained his composure and held the fishing rod while he reached with his other hand to retrieve a spool of rope.

Due to the putrefaction process, the body was starting to smell as some of the gases began to escape. Despite the smell, he threw the rope over the body, retrieved the loose end with his lighter fishing gear, pulled the rope from under the water and as it circled the body, and was able to tie it off. He tied it to a cleat on the side of his boat.

Another troller he had seen earlier saw him struggling with something heavy. Thinking it might be a sturgeon, he sped over to Jesse's boat. Seeing the bloated body tied to the boat almost made the other fisherman, George Jensen, vomit.

They discussed what to do. Jesse asked George Jensen to get over to the ranger station for help. He also said, "Make it as soon as possible, before I lose my lunch!" Both men were former marines, which helped some, but not entirely. The smell was growing worse.

The ranger on duty called the sheriff's department, informing them he would be in the ranger boat and the sheriff better bring the coroner along with a boat.

The responding deputy coincidentally was Harold Drummond. Harold had been the deputy who responded to the scene when Gloria

Hansen's drowned body had been discovered. On arrival, he was met by Ranger Raphael Jimenez. Raphael had just returned from meeting with the fishermen, Jesse Logsdon and George Jensen. Raphael had established the GPS coordinates of where the body had been found. He then returned to the ranger station. Raphael explained to Harold the dilemma which Jesse Logsdon was facing with the terrible smell coming from the body.

Deputy Drummond asked the sheriff's boat patrol to expedite. On a hunch, he called Detectives and spoke with Lynn Hoover. He had already called for the crime scene technical services to respond.

A grateful Jesse Logsdon met with the sheriff's boat patrol deputies. The deputy coroner on the boat, with help from others, managed to slide the body into a body bag. After presenting approximate identification, Jesse was instructed to report to the Sheriff's Detective Bureau the following morning to provide a formal statement. He was thanked for his help, by not only discovering the body, but having the presence of mind to successfully tie it off onto his boat. Jesse Logsdon was more than happy to get his boat off of the lake.

George Jensen was given similar instructions and departed. Both Jesse and George were finished with any more fishing that day.

This sad day did have a benefit for both men, as they became friends and fishing partners.

Lynn Hoover and Bill Morris traveled to the coroner's facility. Deputy Harold Drummond remained at the scene. He worked with the sheriff's boat patrol, as well as their technical services.

Unknown to Deputy Drummond, he would later receive a Meritorious Service award from the Center County sheriff, Tom Gentry. The award had been suggested by Captain Ron Willis. Deputy Drummond would receive another surprise by being transferred to Detectives. His abilities were being recognized.

At the coroner's facility, Lynn Hoover and Bill Morris consulted with the pathologist, Dr. Luke Evans, and Technical Services leader, Sergeant Mark Conrad. Sergeant Conrad took what he could of fingerprints from the body recovered from Grand Lake. After comparing the fingerprints with his file copy, he confirmed the body to be that of Lester Johnson.

Lynn Hoover called Lieutenant Travis with the positive identification of Lester Johnson by a fingerprint match. She then asked a deputy coroner if she would make the death notification of Lester to his brother, CJ. The deputy coroner merely responded with "Thanks a lot."

The decaying body was continuing to smell, despite Vicks on their noses and masks. The body was dressed in a blue-printed Western shirt, blue Wrangler jeans, and cowboy boots. The torso also had a piece of rope tied around it, suggesting perhaps it might have been tied to a weight of some sort. Caught in the rope and torso was a fishing reel, from which the handle and some monofilament line had apparently gotten tangled with the torso. Sergeant Conrad and Dr. Evans took many photos and extensive video from many angles. The doctor mentioned a small patch of blue material was missing from Lester's shirt, possibly having been torn at the time of death, perhaps in a struggle with the murderer.

Prior to performing the autopsy, an external examination of the body was carefully conducted. The body was then carefully undressed and prepared for the autopsy. Dr. Evans noticed what appeared to be damage to the right rear of the victim's head, and so noted. The doctor said, "This head injury may play a role in how Mr. Johnson died. I am not, however, jumping to any conclusions as to cause of death before we open him up." He additionally noted some scraping on the torso, quite possibly due to the victim's struggling against the ropes.

The overhead camera with audio was activated. The doctor scrubbed up in preparation for the opening. Both Sergeants Hoover,

Morris, and Conrad, despite the odor, were required to remain in attendance throughout the autopsy. Those assembled also included coroner's assistant, Sarah Gardner. They all respected the abilities of forensic pathologist, Dr. Luke Evans. He had, over the years, been a material witness in a number of homicide trials. His expertise had convicted many killers.

The autopsy commenced with the opening of the chest cavity. The contents were removed for dissection and submission for toxicology analysis. Dr. Evans confirmed that drowning was the cause of death.

Upon the doctor opening the top of the skull, he removed the brain. He noted, "As you see, the injury to the right side of the brain is severe. Had he not drowned, he might have survived the injury to the head with prompt medical intervention. Did someone mention that Mr. Johnson was mentally retarded?"

"That is our understanding," said Sergeant Hoover.

"Well, I'm not surprised that was the case," said Dr. Evans. "See this heavy scarring on the brain? It appears that Mr. Johnson suffered a severe blow to the head as a young child. Somebody, most likely an adult, hit him very hard. He had to have sustained a severe skull fracture and brain swelling. I see here, a healed skull fracture. This injury occurred when he was four or five years old. Why he didn't die then is a mystery to me."

"We are not sure, Doctor, he may have had abusive parents," said Sergeant Morris.

"Okay," said Dr. Evans, "it is time to close up the body. Drowning is the primary cause of death, with secondary head trauma, caused by a relatively flat, heavy object, such as a rock. The head injury should have bled slightly. We now have wait for the toxicology results."

They departed.

* * * * *

Sergeant Morris called Lieutenant Travis and asked him to set up a meeting with all of the players. He told the lieutenant that he and Lynn had decided to refrain from any notification to Carl Johnson about the death of his brother, Lester. Travis responded with "I'll bet the lady from the coroner's facility was excited to give the death notification."

"It is actually her job; besides, Lynn and I are getting tired of CJ yelling at us," said Morris.

Surprisingly, everyone including Deputy District Attorney Karen Miller, made it to the meeting within three hours. Sergeant Morris made the announcement. "Lester Johnson's body has been recovered from the middle of Grand Lake." This brought about many comments and grew much dismay.

"I guess we won't be getting to interview Lester" were the general comments and reactions.

"Let's have Lynn give an overview of what we have found," said Jeff Travis.

Ron Adams was attending the meeting. He had already been briefed by Lynn Hoover. Their romance was really becoming very serious.

Lynn explained about the fisherman who had reeled in Lester's body. Their early findings after the autopsy caused them to believe Lester had been murdered. Lynn described in detail the results of the autopsy. "Bill Morris and I feel CJ is quite likely the suspect. Lester, it appears, had been fishing in the deepest park of the lake." They felt he had been weighted down; however, somehow the rope tying him to whatever was weighing him down did not hold. Lynn further explained that Lester's body had been recovered from the deepest part of the lake, extremely deep. "Our question is how did he get out there? He certainly needed a boat. Lester's pickup was found abandoned in the lake's marina parking lot, near the main boat ramp. Neighbors of Lester told us he did not have a boat. His brother, Carl Johnson, took him on Carl's boat when he did go to Grand Lake to fish."

Chief Deputy District Attorney Karen Miller said, "I think we have enough information to seek a search warrant of CJ's boat and, hopefully, his house and property. Lynn and Bill, let's get together in my office. Please start the search warrant, and we will try to find a friendly judge."

* * * * *

Karen Miller was in the chambers of the superior court judge, the Honorable Kent Stephens. They discussed some past criminal cases in which Judge Stephens had presided. The judge admired Karen's ability as a prosecutor and knew she had an unblemished record in trying criminal cases. He was, however, concerned about the application for a search warrant Karen had presented him. Also present were Detective Sergeants Bill Morris and Lynn Hoover.

The judge spoke first. "Counselor, you and the sergeants here must know you are treading very lightly on evidence with this search warrant application. I'm usually pretty much a soft touch on these matters, but this is very borderline."

"We agree, Your Honor, it is rather weak and lacking the usual protocols; however, Judge, we are dealing with a very bad individual who doesn't leave many clues."

"I see that one of the alleged victims is Alice Fleetwood. Alice and her late husband, Len, and I were the very best of friends. I was a pallbearer for both of their funerals. Len and I grew up together and were roommates during our college years. I was best man for Len when he and Alice married. I suppose I may very well have a conflict of interest in this case. What more evidence can you give me to sign this search warrant?" said Judge Stephens. "Sergeant Morris, I need to hear more."

"Well, Your Honor, it happened in an interview with Carl Johnson while actually discussing the Alice Fleetwood case with him. Carl Johnson, during our videotaped interview, blurted out, 'I don't know anything about any twenty-five thousand dollars! During that interview, or any prior talks with him, Alice Fleetwood's twenty-five thousand dollars had never been mentioned by anyone. You will find this information a bit later in our search warrant application."

"That's more like it," said the judge.

"Your Honor, Carl Johnson is a vicious killer. He preys on older lonely women who have, in most cases, large financial assets. The Alice Fleetwood case, for example. Mrs. Fleetwood was lonely, which I'm sure, Your Honor, was aware of. We believe Carl Johnson, who goes by CJ, purposely engaged her in conversation at the supermarket. He spent several days charming her with his low-key cowboy style. He has been a professional rodeo cowboy, by the way. We believe he lured Mrs. Fleetwood up to The Bluff after getting a large amount of cash from her. As Your Honor is probably aware, Mrs. Fleetwood was quite the amateur photographer."

"Yes, she was," replied the judge. "My wife and I have a number of photos Alice gave to us over the years. Continue, Sergeant," said the judge.

"Alice Fleetwood's camera was pawned to a pawn shop in Allen County. The John Smith who pawned her camera has been identified as Lester Johnson, CJ's younger brother. The pawn shop worker who took in the camera made the identification. We additionally matched a latent fingerprint found in the camera to Lester. We have also learned that Lester was mentally retarded and would likely help his older brother. Incidentally, CJ's brother Lester's body was recently recovered from Grand Lake. Lester had been murdered; we believe by his older brother, CJ."

"My god!" said Judge Stephens. "How many people has this guy victimized?"

"Several women and his brother, Your Honor," said Karen Miller, "it appears our best hopes lie with this search warrant, Judge."

"Give me something more," asked the judge, "maybe from another victim."

"Well, Your Honor, in addition to Alice Fleetwood we have the names of other women we believe are victims of Carl Johnson." Lynn gave a breakdown of the alleged victims and how they all had some connection to a cowboy-looking guy; in some cases they had the name CJ involved.

"It is our firm belief that he is responsible for the disappearance of his wife, Melba Johnson. She went missing five years ago. Johnson gave us a story that his wife was kidnapped from their home. His story was felt to be suspicious by the investigators. After five years, there has been no trace of Melba. We do have information from

Melba's sisters that CJ was beating her severely, and she planned to leave him when the opportunity arose."

"The next victim is Sylvia Robinson, Your Honor," Lynn continued.

"Yes, I knew Sylvia very well. Her late husband, Jack Robinson, and I were golfing buddies. A number of years ago, Jack and I won our club's golf championship. I was very proud of Sylvia after Jack's death, when she stepped right up and took over managing the business as well as Jack had ever done. I will tell you that I tried very hard to convince both Sylvia and Jack to not build that cabin on that steep curvy road. Don't tell me this Johnson guy was responsible for Sylvia's death."

"I'm afraid so, Judge. We believe he cut the brake lines on Mrs. Robinson's vehicle. He was giving Mrs. Robinson riding lessons at the time. She withdrew thirty-five thousand dollars."

"Good Lord, Karen, this guy needs to be put away forever."

"We couldn't agree more, sir."

"What else?" asked Judge Stephens.

"Seventy-nine-year-old Dottie Lambert. Her son reports his mother as a very stable, sensible woman. She taught in elementary schools for over forty years. Mrs. Lambert was last seen dancing at the senior dance with Carl Johnson. She has not been seen since. He told us they went to Denny's after the dance and he never saw her again. She withdrew twenty-eight thousand dollars.

"Maxine Farrell, age sixty-seven, a retired registered nurse. She was last seen dancing with Carl Johnson at the senior dance. Her body was found near here in a garbage dumpster. She had been strangled to death. Carl Johnson admits to dancing with her but never saw her again. She withdrew forty-six hundred dollars."

"Is there more?" inquired the judge.

"We have already discussed Alice Fleetwood, Your Honor, which is probably our best evidence thus far.

"Next, we have Gloria Hansen, a retired high school teacher. Her drowned body was found in the river below the Equinox Falls. She had been hanging around CJ's ranch, helping out with chores. She felt the work was doing her some good physically. According to her sister, she had given CJ twenty-five thousand dollars to invest in some stud horse scheme.

"I think that pretty much sums it up, Judge"

"But," said Karen, "he seems pretty clever and doesn't leave much in the way of physical evidence. Now we have found the body of Lester Johnson, CJ's brother. Lester has clearly been murdered.

In our search, we intend to search CJ's boat, from which we believe Lester was hit in the head, tied to a weight, and thrown into the lake, where he died from drowning. We are sorry, Your Honor, this is all we have to offer in way of evidence to support a search warrant.

"Additionally, Your Honor, we are seeking, with this other affidavit, a search warrant for the home, property, vehicles, and financial records of Lester Johnson, Carl Johnson's deceased brother. The language in this affidavit is very similar to what we listed in the other search warrant application."

Judge Stephens said nothing for a few minutes, obviously thinking of the possible ramifications of signing the search warrant. "Well," said the judge, "I have always approached the decisions I make from the bench, as 'I may be in error, but am never in doubt.' I truly understand the frustrations which you have encountered trying to catch this evil guy. I am finishing my last term and plan to retire soon. I'm going to sign your search warrant and wish you great success."

Grateful for a signed search warrant, Lieutenant Jeff Travis coordinated the teams for execution of the search warrant.

CHAPTER THIRTY-FOUR

C J had already been contacted by a woman who said she was from the Center County Coroner's Office and that she had bad news about his brother, Lester Johnson. "Lester's body has been found in the water in Grand Lake," she said. She asked if he was the next of kin.

CJ said, "There's just the two of us. I knew those damned detectives would cause this; I knew it when they threatened to put him in prison. They just about scared him to death. Now look what happened."

"Sir," said the lady, "I'm sorry for your loss. It is my duty to also tell you how to proceed from here. You can claim the body at the coroner's facility. If you have a mortuary in mind, you can instruct them to pick up your brother's body. You probably do not want to look at the remains, as he had been in the water for a while."

A stunned CJ seemed overcome with grief and was barely able to speak, when in fact he thought, *How in the hell did Lester's body come up?* He had weighted his body with that heavy piece of railroad track. The indigestion returned. He grabbed a handful of Tums, which sometimes helped.

Now CJ thought, *I have to pay for Lester's burial. Maybe the county would pay for it.* CJ called the coroner's office and asked what he should do with his brother's body. The lady who answered his call explained that his brother's body needed to be removed for burial and asked if his brother had an advanced directive. CJ had no idea what she meant, but was sure whatever it was, Lester didn't have one. He asked how he could he get the county to pay for the burial. She explained that she was not allowed to answer legal questions. This upset CJ, who began cursing at the woman who abruptly hung up on him.

Now what? he asked himself. He had an old telephone directory in which he looked through the yellow pages. He called the mortuary that advertised low-cost burials. After listening to a boring guy from the mortuary explain his options, he decided that cremation would be the cheapest way to go. No, he didn't want a preacher and didn't want the ashes buried, he would take them himself.

He spent the rest of the day going to the coroner's office and signed the release of his brother's body to the mortuary. He gave the dirty overcharging bastards at the mortuary $575 to cremate Lester's body. He told them he wasn't buying any urn and a cardboard box was just fine for the ashes.

Returning home, he thought about his brother. He had mostly raised Lester and fought with those who bullied and tormented him. He remembered when he took care of the bully, Oscar. Oscar never bothered anyone ever again. The bullying, however, never stopped even through his brother's teenage years. He had actually shown Lester how to defend himself.

He recalled Lester coming home with another swollen eye. His brother was about twelve at the time. "Who did this to you?" asked Carl.

Lester, with a big smile, said, "Jimmy McDonald, but you don't have to go beat him up, he went to the hospital. I did what you told me to do, Carl," he said, still smiling. "I kicked him in the balls, and when he went down screaming, I kicked him in the head." Carl was never more proud of his little brother. Sure, there were still bullies, but not nearly as many. Jimmy McDonald nearly died.

CJ was able to convince himself that Lester was better off. CJ didn't really have such a big problem with the $575 for Lester's cremation. After all, while searching his brother's trailer, he had found nearly $4,000 beneath his mattress. *Just like Lester,* thought CJ, *believing his money was safe under the mattress. Poor foolish Lester, but he was a good saver of his money.*

CJ had been hopeful to hear from Christine this morning telling him that she was ready to go to Nevada. He needed to get this plan moving.

Christine had seemed sincerely sad when he had explained that his brother had gone missing. He failed to mention the circumstances surrounding Lester's disappearance and his clashes with the Sheriff's Detectives. Once he told her that Lester's body had been found, Dr. Lawrence offered to help in any way she could. Although she had never met his brother, Christine had offered to attend the funeral and any planned services.

CJ explained that it appeared that his brother had committed suicide by drowning himself in a lake. Lester had been very depressed after his girlfriend had recently been killed by a hit-and-run driver.

Christine mentioned that her husband, Ben, had also died after being struck and killed by a hit-and-run driver. CJ pretended to be saddened by that information.

He told her that his brother had been a very private person and that his services would be private. He also asked that she not send any flowers. If Christine wished to donate any money, she could give it to CJ, who would donate it to his brother's favorite charity. So far, she had not made any offer to do so. *Stingy bitch*, thought CJ.

CHAPTER THIRTY-FIVE

S hortly after moving his steers to another fenced pasture, CJ's thoughts were interrupted by the sudden arrival of several police and sheriff's cars driving onto his property. He immediately felt that familiar heartburn, which this time was not going away.

Detective Sergeant Bill Morris stepped from his unmarked car and shouted to him, "Carl Johnson, we need to speak with you."

There must have been at least a dozen cops getting out of their cars. This included that female detective, Hoover, he observed. CJ shouted, "What the hell are you doing trespassing on my property? I told you last time not to come back here without a warrant. Get off of my property!"

Sergeant Morris continued, "Carl Johnson, we have a search warrant for you and your property, here is your copy. I am only going to tell you this one time. Do not interfere with any of these officers, or you will be arrested and restrained. Understand?"

CJ did not respond.

As Sergeant Mark Conrad began walking in the direction of CJ's boat, CJ ran at him, screaming, "Get off my property!"

Bill Morris grabbed CJ and pushed him against a shed and ordered, "Hands behind your back, I already warned you." Lynn Hoover approached with her handcuffs. "Lynn, do you want the honor?"

"You bet I do!" as she roughly snapped the handcuffs tightly on CJ's wrists. Morris and Hoover walked a yelling CJ to an awaiting patrol car. CJ was shoved against the car. "Spread 'em," said Lynn. CJ continued to rant obscenities, while Bill kicked CJ's feet apart and frisked him. Bill removed a pocket knife, but no other weapons were found on him.

As they attempted to place a struggling CJ into the back seat of the patrol car, they "accidentally" bumped his head on the top of the door frame. This seemed to settle him down considerably. "You did that on purpose!" cried CJ.

Both Morris and Hoover said, "Did what on purpose?"

"You know what you did!" he again cried out.

The fact that they immediately went to his boat concerned CJ, as he watched from the back seat of the patrol car. He continued to yell, "I want a lawyer! I want a lawyer!"

The deputy guarding CJ said, "What's your lawyer's name?"

"None of your business, I want a lawyer."

CJ's ranting's continued while the other officers searched his house, barns, and outbuildings, having little success thus far. Four deputies walked CJ's property. This was also making him nervous. He was pretty sure they would not find his safe beneath the concrete lid; nonetheless, he was concerned.

When a deputy from Technical Services came to the car, he, pursuant to the search warrant, told CJ, "We need a hair and saliva sample from you."

CJ replied, "Screw you, you ain't getting nothing from me."

The deputy very calmly said, "It's up to you, Mr. Johnson. We are going to get those samples from you one way or another. Just letting us swab your mouth on a voluntary basis you will find much easier than us taking you to the ground and prying open your mouth to get the sample. People have ended up losing teeth and even getting broken jaws. Up to you, sir."

"Okay, take your fucking samples," replied CJ. He was still watching as the cops got close to the concrete lid. He breathed a sigh of relief as they seemed to walk away from his concealed safe.

Technical Services leader, Sergeant Mark Conrad, was personally processing the boat. His only findings thus far included a dark brown spot below the middle seat. Only a lab examination will determine if is blood. His other significant finding was a few blue threads. They were stuck on what he called a cleat on the starboard side of the boat. This cleat is common on fishing boats, to tie off the boat at a landing. He placed the threads into an evidence bag and made the determination to cover and tow the boat to the sheriff's secure storage compound. They could conduct further tests at that facility.

CJ's house was thoroughly searched. He couldn't tell from the back seat of the patrol car what they were removing or if they were finding any of the things listed in the search warrant.

CJ was again cursing, complaining the handcuffs were too tight. His yelling seemed to draw very little attention. Finally, Sergeant Lynn Hoover came to the patrol car. She opened the rear door and said, "CJ, if I loosen those handcuffs, will you stop yelling and cursing?"

CJ said, "Yeah, these things are too tight and hurting me."

"Answer my question, if I loosen the cuffs, will you stop cursing and yelling?"

"Yeah," he said.

Lynn had another deputy stand by while she loosened the handcuffs. She said to the deputy, "If he tries anything while I'm loosening these, shoot him in the head." The incredulous deputy caught her wink.

CJ screamed, "I won't do anything! Please just undo these things some."

Lynn released the cuff's a little and did notice CJ's hands had turned purple. *Too bad, poor guy,* she thought. Now she told him, "Any more yelling while we do our work will mean those cuffs get cranked up tighter than before, understood?"

"I understand, but you have no right treating an innocent man like this!" he said, while noticing one of his arms had gone numb for no apparent reason.

"It's time for our saliva sample, CJ," said Sergeant Morris.

A deputy from the Technical Services Unit approached. "I am going to swab your mouth, Mr. Johnson. I am asking that you cooperate. This will not hurt a bit."

Bill Morris was holding a very large set of pliers and winked when he asked the deputy, "Are you going to need these?"

This resulted in CJ yelling, "I thought you said it wasn't going to hurt!"

"No thanks, Sergeant, I don't need them unless Mr. Johnson here won't cooperate."

"I'll cooperate, I'll cooperate!" said a very nervous CJ.

The technician swabbed CJ's extremely dry mouth. He thanked him for not resisting.

As Morris walked away, CJ was very worried. Did he leave something in the boat which they could use? He later became even more concerned when he saw one of the deputies back up a county SUV to his boat and hooked it up. That guy with sergeant stripes was placing a cover over his boat and tying the cover securely.

It was becoming nerve-racking for CJ as he watched boxes and bags of stuff being hauled from his house and barns. He knew now, if they didn't arrest him, he really had to hurry convincing Christine Lawrence to go through with his plan. If he could get the $250,000 cash from her, added to what he had buried in his safe, he was heading to South America where they would never find him.

His plan was still Argentina. Argentina was famous for its cowboys. They were called gauchos and did things the way American cowboys still do. CJ felt he would be right at home in Argentina. Maybe he might even buy himself a ranch, known as *estancias*. The gauchos dressed differently than him. They wore baggy pants and drank lots of wine. CJ romanticized being a gaucho. Maybe he could teach them to wear jeans. He suddenly realized he had been daydreaming.

He had in his safe a fake passport he had purchased in Mexico, along with several other fake types of identification, also bought in Mexico. He also had similar forgeries made for his brother, Lester. *They would no longer help poor Lester,* he thought to himself.

It continued to be nerve-racking for CJ, as he continued to watch stuff being removed from his house and barns. He was grateful they had walked by his buried safe. Should that be found it was probably all over for him. CJ watched as his boat was towed away by a deputy towing the boat with a sheriff's department SUV. His anxiety was growing by the minute. He had even forgotten about the handcuffs holding his hands behind his back.

After what seemed like hours, Detective Sergeant Bill Morris approached the patrol car and told a quiet CJ, "I am going to open the car door." Bill Morris opened the door to the back seat and told CJ, "Get out of the car." CJ found moving difficult as he pushed with his feet. After successfully getting out of the car, he found he was surrounded by cops. Sergeant Morris said, "We are finished here for the time being, Carl. Most likely we'll be back as soon we have evaluated the evidence we've recovered. I will tell you, as you have probably seen in the bad-guy movies, don't leave town. Turn around, I'm going to remove the handcuffs. I advise you to not make any sudden moves as it would give me great pleasure if you want to try and attack me or any of these other officers."

"I'm not going to cause any trouble," said a subdued CJ. "Please just take these things off my wrists."

Morris removed the handcuffs and watched CJ rubbing his wrists. Then CJ said, "Just remember, each and every one of you, sons of bitches, are going to be sued. You have violated my rights." as he walked away, much quieter than when they had arrived. He watched as all the cops drove away, grabbing for his Tums. His heartburn was about the worst it had ever been.

* * * * *

After everyone had driven away, CJ began walking his property, paying close attention to see if anyone was left behind to spy on him. Satisfied that was not the case, he walked across to the southwest end of his property. There, he checked for any evidence the culvert cover covering his safe had been disturbed. Nothing appeared to have been moved.

He returned to his home where he checked the area from which his boat had been towed. He asked himself, *What on earth did they want from my boat?* In looking around, he felt something was not quite right. It was then he remembered he accidentally left the rock in the boat after hitting Lester with it. When he returned home, he had removed the rock from his boat, washed it off with a garden hose, then tossed it. He had tossed the rock twenty-five feet or so from the boat. Now the rock was missing. He did a search, making circles from around the area where he remembered he had tossed the rock. His indigestion, accompanied by chest pains, began again.

He read and tried to understand what written information was in the affidavit for the search warrant. As he read more in depth, he found another search warrant affidavit authorizing the cops to search his brother Lester's home, vehicles, and any financial records. CJ was stunned to see that the cops had also searched his brother's property.

These revelations hit CJ like a ton of bricks. The affidavits mentioned several possible homicide victims. He began shaking as he read Melba Johnson, Dottie Lambert, Alice Fleetwood, Sylvia Robinson, Gloria Hansen, Maxine Farrell. CJ was truly beginning to worry that his plan might fall through if Dr. Lawrence didn't follow up on this soon.

CJ went to sleep that night thinking about getting away to Argentina. Rather than dreaming of Argentina, he began having terrible nightmares. He was under water, facing Lester. Lester was saying over and over, "Carl, why did you drown me?" CJ could not speak because he was drowning. Lester had the piece of railroad track with a rope attached. He placed the rope's noose over CJ's head, which immediately took CJ to the bottom. All the way down, he heard Lester's sorrowful voice, "Carl, why did you drown me?"

When he reached the bottom, he was met by Melba. She said repeatedly, "Why did you murder me, Carl?" She was speaking to him, as Lester had been. Melba was holding the anchor and rope he had placed around her. Melba took a noose from the rope and anchored it to CJ's neck. CJ was now on the bottom, completely weighted down. He awoke with a start, gasping for breath, his body drenched, his heart pounding. He got up and took some more Tums.

He fell back asleep, finding himself at the bottom of the water, again unable to breathe. He was met by Sylvia Robinson's horribly burned body with broadly smiling skeletal teeth. Sylvia asked, "Why, Carl? Why, Carl?"

Next, he saw Alice Fleetwood holding her camera, taking his picture. "Carl, now everybody will have your picture, CJ the killer."

Still unable to breathe, he next saw the horribly rotted decomposed body of Maxine Farrell, with her skeletal smile.

Finally, when he could no longer hold his breath, he discovered Gloria Hansen, her body badly beaten from the turbulence of the falls. "How is the stud horse investment coming along, CJ?" she asked.

CJ frantically tried to swim toward the surface, but the weights were unyielding, and just when his air gave out, he awakened, sucking great amounts of air. Again, he was completely drenched when he awoke.

He attempted to get out of bed, but again fell asleep. This time he found himself at the bottom of the water where Dottie Lambert awaited him. "CJ!" she cried out. "I trusted you! You took my money, you took me fishing, strangled me, and put me down here! Why, why, CJ?"

Appearing from behind Dottie was David Johnson, CJ's father. David had his arm around Carl's old girlfriend, Amy. Amy was holding a baby, and she kept saying again and again, "Why did you kill me and your baby girl?" He now knew he was drowning, swallowing great volumes of water as his vision blurred.

He suddenly was awake again, choking and gasping. This time he was able to stand, telling himself he shouldn't try to sleep. Still trying to shake those terrible nightmares from his brain, he found himself unable to concentrate on the legal papers sitting in front of him.

On his kitchen counter was a copy of the search warrant with an attached receipt of items which had been seized. It looked as though they had taken a bunch of stuff, including some of his clothing and his business records which contained names of his hay delivery clients.

On the last page they had described taking a rock, basically flat, approximately eight inches in length and seven inches in width. CJ knew he had washed out the blood from the boat as well as the rock. Could they possibly trace that rock as the one he had hit Lester with? He had to discontinue reading, as his hands were shaking so hard, he couldn't hold the papers still.

A frantic CJ knew they would be coming for him soon. He must get that money from Christine, *now*.

CHAPTER THIRTY-SIX

S ergeant Mark Conrad was going over CJ's boat at the sheriff's secure impound lot. What the presumptive test showed as blood that was found in the bottom of the boat while he was at the ranch searching the boat had given him a positive confirmation, using the Fluorescein Method. He now needed to submit all of the evidence, including Lester's shirt and the blue threads he had removed from the boat. He was careful to retain the chain of custody of evidence.

What he had not mentioned to anyone was the hand-sized flat rock that he found not far from the boat. He found, once again using the Fluorescein Method of testing for blood on the rock, another positive test. He had seen the back of Lester Johnson's head when attending the autopsy. He felt, with blood on the rock, it could be what had been used to strike Lester's head. Conrad called the pathologist, Dr. Evans, about the rock. Dr. Evans asked him to bring it over. They still had Lester's body at the county morgue.

Sergeant Conrad called Bill Morris and told him what he had found. Bill Morris called to Lynn Hoover. "We need to go to the morgue ASAP."

As they stood by, Dr. Evans examined the rock. "I'll be damned, this pretty well matches the impressions on the victim's head. Great work," he said to Conrad. Dr. Evans began testing the rock. He had made some impressions of the injury to the back of Lester's head, along with a number of his own photographs as well as a video. The measurements of Lester's head injury corresponded very well with the impressions from the rock. As a forensic pathologist, he felt convinced this rock caused this injury. He felt, however, with the magnitude of this case, especially involving multiple victims, he needed some confirmation from another expert.

He called his colleague, Dr. Gerard Hildebrand, at the FBI Lab in Quantico, Virginia. They caught up on personal and professional matters for a while, then they got down to business. While speaking about the rock, Dr. Evans faxed photos, measurements, and everything he could submit by fax.

Dr. Hildebrand told his longtime friend, "I trust your opinion on this, Luke. In going over your faxed material, my first thought is that you are absolutely correct. I do understand, with our advanced technology, we can certainly corroborate your findings. I don't recall a time that you have ever been wrong on this type of analysis. I do remember some mistakes while over-imbibing when we were in medical school, however."

"I try to forget those days, Gerry," said Luke Evans, chuckling. "I'll be in touch, thanks for your help." He ended the call.

"I want to submit this rock to a friend of mine at the FBI's Forensic Lab in Quantico, Virginia," Dr. Evans told the group in the lab, "The FBI lab is the finest in the world. Their largest problem is caseload. They are always backed up for months, even on high-priority cases. My friend owes me a couple favors. I think this is an appropriate time to call in those favors. I know it will be expensive to fly someone back, but will be worth it. I am going to call Captain Willis and ask him to get this rock to Virginia. Quantico is only an hour or so from Washington, DC. This will also preserve the chain of custody, having our own officer take it in his or her custody."

The excited trio, Hoover, Morris, and Conrad, left the coroner's facility, barely able to contain their enthusiasm. Lynn spoke first,

"Mark, your finding that rock just might be the key to undoing Carl Johnson."

"I agree," said Bill Morris, "it will be, by far, the biggest piece of this puzzle, at least with the murder of Lester Johnson."

When they returned to the Detective Bureau, both Captain Willis and Lieutenant Travis were waiting for them. They assembled in the captain's office.

Lynn Hoover did the overview, beginning with search warrant for Carl Johnson's home, boat, and property. The most encouraging results of the search were from CJ's boat. She went on about recovering some blue threads from the side of the boat, which they have hopes will match the blue Western shirt removed from Lester Johnson's body. "A suspected blood stain had also been taken from the boat and is being analyzed. The stain had given a presumptive positive for blood. Even if it is positive for Lester's blood, I'm sure CJ has taken Lester out on the boat before and will claim his brother cut himself somehow leaving the blood stain. Most interesting," she said, "is a flat rock found by Mark Conrad near CJ's boat. Dr. Evans is very interested," she explained. "In his opinion, the rock may have been used to cause the injury to the back of Lester's head."

Captain Willis interrupted, "Excuse me, Lynn, but Dr. Evans called me. I've already called the CEO'S office for out-of-state travel authorization which has been approved. I've spoken with Detective Doyle and am planning to send him to Quantico with this rock. My secretary is arranging for Doyle's flight to Ronald Reagan Airport in Washington, DC. He will have a rental car to get him to Quantico. He will need his complete ID to get into the FBI facility. Since I am a graduate of the FBI National Academy, they, as a courtesy, will arrange for Doyle to stay in one of their visitor's rooms with full cafeteria privileges. It's a pretty nice facility."

Captain Willis called Detective Doyle into his office. "Ralph," he said, "we hope that this trip is successful. I believe the FBI folks will treat you well. One word of caution, don't try to outdrink them. I know from personal experience that it can't be done. Just remember, we are going to the front of the FBI's forensic line. If anyone asks how we are taken out of turn, just tell them you are only the messenger."

"Got it, Skipper," replied Doyle.

"Please keep in touch, as you know the importance of this case," said the captain.

"This may be the break we've been waiting for," said Bill Morris. "While we wait for Ralph Doyle's report, Lynn and I will put together the affidavit for a murder warrant for CJ. This will be for the murder of his brother, Lester. Maybe, if he lets us talk with him, he will give us something on his other victims."

"We won't hold our breath," said Lynn.

* * * * *

Detective Ralph Doyle was enjoying his flight to DC. He had never been to Washington, DC before. He wasn't sure how long he would be there but planned to make the best use of his time sightseeing. He was watching the city below him from his window seat as they approached for landing. Just seeing the Washington Monument and the US Capitol from the plane told him there was lots to see here.

He rented the car and drove about forty-five miles to the exit for Quantico. He then drove toward the FBI facilities. Ralph, being a former marine, had known about Quantico, but this was his first visit. As he approached an entry gate, huge concrete barricades had been placed outside the gate forcing him to drive slowly in a staggered maneuver to the gate. There were several heavily armed marines halting him, and he was asked to step from his car and open the trunk. He presented his credentials, and a marine checked them with what looked similar to a large phone. Apparently, he was expected. His car trunk was closed, and the automated search beneath his car was completed. He was given directions by the guard, and a visitor tag was placed inside the car's windshield.

Doyle was checked in and given his guest room, which seemed fairly spartan but comfortable enough. He was directed to the forensic lab located near the bottom floor of the building. He was met by a gentleman who appeared to be in his middle to late fifties, who introduced himself as Dr. Gerard Hildebrand. Ralph Doyle was momentarily stunned. He immediately recognized Dr. Hildebrand as the author of many books commonly used to teach advanced investigative classes. Dr. Hilterbrand was a legend, and he had just shaken Ralph's hand!

"Please call me Gerry or Doc," he said to Ralph. "Detective Doyle, I believe you have brought something for me."

"Yes, sir, I've brought this rock for you to examine."

"Yes, Luke Evans called me and sent me a great number of reports and photographs. Did Dr. Evans tell you that we attended medical school together and have become very good friends?"

"Not exactly, sir, I do know that he has great respect for you, Doctor."

"Gerry, please. Come with me, Ralph, we need to log in this piece of evidence." Ralph noticed the rock was carefully wrapped in a soft cloth, maybe linen. After signing off the rock to the FBI Forensic Lab, getting a receipt, and being told to sit and be comfortable, the identification comparison began.

Shortly, Ralph was directed into a room containing many what appeared to be electronic instruments. He was met by Dr. Hildebrand who told Ralph to have a seat. When asked, Ralph tried to explain the murder of Lester Johnson and that Dr. Evans had compared the rock to the injury to the right rear of Lester's head. Ralph then said, "That's why I'm here with the rock. In addition to Lester Johnson, we believe his older brother, Carl Johnson, has murdered several older women. As far as I know, Doc, sorry, Gerry, this case with the rock is the best evidence we have against this Carl Johnson. That's why the captain had me fly it out here."

"I understand, and I'll do everything I can to help. By the way, Ralph, are you interested in observing our processing of this piece of evidence and hopefully connecting it to the death of Lester Johnson?"

"Yes, sir!" replied a jubilant Ralph Doyle.

"Okay, then you will have to scrub and be gloved and gowned," which Ralph immediately did, happily.

Dr. Hildebrand began by laying out photographs of Lester. Next to the photos were what looked like vinyl casts of the injury to the back of Lester's head. Several machines were starting up, none of which Ralph understood.

As Dr. Hildebrand fed photos in to one machine, he placed the casts into another. The first machine began making something of a squeaking noise. The doctor began cursing, saying very angrily, "We just had this damned thing serviced! I'm sorry, Ralph, we have to get our technician back here before we go any further. We don't want to proceed with this processer acting up. It could take a while; it was two days last time." The doctor stopped the machine in which he had placed the vinyl cast. "We are stuck until we can get the tech here. Have you been to DC before?" he asked the disappointed Detective Doyle.

"No, sir" was his reply.

"Then my suggestion is that you take a tour of the downtown area. I'll arrange for a private tour of the FBI building. That, I think, will be of interest to you. The Smithsonian is great. You can return to your housing here as late as you wish. I'm hopeful we can continue our testing in the morning. Our receptionist will provide you with brochures of points of interest in DC. I'm sorry for the inconvenience, Ralph."

"No problem, Doctor, I was hoping to have some time for sightseeing."

Ralph called Captain Willis and explained the equipment malfunction. The captain told him, "Take some time sightseeing in Washington. Keep us posted."

"Yes, sir," said Ralph.

Ralph had a great time. The FBI's Hoover Building, dedicated to its founder, the late J. Edgar Hoover, was a special treat, especially with the private tour. Photos of the old gangsters, like John Dillinger, Pretty Boy Floyd, and many others, were very impressive. Ralph, being something of a gun nut, enjoyed visiting the FBI's armory and speaking with the gunsmithing experts. With limited time remaining, he saw what he could of the Smithsonian Natural History Museum. There was so much for him to see, with so little time.

Upon returning to the FBI Academy, he found a message from Dr. Hildebrand telling him that the equipment was still not repaired. Disappointed but not entirely displeased, he looked forward to another day in Washington, he really wanted to see the Air and Space Museum. At the end of his second day of sightseeing, a thoroughly tired Ralph Doyle returned to the academy and found a note from Dr. Hildebrand proclaiming, "Finally, we are good to go in the morning at 0800."

After the cafeteria breakfast, Ralph walked the grounds. Already, firearms training was in progress. He walked by the corner of the building and saw the legendary Hoover Road where a number of men and women were running.

He arrived at the lab at exactly 0800 hours. Dr. Hildebrand wished him a good morning. After prepping, Ralph observed Dr. Hildebrand begin testing the rock with the impressions he had received from Dr. Evans. This time, when the machines began to operate, there was no longer the previous squeaking noise. "As you see, Ralph, these machines are doing in a matter of minutes, even seconds, what would previously have taken us many days. Thank God for technology," proclaimed Dr. Hildebrand. No sooner had those words been uttered, a high-pitched beeping interrupted them.

"Success, Detective Doyle, we have a match. In other words, this rock is the rock that caused the injury to the back of Lester Johnson's head."

"Thank you, Gerry," said Ralph.

"You're welcome. Also, thanks to forensic science."

"What now?" asked Ralph.

"Well, you are safe to report to your office, along with your district attorney, the results of my findings. I will call Luke Evans with our findings. It will take, due to our bureaucracy, several days to provide the reports. I will, however, sign an affidavit of my findings. Our match is completely solid." Ralph was happy to be flying home with good news. He called Captain Willis with the positive news.

* * * * *

Captain Willis hurriedly set up a meeting of the task force. It still took some time, as all of the detectives had other case assignments, including Sergeants Hoover and Morris. There was palatable excitement in the room as Captain Willis made the announcement that FBI Forensic had a positive match on the rock taken back by Detective Ralph Doyle. In fact, Ralph was in the air right now returning from Quantico.

Chief Deputy District Attorney Miller stated, "With a match of the rock, I am issuing an arrest warrant for Carl Johnson for the first-degree murder of his brother, Lester." This drew some high-fives.

Lieutenant Travis said, "This is great news. We may solve the murder of Lester Johnson. We are left with several other people we believe were murdered by Carl Johnson. Anyone have an idea how to proceed? Once we arrest CJ, he will most probably invoke his right to an attorney. Is there a rush to make the arrest? We are awaiting DNA tests results on at least the Alice Fleetwood and Maxine Farrell cases."

Lynn Hoover spoke up, "It seems probable that, with the recovery of Mrs. Fleetwood's camera, DNA may help. I have continued to request that the State Lab at least give us a progress report."

Sergeant Morris added, "The DNA from the camera has been established as coming from Lester Johnson. If we can get just one little trace of CJ's DNA, we have another case for CJ's arrest."

Sergeant Ron Adams replied as well. "Maxine's DNA was very compromised with her body being left in the dumpster amid all of the garbage. The state laboratory is trying their best with DNA in that case. Dr. Evans has done a number of measurements of the strangulation marks on her throat. He can only tell us CJ's hand and finger size could have left the marks on her neck. But he said it was only his guess, not scientific."

"Okay," said Captain Willis, "it seems to be our best evidence against CJ is the murder of his younger brother. Does anyone have anything stronger by way of evidence in any of the other cases we believe were committed by CJ?" Headshakes all around. "Let's face it, we have a very vicious criminal who is suspected in multiple killings of people in our community, yet all we have to charge him is in the killing of his brother."

Before they broke up the meeting, one of the detective receptionists said, "Excuse me, Sergeant Adams, you have a message to call your office."

Everyone was still nearby when Ron Adams returned. "Let's rejoin," he said, "I have some news." When all were assembled, Ron proclaimed, "We have a DNA match in the Maxine Farrell case. Positive match with the finger impressions on Maxine's throat to one Carl Johnson. It was just confirmed by the State Lab."

After high-fives all around, Karen Miller said, "I'll prepare the arrest warrants for CJ. Since it is late on Monday afternoon, let's plan on the arrest tomorrow morning. I think it might be wise to use SWAT, as he has likely been expecting us to return."

CHAPTER THIRTY-SEVEN

———————— • • ○ • • ————————

Christine was pretty much packed. They had planned on departing for Nevada at nine in the morning. She began thinking about traveling all over the country with Ed as he campaigned to become the next president. Just thinking about it was giving her goose flesh. *I may become the future wife of Congressman Ed Hunter.* That sounded like a nice life to live. She couldn't allow her thoughts to project too far into the future. One thing at a time. Tomorrow, she will be able to assist Ed with a huge charitable donation.

At eight thirty the following morning, she locked all of her doors and opened her safe. She counted out twenty-five packs of $10,000 each. She carefully and neatly placed the cash into her attaché case, closed, and locked the case. She also removed from the safe a .45 caliber Colt pistol. It had belonged to her late husband, Ben. He had shown her how to shoot, load the clips, and keep the pistol clean. She inserted a full clip into the pistol and took a second clip from the safe. She would have to remember to remove the pistol from her purse before entering the casino the following day. That shouldn't be a problem as the pistol felt like it weighed a ton.

She reread the list of instructions, which included taking the Valium before she played Black Jack. She had her confirmed hotel reservation. She reread the instructions on how she was to go to the high-stakes table: Tell the dealer she wished to speak to the pit boss. After introducing herself, she would unlock her attaché case, display-ing to the pit boss the cash, and express interest in her cash being secure while she gambled. Thinking about the game, she thought she may have to take two of the Valium. A colleague had prescribed the Valium, as her friend believed it was necessary for any claustrophobia she might have during an upcoming MRI.

* * * * *

Roberto arrived at CJ's ranch early on Tuesday morning with a "Buenos días, Señor Johnson."

"Let's speak English here at my ranch, Roberto," said an irritated Carl Johnson. "We don't speak no Mexican here, understand?"

"Yes sir," replied Roberto.

CJ saw what seemed to be a quick flash of anger from Roberto's eyes and quickly added, "I do appreciate you helping me out while we are gone. We should be back tomorrow by about four or so. Got that, Roberto?" CJ had not sleep well. His heartburn was worse than ever during most of the night. No amount of Tums seemed to help. When he did occasionally doze off, he had the recurring dreams about Lester and being under water. He would be glad when he got rid of Christine and had her money.

"Si, señor," replied Roberto, who tried his best to conceal how much he disliked CJ. He would help this man only because Dr. Lawrence had requested that he do it. As he drove back to Dr. Lawrence's ranch, he was hopeful that CJ was not going to harm his employer. He suspected that CJ was doing something that was not proper and he was involving the doctor in it.

Roberto had been suspicious the first time he had been asked to take care of CJ's ranch. Unknown to her, Roberto had overheard the doctor speaking to CJ on her phone in the horse barn. He wasn't exactly sure what they were talking about. He did hear her say, "Are you sure that this thing is legal? Okay, CJ," she had said, and, "Yes, of course I trust you."

He owed the doctor a great deal. She had hired him, knowing he was in this country illegally. She had hired a tutor to teach him English. Most important to him, Dr. Lawrence had helped him to become a United States citizen. He had been sad when he learned that Dr. Lawrence and Congressman Hunter had broken off their engagement. The congressman had always treated Roberto well. In fact, Congressman Hunter had assisted Roberto's mother in her move to this country, and she became a citizen as well. Now he, Roberto, was foreman of the ranch and also a citizen. He was also very concerned for his jefa, Dr. Lawrence. He thought, *I just might have to have a man-to-man talk with CJ.* He would not allow CJ, or anyone else, to bring harm to his friend and boss lady, Dr. Lawrence. That is, not if he could help it.

When Roberto returned home, he saw Dr. Lawrence loading some things into her car. He offered to assist her, but she declined, saying, "I'm only going to be gone overnight, Nevada isn't that far." She seemed to be thinking to herself. She said, "I'm sorry, Roberto, I wasn't supposed to tell anyone I'm going to Nevada. Please don't tell anyone that I mentioned that state."

"Certainly, Señora Lawrence. Is everything okay?"

"Everything's fine. Please honor my request."

"Si, señora."

* * * * *

CJ was also now packing for the trip. He emptied an old duffel bag. The first thing he packed was a baseball bat. He chuckled to himself when he thought, *I'm surely not likely to be playing any baseball at that view area.* He added an older .38 caliber Colt revolver, which, on second thought, he placed beneath the seat of his pickup, in case he might need to quickly get to it. He added some lengths of rope, some towels, bottles of water, and a change of clothes, just for effect.

That's when he thought again about Roberto. *How much did he know?* he asked himself. Getting rid of that big Mexican guy would take some planning. He was not a problem at this time, but could become one if something happened to Dr. Lawrence.

CJ was packed and left his ranch at eight thirty in the morning. He wanted to be waiting at the view area when Christine pulled up to see the view with him. The thought of this big score had him already excited. He was having those same indigestion pains which he had during the night. He placed another handful of Tums into his mouth and felt he was getting a little relief. This will soon be over, and the stress would be gone.

He had covered his trail perfectly, he felt. No one knew they were traveling to Nevada, except for his nonexistent cousin. It would have been better if he had Lester to take Christine's car away. It would have to be done without Lester's help.

Just before the view turnout, there was an old abandoned logging road. Immediately after he threw Christine over the cliff to her death, he would be sure he had her car keys and drive her car to the logging road. It might not be found for days or weeks. If by chance someone stopped at the overlook, it was unlikely they would stroll down to the logging road. Well, he hoped that didn't happen. If they stayed too long, or Christine was growing impatient, he had his Colt under the seat. He thought, *Naw, it was not likely anyone would be stopping at the overlook at this time of year.*

Once he had Christine's money, along with the cash he had in the underground safe at his ranch, he figured he had a short time to get ready for his flight to Argentina.

CJ arrived at the overlook at ten o'clock. This gave him time to check the best spot to throw Christine from the top. He settled on a spot that was pretty much vertical; there were only a few scrub pine trees from top to bottom. He then drove down and checked out the logging road. He found a spot which could conceal Christine's car very well. He drove back up to the overlook and waited.

* * * * *

All of the regular roundtable members were assembled in the detective conference room. The new attendees were members of the sheriff's SWAT team. They needed to be briefed as to where they would be arresting Carl Johnson, a.k.a. CJ. Captain Willis, introduced Lieutenant Jeff Travis.

Jeff Travis provided an aerial map of CJ's property, building plans had been obtained from the county building inspector. Lieutenant Travis mentioned prior visits to Carl Johnson's had been met with considerable hostility, so that could be anticipated again.

Jeff Travis explained to the SWAT members, "We have two arrest warrants for CJ, the first is for the murder of one Maxine Farrell. The second warrant is for the murder of CJ's younger brother,

Lester Johnson. CJ is suspected in the murder of several other local women," continued Travis. "Use all caution, as he has nothing to lose. He most likely anticipates our revisiting him at any time." A few questions were asked and answered. Photos of CJ were handed out to those present. "This guy can come across as something of a hillbilly, but do not underestimate him."

Captain Willis said, "Okay, everyone, be safe. We plan on hitting him shortly after nine, let's go."

They arrived at CJ's ranch at 9:10 a.m. The SWAT team pulled their vehicle into Carl Johnson's driveway. They spilled from the massive truck, deploying in several directions. When in place, their leader announced over a bullhorn, "Carl Johnson, this is the Center County Sheriff's Department. Come out with your hands up."

After a short while, the leader repeated the pronouncement. A large Hispanic-looking man wearing a cowboy hat emerged from a rear barn with his hands up. "Please, señores, do not shoot, I am not Carl Johnson. Señor Johnson is not here. Please do not shoot me."

"What is your name?" the SWAT leader asked.

"Roberto. My name is Roberto, señor. I am just helping out Señor Johnson who is away. Please don't shoot me, I am unarmed. I have a family and children. Please, por favor."

"Roberto, are there any other people here?"

"No, señor, I am here alone. Señor Johnson is not here."

"Roberto, come toward me with your hands up. Understand?"

"Si, yes, señor. I am walking toward you; my hands are up."
Shortly, Roberto was handcuffed and visibly trembling. "Señores, I
have done nothing wrong."

"We believe you, Roberto," said the leader.

The SWAT team searched the house, buildings, and property.
All clear was announced. Sergeant Bill Morris and Sergeant Lynn
Hoover sat down with Roberto, whose handcuffs had been removed.

"What are you doing on Carl Johnson's property?" asked Bill
Morris. "Do we need an interpreter?"

"No, sir, my English is pretty good. I am a US citizen," proclaimed Roberto, very proudly.

"Roberto, you are not in any trouble," said Sergeant Hoover.

"Gracias, Señorita Detective."

"How well do you know Carl Johnson, CJ?"

"Not very well, my jefa, sorry, my employer is Dr. Christine
Lawrence. She has gone away, just overnight to Nevada, I think."

"What do you mean, you think?"

Roberto told the story about how his female boss lady had asked, on two occasions, for him to take care of CJ's property and his cattle while CJ was away.

"Roberto, this a very serious matter," said Lynn Hoover. "Carl Johnson is a very bad person. We have come here to arrest him on two counts of murder. Roberto, do you understand how important it is that we find CJ?"

"I think so, but how can I help you? I don't know where CJ has gone. He left here about eight thirty this morning and told me he will return tomorrow afternoon. I only take care of his ranch because my boss lady, Dr. Christine Lawrence, asked me to do so."

"Where is Dr. Lawrence right now?" asked Bill Morris.

"I am very worried that Dr. Lawrence is with him. I am sorry to say this about this lady who has given me a home, food, and helped me, Roberto, and my mother become US citizens. Dr. Lawrence is a great, great, lady. I'm sorry, I heard Dr. Lawrence speaking on her phone to, I believe, CJ, about going to Nevada, and she asked him if he was sure it was legal. I feel badly by betraying the doctor. I truly hope she isn't in any danger. She was packing for a trip when she accidentally told me it was Nevada where she was going, just overnight."

"We really need your help, Roberto," said Lynn. "The doctor may be in grave danger right now."

"Mr. CJ left at about eighty thirty this morning, driving his pickup."

They left several officers at the ranch to finish the search and also in case CJ returned home.

Part of the SWAT was directed to travel toward Nevada with Sergeants Morris and Hoover. In all, four vehicles were traveling east at high speed on the only highway from the area which connected with the state of Nevada. The Highway Patrol was alerted to be looking for both Carl Johnson's pickup and Dr. Lawrence's Mercedes. Johnson, they noted, could likely be armed and dangerous.

* * * * *

Christine began driving at exactly nine in the morning. The trip was about three and a half hours. The view area shouldn't take more than ten minutes. For some odd reason, CJ seemed intent on her seeing the view. He'd never seemed like someone who would be interested in that sort of thing. She just didn't like the idea of stopping anywhere with all that cash she was carrying. She will indulge him this one time.

Her drive was uneventful, there was hardly any traffic today. She had many happy thoughts while listening to CDs of her favorite music. She was engrossed in her thoughts when she suddenly saw a frantic CJ waving from the overlook parking area. She quickly stopped and backed up into a parking place.

"I'm sorry, CJ," she said, "I was listening to music and almost missed the viewpoint."

"That's okay," said a visibly shaken CJ. "It's just important that you're here. You have the money, right?"

"Of course, why else would we be making this trip?" she replied.

"Okay, let me show you this beautiful view." Carl's heart was pounding and his chest was hurting. *Must be the altitude*, he thought.

They stepped to the edge, and CJ remarked, "Have you ever seen anything so beautiful, Christine? Here, let me take your car keys because you sure don't want to drop them down there."

With a puzzled look, she handed him the keys. "Okay. Let's just get this over with," she said, "I've seen enough."

"Take my hand, we just need to step on that flat rock."

"CJ, I'm scared to look down," said Christine as CJ suddenly gave her a violent shove. He could hear her screaming briefly, then it stopped.

CJ's heart was pounding as he approached his pickup. He intended to get an axe to take in Christine's car. He planned to cut some branches along the logging road to cover her vehicle from an overhead view. As CJ touched his pickup door handle, he had the worst possible chest pain. He didn't have any feeling in his hand. The surroundings became black, and CJ went down to the pavement.

Carl Johnson, the vicious killer, lay dead from a massive heart attack.

There was nothing but silence. Then, had there been anyone to hear them, sirens were approaching in the distance.

* * * * *

The detectives along with SWAT members had been traveling as fast as they deemed safe, often using their built-in sirens and red lights when they thought it necessary. They were nearly at the summit, when Lynn Hoover said, "Slow down, something's going on at this view spot."

They slowed, saw a pickup which looked like CJ's, with a man lying on the pavement next to the truck. To the right was parked a late model luxury Mercedes sedan. They cautiously exited their vehicles.

Bill Morris said, "I'll be damned, this guy is a very dead Carl Johnson." Next to CJ's hand was a set of car keys which would be determined to belong to the Mercedes that Dr. Lawrence drives. They were all pretty quiet trying to determine what had happened.

Suddenly, they heard what sounded like a very faint "Help me." Looking over the side of the viewpoint, they heard another weak "Help me."

One of the SWAT members brought over a pair of binoculars. He scanned down the side of the cliff, when he exclaimed, "Son of a bitch! Here, look straight down, the third scrub pine. There's someone hanging on, and it's probably Dr. Lawrence!"

Finding several lengths of rope in the bed of CJ's pickup, a SWAT member connected the ropes and found enough length to rappel down and secure a hysterical Dr. Lawrence to his body, should the tree break. They radioed for a rescue team to assist at the summit. Within an hour, a Highway Patrol Helicopter Rescue Crew arrived and safely brought her up from the cliff.

After first bringing up a much-calmed-down Dr. Lawrence, they were then able to pick up the SWAT member who had spent a great deal of time making the much-appreciative doctor regain her composure. When she was back at the parking area, the doctor was immediately placed in an awaiting ambulance to be transported to a Layton hospital. Sergeant Lynn Hoover accompanied her in the ambulance. Before they departed, the doctor requested that she take her attaché case from her car. She said she had some personal items she wished to take with her.

Sergeant Hoover received a pretty bizarre report from Christine Lawrence during the ambulance ride.

CHAPTER THIRTY-EIGHT

fter the sheriff's Technical Services Unit finished processing the vehicles and crime scene, the vehicles were released. The Mercedes was driven by a detective to the doctor's home. CJ's pickup was processed and towed to the sheriff's evidence lot.

When everyone was back at the office, Captain called for a team meeting and debriefing. Detective Sergeant Lynn Hoover gave a summary of her interview with Dr. Christine Lawrence, in a sort of tongue-in-cheek manner. "It seems the doctor has been a customer of CJ for several years. She buys hay from him. Lately, he had been coming around unexpectedly. He was always bringing up the story of his wife Melba's kidnapping. He always sounded so sad, she felt somewhat sorry for him. She, in fact, had taken him to lunch and dinner a couple of times. She told me she had been going through a bad patch herself. She had broken up with her fiancé, the congress-man, and maybe CJ felt she had some attraction to him. Anyway, CJ once tried to kiss her and she rejected him. He had tried further advances toward her, which she continued to reject. She threatened to stop buying his hay, which she thought made him very angry.

"He told her he had needed to get away for a short time and she had her ranch foreman take care of CJ's ranch, hoping this might get him to leave her alone. In fact, he had requested Roberto's help again just yesterday. She consented to his request but told him this would be the last time. She was planning a short trip to Nevada and needed Roberto taking care of her ranch.

"She told me that she and the congressman were making up and were to be married. She admitted to me that she is addicted to gambling. Her trip yesterday was to be her last trip over to Nevada, at least to play Black Jack. On the way, she decided to stop at the viewpoint. CJ had told her that it is a magnificent sight. She had gotten out of her vehicle and walked toward the viewing area. She heard another vehicle pull in, looked, and saw it was CJ. He had fol-lowed her. She was shocked to see him. 'Are you following me?' she asked him. He came up to her, telling her how much he loved her. She tried to push him away. He continued to rant like a madman.

This continued for several minutes, when he suddenly yelled, 'If I can't have you, no other man will either.' CJ suddenly pushed her off of the cliff. She knew she was going to die, when suddenly her arms felt the pine, which she grabbed and held on with all of her might.

"When asked, 'If someone overheard you talking with CJ, on the phone about whether something was legal, would that be true?' she said, 'It must have been Roberto. Yes, CJ was telling me about some Black Jack system called slip card. Yes, I remember asking him if it is legal. We never discussed it again. I must be careful what I say around Roberto,' she had said, laughingly."

"That's quite a story, Lynn," said Captain Willis.

"She sounds very convincing. I almost forgot, she had observed CJ eating Tums by the handful and as a physician told him he should get a checkup. She isn't sure if he ever did."

"I'm sure we have a number of questions," said Captain Willis. "I want to ask the first one. Where is the money CJ stole from his victims?"

Sergeant Morris said, "I'll take that one. We have been unable to locate any evidence that CJ had any bank or safe deposit box rentals. Between his known victims, he must have a good deal of cash stashed somewhere, but where?"

Sergeant Hoover said, "We still have an active search warrant, I think we need to do another search of his property."

The team arrived at the late Carl Johnson's ranch. They found Roberto returning from watering the horses and cattle. "Dr. Lawrence asked that I continue to feed and take care of CJ's stock until the courts give this job to someone. I hope it is soon," said Roberto, "because I am getting behind at Dr. Lawrence's ranch."

Lynn asked, "Roberto, we cannot locate the money CJ stole from his victims. Do you have any ideas?"

"Si, Señorita Detective, perhaps one idea, I do not know if it's correct. We need to go out to the southwest corner of his land." Roberto hitched a wagon to CJ's tractor. Everyone loaded onto the trailer. Roberto slowly drove them to the concrete irrigation cover. Roberto announced, "I do not see why this cover is here, there is not any water connection nearby."

Some photos were taken, and Roberto pushed the tip of a shovel under the cover and lifted up the cover. What was found beneath was about two inches of dirt over some heavy-duty plastic tarp. Soon, CJ's safe was discovered.

About two hours later, a locksmith came to the site of the safe. The safe was found to be too large to lift. Roberto used a tractor blade to dig down in the dirt, where he was able to lift out the safe with the tractor blade. The locksmith suggested Roberto carry the safe on the tractor blade up to CJ's house.

A large Center County truck with a trailered forklift arrived. The safe was moved to the sheriff's headquarter evidence room. With several excited witnesses watching, the locksmith used a variety of tools and was finally able to open the safe.

There were several gasps as the contents of the safe were removed, revealing large stacks of $100 bills. What was helpful was the packets of bills had been left in the exact amounts taken as withdrawals of the victims.

Sergeant Burris breathed a sigh of relief. At least CJ was responsible for Dottie's disappearance, as her labeled packet included matching serial numbers as had been recorded by the bank when she made the withdrawal.

Alice Fleetwood's bills were labeled, as were Sylvia Robinson's, Gloria Hansen's, and Maxine Farrell's (on which he had also written "Stingy Bitch") and a final empty label.

Detective Sergeant Ron Adams was able to clear the Maxine Farrell case.

James Cordley, CJ's attorney, was asked to come into the Detective Bureau for a statement. Sergeants Hoover and Morris interviewed him. Mr. Cordley, they found, barely knew Carl Johnson. CJ had retained him to handle the matter of Melba Johnson. In about two years, Mr. Cordley had Power of Attorney to file that Melba Johnson be declared dead. She had left a sum of $100,000 which she inherited from her father. Mr. Cordley had nothing else to offer. Carl Johnson said he would be in contact with him in two years and give him an address to send Melba's money. Cordley explained to him the legal process and how to proceed.

Karen Miller was able to obtain help from the National Oceanic Underwater Research Bureau to assist by sending a robotic device to dive to the bottom of Grand Lake. It wasn't long before two bodies were discovered and brought to the surface. The skeletal remains were identified as Melba Johnson. Her previous dental work was a match.

Dottie Lambert's remains were still somewhat intact. She was identified by her fingerprints. As a former teacher, her prints were on file with both the state and federal government. Sergeant Bill Burris cleared the Dottie Lambert case.

It would take some time for the cash to be returned to the victim's families.

Lynn Hoover made a visit to Dr. Lawrence's home. She sat in a very nice dining area, drinking coffee. Lynn asked the doctor if they could speak off of the record.

Christine said, "My story seems to be missing a few details? I don't mind talking about it if is between just the two of us."

"Doctor,"

"Please call me Chris."

"Okay, and I'm Lynn."

Christine retold her story. Lynn found what she told her believable. She hadn't done anything illegal. The monster CJ was dead. Lynn did share with Christine that the results of CJ's autopsy revealed death by heart attack. He had two major arteries 100 percent occluded. Dr. Evans said he must have had severe symptoms for some time. Lynn wished Chris congratulations on her upcoming wedding to Congressman Hunter.

The detectives had many other cases and had moved on.

EPILOGUE

———•·•·○·•·•———

Sheriff Tom Gentry was reelected for his last term.

Lynn Hoover and Sergeant Ron Adams were now openly dating and were planning on announcing their engagement soon.

The press had a field day and reported on the Carl Johnson case for many weeks. The most-asked question from the media focused on how many other people Carl Johnson had killed.

Unfortunately for the family and friends of CJ's other victims, Oscar Ripone; Carl's pregnant girlfriend, Amy; CJ's father, Dave Johnson; CJ's roping partner, Brent Marshall; and Melba's father, Jack Conner, the likelihood of these cases ever being solved is remote.

Dr. Christine Lawrence is the only surviving victim of CJ. She recognized how fortunate she had been to be a survivor. She completely gave up gambling. The $250,000 of her personal money which was to be used in CJ's nonexistent slip card scheme was donated to charity, which pleased her soon-to-be husband, Congressman Ed Hunter.

ACKNOWLEDGMENTS

Many thanks to my great friends in Seaside, Oregon. Your support and encouragement have been invaluable. (You know who you are.)

Thanks to my best friend since childhood, Dr. Tom Walters, a fellow author, for all of the advice, insight, and expertise.

ABOUT THE AUTHOR

Rod Wells is a retired sheriff's captain. He spent thirty-two years with the Stanislaus County Sheriff's Department in Modesto, California. He has a BA degree from the University of San Francisco and is a graduate of the FBI National Academy. He and his wife Diane, along with their yellow Lab, Lulu, live in the Pacific Northwest.

Printed in the USA
CPSIA information can be obtained
at www.ICGtesting.com
LVHW040918280723
753392LV00001B/81